PRAISE FOR TAMMY L. GRACE

"*A Season of Hope* is a perfect holiday read! Warm wonderful and gentle tale reflecting small town romance at its best."
— Jeanie, review of A Season for Hope: A Christmas Novella

"This book is a clean, simple romance with a background story very similar to the works of Debbie Macomber. If you like Macomber's books you will like this one. The main character, Hope and her son Jake are on a road trip when their car breaks down, thus starts the story. A holiday tale filled with dogs, holiday fun, and the joy of giving will warm your heart.
— Avid Mystery Reader, review of A Season for Hope: A Christmas Novella

"This book was just as enchanting as the others. Hardships with the love of a special group of friends. I recommend the series as a must read. I loved every exciting moment. A new author for me. She's fabulous."
—Maggie!, review of Pieces of Home: A Hometown Harbor Novel (Book 4)

"Tammy is an amazing author, she reminds me of Debbie Macomber… Delightful, heartwarming...just down to earth."
— Plee, review of A Promise of Home: A Hometown Harbor Novel (Book 3)

"This was an entertaining and relaxing novel. Tammy Grace has a simple yet compelling way of drawing the reader into the lives of her characters. It was a pleasure to read a story that didn't rely on theatrical tricks, unrealistic events or steamy sex scenes to fill up the pages. Her characters and plot were strong enough to hold the reader's interest."
—MrsQ125, review of Finding Home: A Hometown Harbor Novel (Book 1)

"This is a beautifully written story of loss, grief, forgiveness and healing. I believe anyone could relate to the situations and feelings represented here. This is a read that will stay with you long after you've completed the book."
—Cassidy Hop, review of Finally Home: A Hometown Harbor Novel (Book 5)

Killer Music and Deadly Connection are award-winning novels, earning the 2016 & 2017 Mystery Gold Medal by the Global E-Book Awards

"Killer Music is a clever and well-crafted whodunit. The vivid and colorful characters shine as the author gradually reveals their hidden secrets—an absorbing page-turning read."
— Jason Deas, bestselling author of Pushed and Birdsongs

"I could not put this book down! It was so well written & a suspenseful read! This is definitely a 5-star story! I'm hoping there will be a sequel!"
—Colleen, review of Killer Music

"This is the best book yet by this author. The plot was well crafted with an unanticipated ending. I like to try to leap ahead and see if I can accurately guess the outcome. I was able to predict some of the plot but not the actual details which made reading the last several chapters quite engrossing."

—0001PW, review of Deadly Connection

DEADLY CONNECTION

A COOPER HARRINGTON DETECTIVE NOVEL

TAMMY L. GRACE

LONE MOUNTAIN PRESS

Deadly Connection
A novel by
Tammy L. Grace

www.tammylgrace.com
Facebook: https://www.facebook.com/tammylgrace.books
Twitter: @TammyLGrace

Published in the United States by Lone Mountain Press, Nevada

ISBN 978-1-945591-26-6(paperback)
SECOND EDITION
ISBN 978-1-945591-02-0 (eBook)
FIRST EDITION
Cover design Elizabeth Mackey Graphic Design

ALSO BY TAMMY L. GRACE

COOPER HARRINGTON DETECTIVE NOVELS

Killer Music

Deadly Connection

Dead Wrong

Cold Killer

Deadly Deception

HOMETOWN HARBOR SERIES

Hometown Harbor: The Beginning (Prequel Novella)

Finding Home

Home Blooms

A Promise of Home

Pieces of Home

Finally Home

Forever Home

Follow Me Home

CHRISTMAS STORIES

A Season for Hope: Christmas in Silver Falls Book 1

The Magic of the Season: Christmas in Silver Falls Book 2

Christmas in Snow Valley: A Hometown Christmas Book 1

One Unforgettable Christmas: A Hometown Christmas Book 2

Christmas Wishes: Souls Sisters at Cedar Mountain Lodge

Christmas Surprises: Soul Sisters at Cedar Mountain Lodge

GLASS BEACH COTTAGE SERIES

Beach Haven

Moonlight Beach

Beach Dreams

WRITING AS CASEY WILSON

A Dog's Hope

A Dog's Chance

WISHING TREE SERIES

The Wishing Tree

Wish Again

Overdue Wishes

SISTERS OF THE HEART SERIES

Greetings from Lavender Valley

Pathway to Lavender Valley

Sanctuary at Lavender Valley

Blossoms at Lavender Valley

Comfort in Lavender Valley

Reunion in Lavender Valley

Remember to subscribe to Tammy's exclusive group of readers for your gift, only available to readers on her mailing list. **Sign up at www.tammylgrace.com. Follow this link to subscribe at https://wp.me/P9umIy-e** and you'll receive the exclusive interview she did with all the canine characters in her Hometown Harbor Series.

Follow Tammy on Facebook by liking her page. You may also follow Tammy on book retailers or at BookBub by clicking on the follow button.

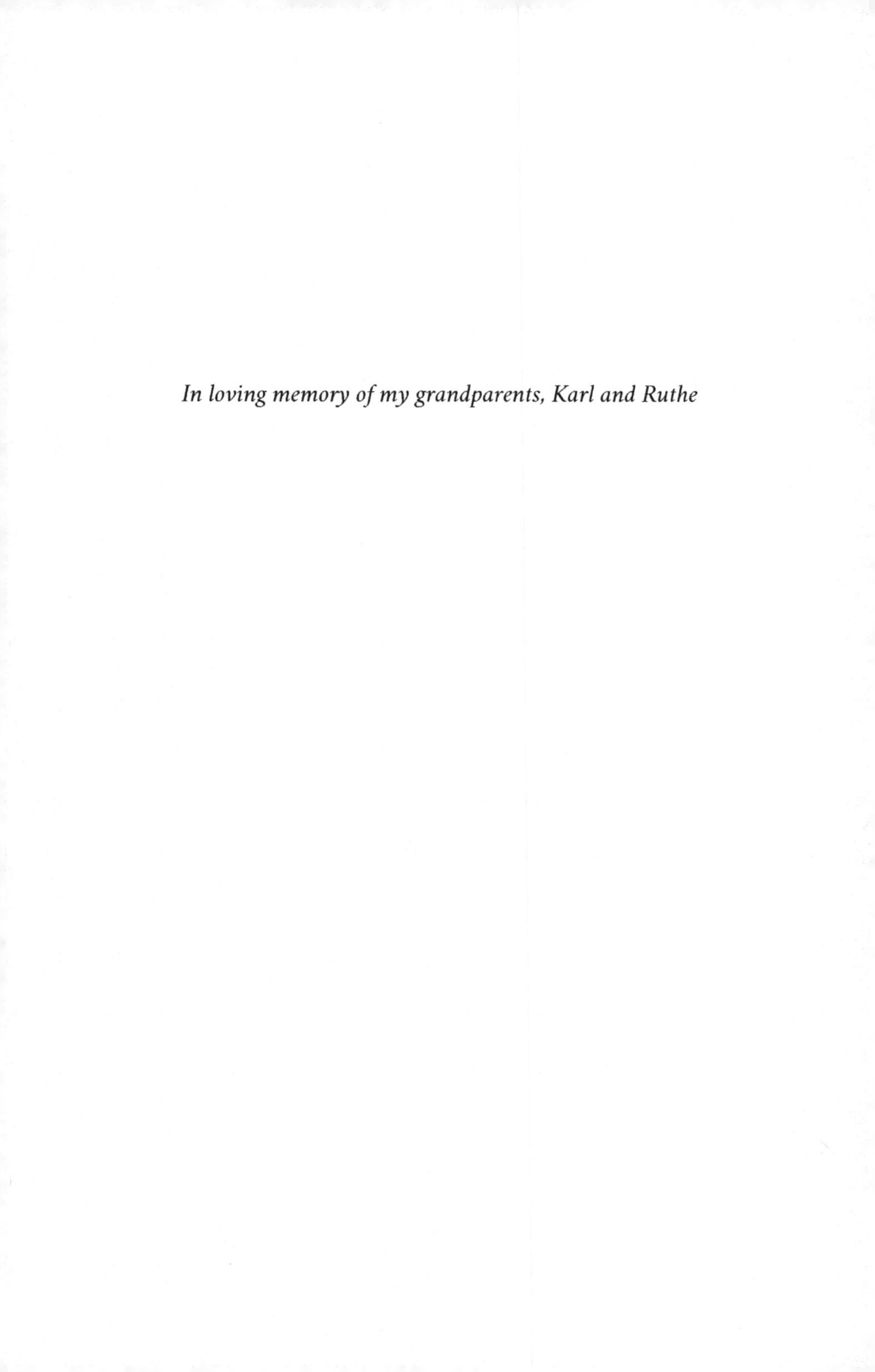

In loving memory of my grandparents, Karl and Ruthe

DEADLY CONNECTION

A COOPER HARRINGTON DETECTIVE NOVEL

Book 2

1

Callie waited at the reception desk for the serious looking woman to finish her call. She rubbed her gloved hands together while she gazed out the sixth-floor window of the outer sanctum of Judge Reese Hunt. The light rain she had endured on the walk from the office had transformed into a heavy pelting against the windows overlooking the grey Cumberland River. She shivered in anticipation of the cold walk back to her car at the Law Offices of Brandon King. This was her third trip of the day to the courthouse. The traffic and parking situation had been a fiasco earlier in the day, so she hadn't bothered to drive, thinking the walk would be quicker, but now wished she had taken the time.

Callie listened to the receptionist end her call and attempted to catch her eye as a bicycle messenger approached the counter. Beads of water danced atop his reflective jacket and his shoes squeaked on the polished floor. "Hey, Miss Sadie," said the cheerful young man.

Sadie's stern face softened as she placed her reading glasses atop her nose and grabbed a pile of folders from the counter. "Here you go, Billy. Stay dry out there."

He glanced at the labels and scanned them with a handheld device before he slipped the items into a protective envelope in his bag. “See y’all tomorrow.” He turned and nodded at Callie. “Have a good day, miss.”

The hint of softness disappeared, transforming Sadie’s face to that of the harsh guardian behind the counter. “How may I help you?”

Callie smothered the urge to ask Sadie why she couldn’t bother to remember her since she’d been in several times this week, but instead summoned her polite voice. Callie explained she was from Brandon King’s office and Sadie plucked a small bundle of folders from a slot. Callie signed for them and stashed them in her oversized tote bag. “Thanks, Sadie. Have a pleasant evening,” she said as she made for the door. “One of these days she’ll remember my name,” muttered Callie once the door closed.

With reluctance she left the warm shelter of the building and hurried onto the sidewalk. She was drenched, cold, and cranky by the time she reached the office. With it being minutes before five o’clock, she discarded the idea of trudging all the way into the building and tossed her tote in the passenger seat of the car. She turned up the heat and sat in the car watching the blades swipe the water from her windshield, while she huddled in her coat.

The warm air thawed her toes and fingers. She spied her limp hair in the rearview mirror and shook her head. With the blower on full blast, she steered for home. The three miles to her house near Green Hills took thirty minutes with the deluge of rain and traffic. She eased her car under the carport and lugged her tote bag up the steps. Dry leaves skittered across the walkway as a fresh blast of cold air found its way inside the scarf around her neck. Warmth greeted her when she opened the door. After shedding her shoes and coat, she made for her bedroom and changed into her warmest pajamas.

She stuck some leftovers in the microwave and flicked the remote to her favorite news station. She was a news junkie and always had it on at work and at home. She found the incessant droning of the voices in the background comforting. Despite Christmas being only a few weeks away, she had no tree or decorations. She planned to spend the holiday with her family in Virginia and didn't have the energy to deal with the task of decorating. Her tiny cottage on a quiet street was comfortable and cozy, but far from what she was used to for living accommodations. She plated her meal and snuggled into her chair to watch television.

She longed for a roaring fire, but had to make do with the furry throw her mother had given her. She knew she had made a mess of her life and starting over in Nashville was her best hope for a future. It had been three short months since her move, but she was making progress. She was a forty-something year old associate, but it was better than being disbarred. Instead of a partner with a plush office, she was in a cubicle next to kids fresh out of school. And she was lucky to have a job. If her parents hadn't been connected, she would have been fortunate to land a job in a convenience store. She rolled her shoulders and rotated her neck, trying to dislodge the incessant cramp that had taken up residence.

To divert her mind from the loneliness of the quiet house, she scanned the neighborhood newsletter. Articles summarizing holiday events, garbage reminders, and safety tips were prominent. The pet section featured lost and found animals as well as those for sale. She uttered a soft "ahh" when she studied the photos of the puppy faces. "If I had a dog, I wouldn't feel so lonely." She shook the thought from her mind, realizing how unfair it would be to leave the dog alone all day.

After putting her dishes in the dishwasher, she grabbed her tote and took out the folders she'd picked up from the courthouse. She perused the papers and made a list of notes for tomorrow. She had to prepare a response and wanted to impress Mr. King.

She finally finished and turned up the volume to catch the late edition of the local news. She was tidying the folders when she noticed a slim manila envelope in the bundle. The messenger service label had uncurled from the envelope and stuck to the back of her folder, joining the two pieces of mail. She tried to peel the label to unstick the folder and, in the process, ripped the envelope open. "Crap," she muttered.

She noticed it was a plain envelope without the return address of the Justice AA Birch Building. It was addressed to H. Featherstone at an address downtown. She didn't know what to do with the mess of the envelope and didn't want to get on the bad side of the court. She hurried to the second bedroom and found a manila envelope. She addressed it, taking care to copy the plain handwriting from the original envelope. There was no way to salvage the entire delivery label.

A news segment flashed on the television and she listened to the anchor report on a fatal hit and run accident downtown. She perked up when she heard the victim was a bike messenger named William Corey, known as "Billy" to all his clients. The owner of the bike messenger company was interviewed and had a hard time maintaining when he talked about what a kind young man Billy had been.

Callie put her hand to her throat when she viewed a photo of Billy, smiling in his uniform, as she had seen him only hours ago. The police were investigating and asked anyone with information to contact them.

Although Callie didn't know Billy beyond her encounter with him at the courthouse, she felt a lump in her throat and sadness for the young man and his family. She went back to transferring the contents from the ripped envelope to the new envelope.

As she unearthed the papers, her curiosity piqued. She didn't intend to snoop, but couldn't help noticing the envelope contained several photos of a man, who appeared to be in his fifties. Some photos were close-up and others were from a distance in front of a house. Included with the photos was a typed sheet with the name "Avery Logan" and a Nashville address at the top of the page. Below Avery's name was a list of additional names of people with the surname Logan and photos of two vehicles. The following page showed dates and times along with a variety of locations in Nashville.

Her forehead crinkled as she perused the list and photos again. "This is weird." She removed some of the loose label from the original envelope and applied it to the new one. "I should take this back to Judge Hunt's office." She shrugged and looked at the address again. "Or, I could just deliver it myself tomorrow. It's not far from the office." She admired her work and compared the handwriting one more time. "It looks the same." She scraped the remnants of the messenger label from her case folder and stuffed the new envelope and the torn one into her tote.

She turned off the television and went to bed, guilt ridden for not going to her meeting tonight. She had been faithful about attending Alcoholics Anonymous meetings as part of her efforts to rebuild her life. She liked going to the evening meeting in Belle Meade. With the fundraiser at Vanderbilt tomorrow night, she'd have to do a lunchtime meeting downtown or risk skipping two meetings. She punched her pillow and repositioned her head. "I'll go downtown tomorrow. I'll need the meeting to get through the party."

As soon as she got comfortable in bed, she bolted upright, remembering her cell phone. She'd been in such a snit when she got home, she forgot to charge it and hadn't checked it all evening. She shook her head when she saw three missed calls from Ollie, her ex-boyfriend. He'd been trying to contact her for a few weeks and she'd been ignoring him. Her eyes brightened when she saw a text from Annabelle, reminding her about the fundraiser and telling her she was looking forward to the evening.

Annabelle, or AB as she was known to most of her friends, had always been there for Callie and her friendship was one of the best things about being back in Nashville. Callie had rekindled the college friendship the two had developed and AB accepted her without reservation. Callie had told AB about the disaster she'd made of her life and career in Virginia and AB had never judged her. She was a true and loyal friend. They'd been getting together every couple of weeks since Callie had moved back. Although Callie hadn't had a relationship with AB for years, she never made Callie feel guilty. She welcomed her back with open arms and few questions.

Annabelle worked for Coop Harrington, a lawyer and private detective. The three of them had gone to school together at Vanderbilt. Callie had worried AB might share her failures with Coop, but AB assured her she would keep their conversations confidential. Callie trusted her and knew AB would guard her secrets. Callie tapped in a short reply and a happy face before plugging the phone in to charge for the night.

Friday morning, Callie got up late. She rushed to get to the office on time and nixed the idea of delivering the envelope on her way to work. Being late could jeopardize her job and she wasn't about to risk it. She took the case folders from Judge Hunt out of her tote leaving the envelope behind, with a plan to drop it off later. She smuggled the ripped envelope to the copy room and ran it through the shredder. Instead of sleeping she had used the dark of night to contemplate her best course of action. She concluded it was better to deliver the envelope to the recipient and be done with it. She intended to fly under the radar and didn't want to draw attention to herself at the courthouse.

She slugged down some coffee, turned on the news, and got to work on the response. She finished the final draft at eleven and emailed it to Mr. King's assistant. She had just enough time to make the eleven-thirty meeting a few blocks away. She opted for the car this time, since it was still spitting rain and the church had a large parking lot.

She deposited some cash in the collection box and selected a sandwich from the tray. She'd only come to this meeting a few times, but found the lunch option convenient. She listened as several speakers spoke about their road to sobriety and the struggles they endured. Some of the tension in her chest dissipated as she listened to others and let her own problems fade into the background. Peace and calmness always came over her at meetings. Attending a meeting gave her a sense of accomplishment and she was glad she had made the time for it today.

She didn't feel like sharing and concentrated on summoning the strength she would need to get through the event tonight without drinking. She'd also been a drug addict, but didn't crave drugs like she did a drink. Drugs had led her to the most destructive time of her life. She'd stolen funds from the law firm to feed her habit, intending to put the money back, but never did. Her parents bailed her out and paid back all the money and the firm agreed to keep it confidential if she left quietly. She was on her way to a senior partnership and had destroyed her career. Now, here she was not quite a year sober and still struggling.

There was no time to drop off the envelope and get back to the office before her lunch break was over, so she kept it hidden in her tote, stuffed in the file cabinet in her cubicle. Although her desk was in the cube farm, it wasn't a cheap call center cubicle. It was plush and rather large, with tall walls for privacy and outfitted with a television. Her desk was on the end and afforded her a window view. She was stowing her coat when she heard the name Avery Logan on the television. She turned her attention to the monitor where the anchorwoman described a current murder investigation into the death of a Nashville resident, Avery Logan. He had been found shot in a park early Friday morning.

Callie gasped as she continued to watch the clip. She was tempted to dig out the envelope, but knew the name without checking the papers inside— it was Avery Logan. The sandwich she had just eaten felt like a lead ball in her stomach. She swallowed hard, praying her lunch would stay put. She looked around the side of her cubicle, but nobody was paying any attention to her or the news. She walked to the kitchen to get a cold drink and brought it back to her desk.

She crumpled into her chair, hands shaking as she contemplated what to do. She thought about talking to Mr. King, but then thought better of it. She didn't want to draw any negative attention to herself. It was bad enough she'd walked in on him and his assistant in a compromising position last week. She knew they were both married. In her flustered state, she stumbled as she fled the room. Neither of them had said a word to Callie about the incident and she was fine with pretending it never happened. This was her last chance for a law career and she wasn't about to get in the middle of a workplace affair or anything else. She hadn't told AB or anyone at work about what she witnessed, only her sponsor.

She completed a few more assignments and then stared at the television when a preview for the evening news showed a photo of Avery Logan. She choked on her drink when she saw the same face from the photos in the envelope staring back from the screen.

She drummed her fingers on her desk and checked her email. A note from her boss telling her he appreciated her great work on the response she had drafted lifted her spirits, but only for a moment. To distract herself from the television, she scrolled her calendar and saw the fundraiser at the Vanderbilt Law Library.

That was her answer. She'd talk to AB tonight and get an appointment with Coop. He had been a whiz in school and from what she knew he was an accomplished detective, as well as a successful lawyer. If he was half as talented as AB said he was, he'd figure it out and know what to do.

Her phone vibrated atop her desk. She checked the screen and sensed the tension rise in her shoulders. A text from Ollie begging her to call him. "I really don't need this right now," she whispered as she deleted the message.

2

Friday morning, Coop was ensconced in his favorite booth at Peg's Pancakes across from his best friend and Chief of Detectives, Ben Mason. They had been meeting for breakfast every Friday for the last twenty years, having met in school at Vanderbilt. Although they couldn't be more unalike in looks, with Ben short, stocky, and balding, and Coop tall and lanky, with a full head of dark hair, they were closer than brothers. They were discussing the current state of crime in Nashville, with Ben focused on the hit and run of Billy the bike messenger.

"So, no leads yet?" asked Coop.

Ben shook his head and moved his coffee cup to make room for Myrtle's delivery. She placed two heaping plates in front of each of them. "Y'all eat up now. Anything else for my two favorite men?"

Coop smiled. "Looks delicious. I just need AB's order before we leave."

Myrtle smiled and turned to retrieve the coffee pot. She refilled their cups and said, "I'd never forget that sweet girl. I'll be back with her box in a jiffy."

"No leads. From the camera feeds it looks like a black SUV,

no plates, nothing to identify it, and dark windows. We're trying to enhance everything, but with the rain and the reflection of the lights, the quality is horrible."

Coop shook his head. "Tragic situation all around. Looked like a nice kid."

Ben nodded as he stuffed a wedge of pancake in his mouth. "Nobody had anything negative to say about him. I can't figure out why the car didn't stop though. Speeding away doesn't help your case when you've hit a man."

"A bike messenger is a tough way to make a living. And dangerous."

"Yeah, I wouldn't want to bike through downtown traffic. We found his messenger bag a block away. Papers strewn about. The company is having a fit about it. They do a lot of business with lawyers and want to make sure all the paperwork is collected and they contact their clients. It's a mess."

Myrtle returned with the check and a box she placed in front of Coop. "There y'all be."

Ben's phone rang and he wiped the syrup from his mouth and answered. "Got it. I'll be there in a few minutes." He disconnected and took a swig of his coffee.

"Gotta run?"

Ben nodded. "Homicide in Bells Bend. Guy shot to death while running."

"Another reason I don't like exercise," said Coop, puffing up his chest so Ben could get a look at his t-shirt of the day. It read, *Exercise? I thought you said extra fries.*

Ben smirked and shook his head. He threw some bills on the table. "My turn this week. Give AB a hug from me."

"Catch ya later," waved Coop, as Ben slid out of the booth.

Myrtle came by the table and let out a tsk. "That poor man never gets to enjoy a meal anymore." She filled Coop's cup. "Too many hooligans in the world today."

"There's been a murder. He had to go." He shoved the money and the check to Myrtle. "Keep the change."

She beamed and tucked the money in her apron pocket. "See you boys next week."

Coop gathered the box and took one more gulp from his cup before leaving through the glass doors, festooned with holly and berries for the holidays. He jumped in the Jeep and Gus lifted his head, sniffing the box.

"That's not for you, big guy." Coop petted the golden retriever's head, causing a thumping frenzy of the dog's tail.

He drove the few blocks to Harrington and Associates and parked behind the renovated three-story home that served as his offices. Gus bounded out of the Jeep and waited by the back door. Coop turned the handle and the dog slid across the wooden floor, his paws wet from the rain.

Coop found AB at her desk and deposited her breakfast. He leaned over and engulfed her in a one-armed hug. "That's from Ben."

She jumped in surprise and then laughed. "How's our favorite Chief of Detectives this fine rainy morning?"

"Busy. He's working the hit and run downtown with the bike guy and just got a call for a homicide in Bells Bend."

She popped open her box and eyed the raspberry filled pancakes topped with more raspberry compote and fresh whipped cream. "Poor Ben." She dug into the breakfast and moaned. "This is to die for. Thank you for breakfast."

"Just another perk for being the best lawyer slash office manager in Tennessee. He gave her a sheepish grin. "It was Ben's turn this week." He saw Gus had positioned himself under AB's desk, with only his tail hanging out. The dog knew he could count on a morsel from his bestie. She chuckled as she forked in another bite. "I gave the kids some time off. They're trying to study for finals next week." She glanced at the empty office where two interns from Vanderbilt were usually housed.

"What's on the schedule today?"

"Not much. I've got to finish up a few reports for you to sign. It's always slow this time of year. We're all caught up unless something new comes in. Works out well since we'll be closing for two weeks at Christmas."

"It would be beneficial to get more work. We still have a couple of weeks before we close and need to pay some bills."

"Madison and Ross are still working on the corporate security case. They should finish the analysis up next week." She delivered a wedge of pancake to Gus. "I'll make a few calls to our regulars and drum up something to keep us busy." She finished one last bite of pancake and slipped a forkful to Gus before closing the lid on her breakfast. "I suppose you can't convince your dad to come for Christmas since he was just here for Thanksgiving?"

"Not gonna happen. I tried, but he said he's had enough flying around the countryside to last him."

"He had fun, didn't he?"

Coop grinned. "He had a great time. So did Aunt Camille. She loved doting on him. She had a hard time when he went home. She misses Uncle John so much and Dad did an admirable job of filling in for him."

"He'll spend Christmas with your brother?"

He nodded. "Yeah, he'll have fun with all the kids. I don't have their appeal."

He looked out the front window at the rain. "Aunt Camille invited some of her widowed and single friends to join us this year. Too bad you're going on your trip. You could be my wingman. It does make you feel young, you know, surrounded by Aunt Camille and her friends."

She laughed. "I would love to, if I weren't going to the Bahamas. I still can't believe the whole family agreed to an exotic vacation this year instead of our usual Christmas. I'm excited to go to a sunny beach."

"You'll have a terrific time. I'm jealous. Maybe I should go to the Bahamas." He smirked as he wandered back to the kitchen to retrieve his first of many cups of coffee. It was decaf now, after orders from the doctor a few months ago. Not to mention his bowl of M&M's had been reduced to one small bag a week. It was hell getting old.

He shuffled back through AB's area and wandered to his office. He settled into his chair. He loved the brick, wood, and dark green colors. Annabelle had a fire going in the fireplace and he relished the heat. Being in Uncle John's old office always made Coop feel comforted. He missed his uncle and with a pang of regret knew Aunt Camille wasn't the only one who would have a hard time during the holidays.

He and AB spent the day finishing the pending paperwork and he initiated a background check for one of their regular clients. He perused the accounts receivable file on his computer and scribbled a few notes. He expected the payments by the end of the year, but had a few new clients and wanted to remind them.

He and AB shared a salad she brought in for lunch. "I'm going to take off a little early this afternoon if it's okay?" she asked.

"Sure, it's the annual Women of Vanderbilt Law shindig tonight, right?"

She smiled. "Yep, it's at the law library. It's a fundraiser, but I think it'll be entertaining. Callie's coming. It's her first event with the group since moving back. She's a bit anxious."

Coop nodded as he slogged more dressing onto his plate. "Understandable. You haven't said much about her, but it's clear something happened. You don't go from a partner at one of the oldest firms in Virginia to an associate over at King, unless there's a major problem."

She kept eating and didn't say anything. He continued to

stare at her while he chewed. She stared back. "If you're curious about Callie's career, you'll have to ask her yourself."

"Just sayin'. It doesn't take a rocket scientist to figure it out." He took his plate to the sink. "I always liked Callie. I'm sorry she's having a hard time. It can't be easy with her family."

"They're definitely ingrained in the business. If you aren't a lawyer, judge, legislator, or governor, I think they disown you."

"Is she having a hard time adjusting to being here?"

She nodded. "I think so. She's used to being surrounded by family and all things luxurious. The family estate in McLean is beyond extravagant. I think it's bigger than Aunt Camille's place. Despite going to school here, she's always lived in Virginia. You know what it's like to be away from home."

"Yeah, but I had Uncle John and Aunt Camille. Not to mention you and Ben."

"Exactly. She needs to get a circle of friends. We've been going out after work every couple of weeks, but she doesn't socialize with anyone but me. Maybe I can convince her to an evening with you and Ben and Jen."

"Good idea. You're a true friend, AB. The only girl I know who isn't tempted to gossip. Even when I baited you." He wiggled his eyebrows at her and took her empty plate to the sink.

"I'm immune to your subtleties. I know how you work, Coop. I'm not going to violate Callie's trust. I also know you're plenty smart enough to figure out something bad happened. It's not my story to tell."

He finished drying the plates and wrapped his arm around her shoulder. "You're a good man, AB. Now get out of here and have fun at the party."

She gave Gus a substantial nuzzle and gathered her things. Coop watched her drive away in her bright green Beetle, which brought to mind a tropical gecko.

The theme for the Women of Vanderbilt Law event demanded some serious swank. The classmates were asked to dress in styles of old Hollywood glamour actresses. Callie's upbringing and lifestyle often required lavish gowns and she was happy to share her collection with AB. Grace Kelly served as AB's inspiration and with her in mind AB selected a gorgeous flowing white chiffon strapless number, like the actress wore in *To Catch a Thief.* She was one of the first to arrive at the library and after checking her coat, hung out in the lobby, waiting for Callie.

Callie was channeling Audrey Hepburn and wore an iconic black satin number, complete with gloves and a stunning necklace. She even added a tiara after she did her hair Audrey-style. Callie was greeted with a hug from her friend as soon as she came through the door.

"Sorry, I'm a bit late. I got out a few minutes early tonight, but this hair took forever." She didn't admit to using the extra time to drive downtown to deliver the envelope.

Callie tried to relax and slow the pounding in her chest, but her mind kept replaying what happened when she had left work. Frustrated after driving in circles to find a parking spot, she had given up and parked at the Hilton a few blocks from the address on the envelope. She hurried to make her way to the address, disappointed to face a darkened storefront of a postage and shipping store. She checked the address on the envelope again and saw it listed a number after the street name, which she surmised corresponded to one of the private mailboxes she could see on the wall. There was a twenty-four-hour entrance to the mailbox section, but it required a key.

She let out a heavy breath. "What a pain." She noted, with exasperation, the store was closed on the weekend. "You've got to be kidding me," she muttered through gritted teeth, as she hustled down the street in the direction of the Hilton. She had raced through the streets, trying to make up time and get home to change for the party.

This was why the dreaded envelope was still stuffed in her tote bag.

"No problem. They're checking coats over there," said AB, pointing to an open door. Callie eyes were locked as she stared across the room. She didn't respond, so AB put her hand on her shoulder. "Callie, are you okay? I said you can leave your coat over there."

The sound of AB's voice and the touch from her fingers brought Callie back to reality. She blinked several times and refocused on AB's face. "Sorry, I hate rushing." She took off her furry wrap and handed it to the young woman.

"I'm happy to check your bag," she offered, eyeing the large tote Callie clutched in her hand.

"Uh, that's okay. I need some things in it." She took her ticket and stuffed it into the inside pocket of her tote.

The small beaded evening bag AB carried looked much more glamorous than the worn leather tote, but Callie wasn't letting the envelope out of her sight. As soon as she looked up from stowing the ticket, she was surrounded by several of the women she remembered from her days in law school. They were wearing nametags, so she had no trouble remembering them. After chatting for several minutes, she made her way to the registration table and picked up her own nametag.

She and AB mingled with a number of small groups and AB was kind enough to retrieve club sodas from the bar. Callie smiled when she returned. "Thanks for joining me in my non-alcoholic drink."

They toured the silent auction tables and bid on a few things. The women had a grand time admiring all the other dresses and the variety of items up for auction. Out of the corner of her eye AB saw a woman approaching. "Don't look now, but Trixie's seen us."

Callie emitted a sigh and AB felt the tension it attempted to dispel. "I was hoping she wouldn't be here."

"My heavens, if it isn't Calista and Annabelle as I live and breathe. I haven't seen y'all together for years.

"Callie's just moved back to town and I'm delighted," said AB, extending her hand to Trixie. As luck would have it, Trixie wore a gown similar to Callie's and was doing her best to portray Audrey Hepburn, but falling short.

"How wonderful," Trixie said, sweetness dripping from her words like syrup off a stack of Peg's pancakes. "I assume you're still squanderin' your talents with our favorite private detective, Annabelle?"

"Yes, Coop and I are still hard at it."

"Well, now that I've married Chandler, he insists I stay home and Daddy agreed to let me go. Chandler's a partner in Daddy's firm, you know?" She took a sip of her drink and feigned surprise. "It appears Calista and I share the same tastes in men as we do Hollywood divas. Oh, dear, Calista, I do hope you knew I had married Chandler. I don't have to tell you what a wonderful man he is. It's a pity you gave him up. But, as they say, it was my gain." She batted her eyes as she scanned the room in search of more prey.

"Yes, I had heard. Congratulations to both of you. Give Chandler my best," said Callie, praying for a fire, a bolt of lightning, anything to end the interaction.

"We always shared a healthy rivalry. I'm hopin' you didn't come back to charm Chandler." She narrowed her eyes and whispered, "You'd best remember he's mine and he made his choice. You need to stay away. We don't need you back meddlin' in our lives."

Callie's eye went wide. "Of course not. I'm not interested in Chandler."

"Then what are you doin' in Nashville?" Trixie's eyebrows raised in anticipation.

"I took a position with Brandon King."

AB pointed across the room. "Oh, there's Molly. We promised to meet up with her. Nice to visit with you, Trixie," said AB, taking Callie by the arm and all but hurtling her away from Trixie. She hoped to avoid Callie having to divulge more information about her current employment status to her nemesis.

The two stopped at several groups to say hello and then pretended to be interested in another auction item to escape the gaze of Trixie. When AB and Callie, tired of mingling, took their chairs at their table AB said, "I think we're the most convincing Grace and Audrey in the room."

Callie laughed. "Hands down." She looked across the room at Trixie attempting to be Audrey Hepburn, who, unlike Callie, didn't have the figure to pull off the fitted gown associated with *Breakfast at Tiffany's*. The result was a procession of pudgy satin covered rolls marching down each side of Trixie's back. Callie wedged her tote between her feet under the table.

They saw the president of the group approach the podium and the attendees scurried to their assigned tables. As the women made their way to their tables, Callie gripped her tote tighter between her feet and leaned over to AB. She whispered, "I need to make an appointment and talk with you and Coop as soon as possible. I've got a tricky problem and need some help and advice."

The serious look in Callie's eyes confirmed the anxiety AB heard in her fearful whisper. "Of course. I'll text Coop and ask if he can make something work on Sunday. I know he has plans tomorrow."

"The sooner the better."

"Are you okay?"

Callie's eyes darted around the room. "I think so. I'm just nervous."

"What happened?"

She scanned the crowd of sequined gowns and lowered her voice, "It's something at work. I accidentally came across something. I tried to handle it, but I just don't know what to do. Having it is making me a nervous wreck, but I'm afraid to show it to anyone. This job is my last chance and now...I can't discuss it here. If Coop can meet me Sunday that would be great."

The two were joined by four other women, all of whom commented on their perfect dresses. While they were chatting, AB slipped her hand into her bag and slid her phone onto her lap. She texted Coop and asked if he could make time for Callie first thing Sunday morning.

The servers delivered trays of salads to each table as the president addressed the group. AB felt her phone vibrating and glanced at her lap. Relief flooded through her as she tapped in a short response before snapping her bag closed. She tilted her head close to Callie and whispered, "Coop said Sunday at eight would work for him."

Callie heaved a breath out and gripped AB's hand. "Perfect. Thank you so much, AB. I'll be there."

After the main course, the women were given clues for a scavenger hunt. The teams consisted of tablemates and they were charged with finding a list of items, all of which could be found inside the building. They were promised dessert when they returned, along with prizes for the winners.

Women dressed like Ginger Rogers, Katharine Hepburn, Elizabeth Taylor, and Marilyn Monroe accompanied AB and Callie as they deciphered clues and searched the stacks of law books. Reluctant to leave the tote bag behind, Callie carried it on her shoulder as she helped search. They decided to split up the clues with the hope of making better time if they were lucky enough to each find an item.

The strategy paid off and between the six of them, they found all six items and were the first ones back to their table. While they waited for the others, the discussion turned to their careers. The youngest woman in the group was an associate, but all the others were partners or well on their way to a partnership. Callie didn't reveal much, except to say she was an associate at the Law Offices of Brandon King. Sensing Callie's discomfort, AB jumped in and talked about her own career. She told the group she wasn't practicing, instead doing what she loved as the office manager and paralegal at Coop's law firm and detective agency.

Her description piqued the interest of the women and AB fielded questions about their detective work, including the high-profile case from a few months ago where they helped capture the murderer of record label mogul, Grayson Taylor. The women quizzed her about her role in the process and AB entertained them with the story. The conversation turned to memories of the time they had spent in the law library, until the other alumni returned to their tables.

Dessert was served and the winners all received oversized gift bags filled with classic films on DVD, tickets for movies at local theatres, bath products, and gourmet chocolates. The silent auction winners were announced and the president beamed when she reported the amount of money raised.

It was close to midnight when Callie and AB collected their coats and set out for the parking garage. They lingered outside the entrance saying goodbye to several women. Callie gave AB a hug and thanked her for arranging time with Coop. Callie's grip slipped on the handles of the gift bag and AB helped catch it. "Hey, where's your tote bag?"

"Oh, crap. I must have left it under the table. I'll be right back." She darted into the main room and lifted the edge of the tablecloth and spied her bag. She plucked it from its hiding spot and returned to AB, who was waiting in the lobby. "It was there," she smiled. "I'll see you first thing Sunday morning. I'll stop by and pick up coffees and donuts."

"Excellent strategy when dealing with Coop. I'm going to

guilt him into going to the gym Sunday. Donuts will make a perfect catalyst." She linked her arms in Callie's as they walked outside and said, "You could come and stay at my place tonight, if you're still worried about work."

"Oh, that's sweet, AB. I'm fine. Now I have a plan and I'm better." She paused and added, "Thanks for making me come tonight. It was fun to go back and remember all the hours we spent in the library. I loved my time here." She took another look at the building and waved as she climbed into her car. AB followed her out of the garage, blinking her lights as she turned off for her house.

Callie forced herself to rise early Saturday and attend an AA meeting in Belle Meade. The envelope conundrum nagged at her and she knew stress was a major trigger for her to drink. She had to get through the next twenty-four hours before her meeting with Coop.

After the meeting at the church she went to coffee with her sponsor, Hattie Mae. She was an older woman who had been sober for decades and was an excellent listener. Callie longed to tell her about the envelope, but resisted and instead shared she was stressed with a work situation. After promising to check in next week, Callie left the coffee shop and headed for the mall in Green Hills.

Callie spent the rest of the day running errands and picking up a few Christmas gifts. She indulged in a late lunch at Panera—one of her favorites. After stocking her fridge and cupboards for the week, she settled in for a movie marathon. She loved all the movies in the gift basket, but in deference to her persona from the party, she inserted *Breakfast at Tiffany's*.

She had just opened the box of gourmet chocolates when her cell phone rang. She sighed when she saw Ollie's name on the screen. Another trigger. She wrestled with the decision to press answer or ignore and decided to talk to him, with the hope of getting rid of the pest. She didn't give him a chance to say anything and barked into the phone. "Ollie, I've told you, I'm not interested in talking to you or meeting with you. You need to stop calling and leave me alone."

He dragged his words out when he responded. "Hey, Callie, don't be like that. I love you. I need you. I miss you." His speech was slow and slurred.

"Are you high?"

"No, no," he laughed. "Maybe just a little."

"I'm done with you, Ollie. Don't call me again. Got it? I'll get a restraining order, if I have to."

"A piece of paper won't stop me, babe. I love you. I can't live without you. I'm in Nashville for a meeting next week. I want to see you."

"That's not going to happen, Ollie. I'm starting over here and I can't mess it up."

"Maybe I'll just stop by your office then. I know you work at the King firm downtown."

"Don't you dare come to my office." She paused, fuming. "I'll meet you at your conference. Text me the details."

"That's perfect, Callie. I'll see you next week, baby."

"One meeting, Ollie, that's it. You need to get some help. Stop throwing your life away and leave me the hell alone." She tapped the red button to disconnect the call and tossed her phone on the couch.

"What a loser. How did I ever get hooked up with him?" She ranted as she fingered the remote to start the movie. She was glad Ollie was in Virginia and she was in Tennessee, but a sense of dread saturated her thoughts at the anticipation of meeting him next week.

After sampling a few chocolate truffles, she fixed herself a cup of tea and popped in another DVD. She let the antics of

Katharine Hepburn and Spencer Tracy keep her company until her eyes became too heavy and she fell asleep on the couch.

Several hours later, brisk air drifted over her face and her eyes fluttered open. She raised her head off the arm of the couch and was shoved down by a cool gloved hand clamped across her mouth. Her eyes went wide in terror, but before she could utter a word her neck snapped and she slumped back onto the soft pillows stacked in the corner of the couch.

The DVD had long ended, but a gloved finger pushed the play button and the movie filled the screen. There were no sounds as the intruder's disposable shoe covers glided across the wooden floors. Her tote, files, cupboards, closets, bookcases, and dressers were rifled and the contents strewn over the floors. The murderer pocketed several pieces of expensive jewelry and took all her credit cards and cash from her wallet before leaving through the back door. Callie's lifeless eyes stared at the television screen, but she'd seen her last movie.

3

When Coop arrived at work Sunday morning, he found AB in his office, huddled in front of a roaring fire. "It's nice and toasty in here," he said. Gus followed him and jumped onto his favorite leather chair he had commandeered for his bed.

"I was freezing and figured we could meet in here. Callie promised coffee and donuts so I didn't brew any."

"I knew I liked Callie," said Coop with a boyish grin. He took off his jacket and revealed his t-shirt of the day. *Admit it—life would be boring without me* was lettered across the navy fabric.

She laughed and said, "Yes, it would be boring. Speaking of boring, we have to go the gym today when we're done with Callie."

He scrunched his nose and frowned. "How was the party?"

"It was fun." She dug into her pocket for her cell phone. "I have a few pictures of us." She handed him the phone. "Scroll through starting there."

He smiled as he viewed the photos. "You two look great. You could pass for the real Grace and Audrey."

"Our table won the scavenger hunt and we all got prizes.

Callie enjoyed herself, I think. She appeared much more relaxed at the end of the evening."

Coop glanced at his watch. "Is she usually late?"

"No. And she was anxious for this meeting. I'll give her a call." She touched the icon for Callie and the phone rang and rang and then went to voicemail. She followed with a text in case the ringer was off. They waited fifteen more minutes and didn't receive a reply.

"Does she have a landline in her house?"

She shook her head. "No, just the cell." She paced to the window and looked out at the street. "Maybe we should go check at her house."

"I'll drive," Coop said, Gus on their heels.

Gus gave up his front seat to AB. The dog sat in the back, his head resting on her shoulder. Callie's house was less than five minutes from the office. Coop parked his Jeep behind her late model BMW and told Gus to stay.

"This is weird," said AB, concern edging into her voice. She knocked on the backdoor. It didn't have a window and the blinds were closed in the adjacent windows, obstructing any chance of a view inside the house.

Coop offered to try the front door. It had decorative glass high on the door, designed for ascetics and not for viewing. There was no response to his loud pounding, and like the back door it was locked. He scanned the windows and found all the blinds closed. "Try her phone again."

With shaky hands, AB connected the call. Coop put his ear to the window near the backdoor and tried to listen for the ring. "I think I hear something, but it's faint."

"I've got a key for emergencies. I think this constitutes the use of it." She ran back to the Jeep and dug through her purse.

Coop examined the lock before he inserted the key and saw no visible signs of tool marks or forced entry. He slipped the key in and opened the door. He put a hand in front of AB as she made to dart through the opening. "Stay back and let me check first."

She rolled her eyes, but obliged. He hollered out, "Callie, it's Coop and AB. Are you here?" The door opened into the small kitchen, only steps away from and open to the living area. He saw the television displayed a DVD menu screen. He glanced at the couch and saw Callie's dark hair. He rushed to end of the couch and when he reached her, knew at once she was dead. He squatted and placed a gentle finger on her neck to check for a pulse, confirming what he suspected. Her once beautiful dark eyes were now hazy with death.

He looked up to find AB craning her neck to look into the space. "Stay there, AB...she's gone."

He heard a sharp gasp followed by a moan. "What? You mean she's dead, Coop? What happened?"

He glanced around the space noting the disarray and items strewn about the floor. "I don't know," he said, straightening and retracing his steps to the backdoor. He wrapped AB in his arms and whispered, "I'm so sorry, AB." She shuddered with sobs as he continued to hold her and guide her back to the Jeep. He placed her in the passenger seat and Gus nuzzled her neck.

Coop retrieved his cell phone and put in a call to Ben. "Hey, Ben. I'm at Callie's house with AB. We had an appointment this morning and she didn't show so we came to check on her. She's dead on her couch and her place has been tossed."

He nodded as he listened to Ben. "I know the drill. We'll be here." He recited the address and disconnected.

He saw AB shivering in the seat and shut the door. He hopped in the driver's seat and cranked the engine, turning the heat on full blast. He kept a blanket in the backseat and wrapped it around her. She'd be covered in dog hair, but she'd be warm. "Ben's on his way."

She nodded and sniffed, wiping her nose with the back of her hand. "Callie was worried about something. I should have made her stay at my place." Tears streamed down her face as she continued to shake.

Within minutes, an unmarked police vehicle parked across the street. Coop saw Jimmy and Kate emerge, two of the best detectives on Ben's team. Coop left the Jeep running and met the two in the middle of the street.

"Ben's on his way, but we were close," said Kate. "Tell me what happened."

Coop went through the morning with them, informing them about Callie's request for an emergency meeting. He outlined the timeline and the attempts to contact Callie before they used AB's key to enter the house.

"What did you touch?" asked Jimmy.

"I touched the backdoor, the front door, and checked her pulse. I retraced my steps from the back door to the couch when I left. I made sure AB stayed at the doorway. She didn't come in. I didn't observe any signs of a break-in at either door."

"You wait with AB and we'll go in," said Kate. "The medical examiner is on the way."

Coop stole a handful of tissues from Kate's car and settled back into the Jeep. He took note of Gus panting and turned off the engine. His dog was all but sitting in AB's lap and it was more than warm in the Jeep now. She had her hand on the back of the dog and Coop slipped a wad of tissues between her fingers.

"Thanks," she sniffed and blew her nose. Gus whimpered and put his head across her chest.

"Kate and Jimmy are inside. Ben will be here in a few minutes." He paused and looked at the open back door. "Any idea what this thing was at work that had her so spooked?"

She shook her head. "I've been racking my brain. She said she accidentally came upon something at work and didn't know what to do." She paused and wiped her eyes with the tissues. "It sounded like it was more than just information, an actual object she had. I know she didn't want to do anything to jeopardize her job. She knew it was her last chance."

Ben tapped on Coop's window. Coop opened his door. "I stopped by the Donut Hole and brought you guys some coffee and donuts." He handed the provisions through the opening. "Hey, AB. Sorry about Callie. Are you going to be okay?"

She nodded through her tears. "Yeah, it's just a shock." She wrapped her hands around the warm cup of coffee and inhaled the soothing aroma.

"You two go on back to your office. We'll come by there when we finish up and take your statements and go from there. We'll need to get in touch with her parents."

"I have their contact information," said AB.

Coop dislodged Gus from AB's lap and steadied him in the backseat. "We'll see you in a bit," he said to Ben.

Coop added more wood on the fire when they reached the office. He forced AB to eat a few bites of donut while they waited for Ben. He put a pot of coffee on to brew and called Aunt Camille to let her know he wouldn't be home.

Coop's cell vibrated and he saw a text from Ben asking for the contact information for Callie's parents. After AB retrieved it, he texted it back to Ben and AB stroked Gus's fur while they waited. AB sat in front of the dancing flames, quiet. Her grief palpable.

It was early afternoon when Ben arrived, bearing lunch. He gave AB a hug and deposited the bag of sandwiches and salads on the kitchen table. While they ate, he asked his questions.

After he finished listening to AB recount what she knew, Ben took out his notepad and scribbled in it. "Kate and Jimmy are on their way to talk to Callie's boss. Virginia is handling the notification of her parents."

"AB, Ben's going to need to know everything with regard to Callie's life. Even the stuff she didn't want anyone to know as to why she left Virginia," said Coop. He pointed at her plate of food and tilted his head encouraging her to eat.

She nodded, swallowed a bite, and took a sip of sweet tea. She let out a breath. "Callie was an alcoholic and a drug addict. She'd been sober about a year, but lost her job in Virginia because she embezzled funds. Her parents paid it all back and she got serious about changing her life. She went to AA meetings several times a week. She had an ex-boyfriend, Ollie, who I think was the instigator for most of her troubles. He got her into drugs, I know."

"Do you know how to get in touch with him?" asked Ben.

She shook her head. "He lives in Virginia. He's a banker or something associated with banking."

"We found her cell phone wedged into the cushions of the couch, under her. We're pulling the records and going through her contacts now. We'll look for Ollie. So, besides her substance abuse problems, whatever this thing she discovered at work was, and a deadbeat ex-boyfriend, anything else come to mind?"

"Do you think it was a burglary?" asked AB.

One side of Ben's mouth rose and he said, "I don't think so. No cash or credit cards in her wallet and it looks like there's some empty space in her jewelry box, but the uh, manner in which it looks like she was killed, appears professional."

A soft squeal escaped from AB and her head hung. "What do you mean?"

Ben placed his hand atop hers. "We can't be one hundred percent until Doc Lawrence completes her work, but she said Callie's neck was broken. There were no signs of defensive wounds or even a struggle. It was quick and death was instantaneous. Most burglars don't employ such effective methods. She estimates Callie died around three this morning."

Ben had Coop complete a written statement since he was the one who had entered the premises and found the body. While he was finishing, AB's cell phone rang. She excused herself and answered it.

When she returned a few minutes later, her eyes were filled with fresh tears. "That was Callie's mom. She wants to hire Coop to investigate her death. She said Callie told her what a wonderful friend I was and that I worked for this brilliant detective. She said she wants no expense spared in finding out who killed Callie and why."

Ben looked up from his notebook. "How can I refuse help from a brilliant detective?" He rolled his eyes, but smiled. "Actually, we're swamped. We haven't found anything of substance on the homicide in the park Friday morning. Brilliance aside, I'm happy to have the help."

Coop shrugged his shoulders and gave Ben one of his famous grins. Even AB smiled through her tears. "I told her we'd do it."

"Of course, we'll do it," said Coop.

Ben looked over his notes and said, "You two take the AA meeting connection. We'll pull her finances and phone records and let you know what we learn from Mr. King."

"Did you pull her GPS from her car?" asked Coop.

Ben gritted his teeth through a smile. "Yes, we did. Some of our own brilliant detectives are on it." He put his notebook back in his jacket pocket. "Let's meet tomorrow afternoon and review what we have. Try to get some rest, AB. Again, I'm very sorry."

Ben left and Coop suggested they try and find Callie's sponsor, Hattie Mae. Gus trundled into the backseat and they set out for the church in Belle Meade. On the way, Coop called Aunt Camille, hoping she might know the pastor of the church. As he suspected, she did.

He disconnected and AB couldn't help but smile, recounting the excitement in Camille's voice when she was helping on a case. She persuaded AB to come to Sunday supper and wanted to know all about the developments.

There were a few cars in the parking lot and Coop suspected one of them belonged to Reverend Clark. The two of them opened the sanctuary doors and followed a hallway to the office. The door was open and Coop filled the space. "Reverend Clark?"

The grey-haired man turned his kind face to meet Coop's. "Yes, how may I help you?"

Coop extended his hand and said, "I'm Cooper Harrington. I think you know my Aunt Camille. I'm a private detective and this is my assistant, Annabelle."

Reverend Clark shook Coop's hand with enthusiasm. "I've known Camille for years. She helps us every year on our fundraiser event. Lovely woman. What can I do for you?"

Coop explained they were investigating the death of a former classmate and friend, Calista Baxter. He summarized the events and the fact she was a regular attendee of the AA meetings at the church. "We're hoping to speak with her sponsor, a woman named Hattie Mae."

"Oh, yes, I know Hattie Mae. She's been a sponsor to many and a wonderful role model. She's a member here at the church. Let me get you her information." He thumbed through a binder of papers and scribbled out a phone number and address. "I realize a tenant of the organization is the anonymity, but in a case like this I'm sure Hattie Mae won't mind."

"Thank you, Reverend. We appreciate your time."

"Don't be a stranger. You two are welcome anytime. Give your aunt my best." He waved as they left the office.

"Let's just drive over to her house. I always get more in person than on the phone."

AB nodded in agreement and keyed Hattie Mae's information into her phone. They made their way to a condominium complex on Hillsboro Pike. Coop dialed Hattie Mae's number from the parking lot and when she answered explained he was a private detective working in conjunction with the police and needed to ask her a few questions about Callie.

She agreed without hesitation and invited them to her second-floor condo. She met them at the door, the smell of coffee, baking, and Christmas greeted them. She led them into the living area and offered them fresh cookies, but they declined. When Coop introduced Annabelle, Hattie Mae's eyes brightened. "You're her friend, AB. She always speaks so highly of you. So glad to meet you."

Tears swam in AB's eyes as she smiled and shook the woman's hand. With gentle words, Coop explained why they were there and informed Hattie Mae of Callie's murder. Hattie Mae clutched her hand to her chest in disbelief.

"I just met with her for coffee yesterday morning." Hattie Mae's voice shook when she spoke.

"I'm sorry to bring you such bad news, but we need to find out what you might know that could help. For instance, did she mention anything about a problem at work?"

Hattie Mae looked across the room, lost in thought. After a few moments she said, "Callie was so concerned about keeping her job. She told me she had caught her boss and his assistant in a compromising position at work last week. She was terribly nervous she was going to get in trouble for discovering their dalliance. Yesterday she mentioned she was stressed about a work situation, but when I quizzed her, she said it wasn't about Mr. King and his affair. It was something new. She wouldn't tell me anything specific."

"What about her ex-boyfriend, Ollie?" asked AB.

"I know from listening to her, he's a scoundrel. He was one of the factors that led Callie to drugs. She was already an alcoholic, but the drug addiction brought about more misery." She shook her head. "She's been doing so well."

"Was she close to anyone in the meetings? Did she have any problems with anyone?" asked Coop.

Hattie Mae shook her head. "No, she kept to herself for the most part. I think she was still embarrassed and didn't like to share much of herself. She was open with me, but wasn't close to anyone else."

Coop gave her his card and asked her to call if she remembered anything else related to Callie.

Hattie Mae gripped AB's hand. "She was so thankful for you. She couldn't believe you never judged her and accepted her as you did. You're a wonderful friend."

Tears trickled down AB's face as she hugged the older woman. "Thank you."

"Please pass my condolences to her family," said Hattie Mae, leading them to the door. "She'll be missed."

Coop put his arm around AB's shoulders as they walked down the stairs to the Jeep. "How about we swing by your place and get a bag. You can stay at Camille's tonight."

She rested her head against his shoulder and nodded. He saw the exhaustion in her eyes and made no effort to fill the silence on the ride to her house. Gus parked himself between them and leaned onto her shoulder to let her stroke his neck.

Coop followed AB through the door of her house and waited in her spotless living room while she packed an overnight bag. He admired the small tabletop tree she had on display and the mantle decorations.

She returned holding hangers poking out of a garment bag and carrying a small suitcase. Coop grabbed both of them and stowed them in the Jeep while she made sure the house was locked. She climbed into the seat and said, "Thanks for offering. I could stay here, but I'd rather be around people."

"Anytime, AB. Anytime." He gave her knee a squeeze as he backed out of her driveway.

4

A towering tree filled the space behind her as Aunt Camille welcomed them at the door. She bustled through the house, chattering as she led AB to one of the many guest rooms. It was lit with soft lamps, a plush throw resembling a mink was cascading across the foot of the bed, and a small vase of fresh flowers was on the nightstand, their intoxicating perfume mingled with the scent of Camille's supper. A Christmas tree, adorned with floral themed decorations, stood in the corner. The room was decorated in soft shades of peach, taupe, and beige and was larger than AB's house. Coop hung her garment bag in the closet and set her suitcase below it.

"If you need anything, just let me know. Towels are in the closet in the bathroom and there's a whole drawer of soaps and lotions. Use whatever you want," said Camille, patting AB's arm. "Supper's almost ready, but take all the time y'all need."

Coop followed his aunt out the door and closed it behind him. He noticed Gus wasn't with them and opened the door a crack. "Is Gus in there with you?"

"Yes, he's fine. I'll bring him in a few minutes." He listened to her murmuring to the dog when he closed the door. He smiled with relief when he heard a hint of her usual cheer. Gus was a good boy.

Coop slid onto a chair at the large island and watched his aunt add her own touches to the meal. Mrs. Henderson, Camille's cook and housekeeper was off on Sundays, giving Camille the opportunity to exercise her cooking muscles. While he watched his aunt orchestrate the food, he brought her up to speed on Callie's murder and begged her not to ask too many questions while AB was within earshot.

She frowned. "I know how to behave, young man. I just want to help, if I can."

"You were a big help with Reverend Clark. He said to give you his best."

She perked up as she placed a pat of butter atop a mountain of mashed potatoes. "He's a dear man." She popped biscuits, hot from the oven, into a basket. "Get the oven mitts and carry the chicken out to the table," she said, pointing to the oven.

She soon had the table covered with food and pronounced it ready when AB and Gus padded into the dining room. "Y'all are just in time. Sit down and make yourself comfortable." Camille poured them all glasses of sweet tea before she took her chair.

Coop loaded his plate with helpings from each dish and covered the stuffing and potatoes with steaming gravy. Aunt Camille made the best applesauce. He took a huge helping of it before passing it to AB. He dug into his plate and said, "This is all delicious, Aunt Camille."

She radiated delight in his compliments. After filling her plate, she regarded AB. "Tell us about Callie's family up in Virginia. What do you know about them?"

"They live in McLean and I remember going there when we were in school a few times. I haven't been there since. They have a large estate. I remember the place had ten bathrooms. It's gorgeous, but beyond lavish. I know Callie had been staying on the property in the guest house until she moved here in

September." She paused and took another forkful of mashed potatoes. "This food tastes great, Camille."

"I'm so pleased you like it. I have peach cobbler in the oven for dessert." Camille gave her a conspiratorial wink. "Isn't it one of your favorites?"

AB smiled and she raised her brows. "I'm never going to want to leave if you keep this up." She ate several more bites. "Callie's mother is the source of the family wealth. She's a Campbell. Not that her dad is a slouch, but Carter worked for a living as a lawyer and judge. He's retired now and does some consulting. Her mom's family has deep roots in the Virginia political scene. Lots of senators and governors in her lineage. Callie's the baby, with two older brothers. One is set to be the next counsel to the governor in Virginia and the other is a judge with his eye on the Virginia Supreme Court."

"That must have put a lot of pressure on Callie," said Coop, reaching for another biscuit. "Sounds like a lot of high expectations and competition to contend with inside the family estate."

AB nodded. "I think it's why Callie came back here. She knew she was an embarrassment to her family and it was easier on all of them if she was somewhere else. Her presence there served as a constant reminder of her failures. I know she was lonely here, though." A tear leaked from the corner of her eye and she dabbed it with her napkin.

"Family relationships can be so complicated," said Camille. "It's difficult when a child doesn't fit the mold the parents have made."

"We've got to figure out who would have benefited from Callie's death. The motive will lead us to her killer," said Coop, pushing his empty plate away from the edge of the table.

"Especially to have a professional involved," said AB.

Camille's eyebrows went up and Coop explained about Ben's theory of the killing being carried out by a pro. "Oh, my," she said when he finished.

A frown appeared on AB's face. "I know Ollie's parents are also wealthy, so he'd have access to money to hire someone. I can't imagine Callie's own family, but I don't know them well."

"Do you think she could have been dipping her toe back into drugs?" asked Coop.

Alarm flickered across her face and AB gave her head a vigorous shake. "No, no. She didn't exhibit any signs." She recalled the tight grip Callie kept on her tote and her unwillingness to check the thing. Callie's dress was always impeccable and the oversized tote was like wearing tennis shoes with her evening gown. "She was overprotective of her tote bag at the gala on Friday night. I couldn't believe she brought it with her. She wouldn't check it and kept it with her even on our scavenger hunt."

"Let me look at your photos from the event again." She manipulated the screen and handed him her phone. He enlarged one photo of the two of them and said, "Yeah, I see it there in her hand. Even I can tell it doesn't go with her dress."

Camille was craning her neck to catch a glimpse and her hand, sparkling with diamond rings, extended across the table. Coop looked up and passed her the phone. "Oh, the bag is dreadful. It's more like a work bag, not at all suitable for such a lovely dress. You both look gorgeous, by the way."

Coop texted Ben a quick note to check the tote bag and analyze it for any trace evidence of drugs. "I know you don't want to believe she was using, AB, but we need to look at every angle."

She hung her head and placed her fork on her plate. "I get it, but I honestly don't think she was back into drugs. She told me she was tempted to drink often, but had no interest in drugs."

"It's just one thing to check out so we can eliminate it. Same with her family and the creepy ex-boyfriend. I'm inclined to think it was related to the work issue or problem, but I don't want to get tunnel vision."

Camille went about clearing the dishes, happy to find most of the food on AB's plate eaten. They agreed they were too stuffed to eat dessert and elected to wait. While AB and Camille worked on cleaning up the dishes, Coop slipped into his home office and emailed a contract for services to Callie's mother, Arden Campbell Baxter, via her personal assistant. He expressed his sincere condolences and let her know he and Annabelle were working on Callie's case and would be in contact with an update on Monday.

He rejoined the ladies in his aunt's favorite sitting room, the one that always made him feel like he was inside Barbie's dream house. Camille had installed several Christmas trees throughout the house and this one was decked out in pink and silver. He fixed himself a cup of tea from the tea service on the table and squeezed in next to AB. He was a big guy, a man's-man, drinking out of a dainty flowered cup, surrounded by all things pink, atop a rose brocade settee. Even Gus was humiliated and put his paw over his eyes as he watched the threesome from his fluffy dog bed—a fuzzy pink miniature sofa.

Despite all his efforts with blackout blinds, nature sounds, lavender pillow inserts, and a collection of essential oils, Coop didn't sleep. He had the best smelling bedroom of any bachelor in the Nashville area, but sleep continued to elude him. He had been diagnosed as a chronic insomniac. The symptoms originated in college, when his parents split up, and had worsened over time. He refused to take medication, so suffered through the sleepless nights. He worked most of the night, researching Callie and her family.

He emerged from his wing of the house after an invigorating shower. The appealing aroma of warm cinnamon guided him to the kitchen. He found Mrs. Henderson preparing breakfast and her husband on his way outside to tidy the grounds. "Morning, Mr. Cooper," said the man, tipping his hat as he opened the door.

"Hey, Mr. Henderson. How ya doing?"

"Good day to work the soil after all the rain. You have yourself a fine day, Mr. Cooper."

Coop helped himself to the one cup of real coffee he was permitted each morning. He made sure to use the largest mug he could find. Gus had abandoned him in favor of AB last night and Coop saw no trace of either of them. He took his coffee and the paper and perched at the granite countertop, watching the news as he scanned the headlines.

The police, via a statement from Ben, were asking for help from anyone who may have witnessed activity in the hour around sunrise at the Bells Bend Loop Trail where Avery Logan had been found shot. A number was given for anonymous tips as well as a number to speak with detectives.

He continued to scan and saw a small article again citing Ben, who informed the reporter they were investigating the hit and run death of the bike messenger, but did not have a suspect. Coop flipped through the rest of the paper and said, "Tough week for Ben. Unsolved cases make him nuts and now he'll have Callie's."

He heard Gus's nails on the wooden floors and soon felt him lean against his leg, tail thwacking the chair. "The traitor has returned, huh?" said Coop, looking into his happy brown eyes. The dog's nose edged higher and he sniffed. Coop smiled, knowing Gus smelled the fresh cinnamon rolls in the oven.

By the time he finished the paper, AB emerged from her room and rolled her eyes when she saw Coop's t-shirt. It read, *You are about to exceed the limits of my medication.* She was wearing a blouse and jacket with jeans. "I thought we might have to interview people today. Do you really want to wear that shirt?"

Coop looked down at his chest. "I can put a jacket on over it, if we go anywhere important."

Mrs. Henderson hollered out, "Breakfast is ready for y'all."

Gus understood those words and dashed into the dining room, parking himself at the end of the buffet. Coop eased out of his chair and motioned to AB to go ahead of him. "How'd you sleep?" he asked.

"Like a rock. I think the day caught up with me."

"You look good. I mean like you're rested." He paused and then added, "You always look nice, AB. I just meant you look better than you did yesterday." He winced and gritted his teeth. "Not that you looked bad yesterday." He stopped and then chuckled. "I can't seem to make a coherent sentence, sorry. Where did my dog sleep?"

She grinned and looked at Gus, who was smiling. "Uh, well, he started out on the floor, but ended up on the bed. I think he was cold."

Coop shook his head and eyed Gus. "He's definitely got your number, AB."

"You realize we missed the gym yesterday. We should go today."

"Tomorrow, I'm already dressed." He winked and made a production of showcasing his t-shirt.

"I'm going to hold you to it. Tomorrow, seven o'clock. How about you? Did you get any sleep last night?"

"Maybe an hour or two, not much. I spent the night online researching Callie and her family."

"Learn anything?" AB loaded her plate with fruit, eggs, and a cinnamon roll.

"Not much, except they're more than connected. Lots of hobnobbing with politicians in DC. They host a ton of swanky events in their home and Carter is consulting for the US Department of Justice. The brother appears to be a shoe-in for the counsel to the governor appointment and the other is a well-respected judge. I didn't find anything negative about the Baxter clan. Nothing online about Callie's misadventures, so they have the juice to keep it out of the public eye."

Coop stuffed a piece of cinnamon roll in his mouth and AB slipped a morsel to Gus. She took a bite herself and sipped her coffee. "Mmm. It's been so long since I've had one of these. They taste even more fattening than they smell."

They finished breakfast and left Aunt Camille to sleep in while they made their way to the office. After he got a fire going, Coop sent Ben a text to check on the status of Callie's case.

An hour later his phone rang. Ben told him they'd have the phone data and GPS information from Callie's car in the afternoon, but didn't have the manpower to analyze it, with the other two pending cases. He said the autopsy confirmed the time and manner of death they had suspected. He wanted AB to go through the crime scene photos and determine if anything was missing.

"We can handle the phone and GPS data. I can swing by and pick it up this afternoon. I'll have AB look at the photos and we could get together tomorrow and assess what we know," offered Coop.

Ben's voice did little to hide his exhaustion. "Sounds like a plan. We can't catch a break on the homicide in the park. All the techs are tied up trying to piece together video footage from downtown to trace the movements of the hit and run vehicle."

After he hung up from Ben, Coop kept busy with the background check and AB drafted the preliminary report from the work Madison and Ross were completing. Coop left in the early afternoon, promising to return with crime scene photos and data, plus lunch.

While he was out, AB took a call from Arden Baxter's assistant. She wanted AB to know they were planning a service for Callie on Saturday. It would be a private burial, but AB was invited to the reception and Callie's parents insisted she stay as a guest at their home. She was also welcome to bring a companion. The assistant asked AB to keep her informed of her travel arrangements so the family could send a car to pick her up, should she arrive by plane or train.

After taking notes, AB hung up the phone and searched for flights. When Coop returned with lunch and a folder from Ben, he found her engrossed in her computer screen. She told him about the call from Virginia and the fact she didn't want to drive ten hours, so she was looking for flights.

"Book two seats. I'm not sure if we'll have the case solved by Saturday, but I'd like to go and meet her family, regardless," said Coop.

Relief flooded her face. "That would be great. I was dreading going alone." She selected a flight leaving on Friday and once she had it confirmed she texted the assistant with the flight information. Her phone emitted an immediate ping with a reply to let her know a car and driver would be waiting to collect AB and Coop at Dulles on Friday afternoon.

"Wow, they're on the ball," said AB, relaying the text to Coop.

Over soup and salads, they studied the crime scene photos from Callie's cottage. Ben took deliberate steps to exclude any photos of Callie's body. AB wiped her eyes with a napkin several times while she pored over the details of each shot. While they were still at the kitchen table, Gus made a dash for the back door moments before Aunt Camille came into view. She had a plate of her famous pecan chocolate chunk cookies in her hand and Gus's nose was working overtime sniffing at it.

"Oh, dear, now Gus, go on." She held the cookies higher and out of his reach. "I thought you two could use a pick me up," she said, smiling and placing the plate in the middle of the table. She blew air from her lips which caused the feathers in her hat to flutter. She shucked her fur coat and helped herself to a glass of sweet tea. "It's warm and toasty in here, y'all."

Coop pulled out a chair for her and she busied herself looking at the photos strewn across the table. "Oh, my, what a dreadful mess the scoundrel left behind." She made clucking noises as she went through each photo. "What a shame."

"Except for some jewelry, I can't tell if anything's missing," said AB. "I know she had an elaborate diamond necklace and matching earrings, which I don't see. She also had lovely pearls and a large sapphire pendant surrounded by diamonds, with matching earrings. Her diamond rings and her TAG Heuer watch aren't in the jewelry box. She didn't wear it often, preferring the Movado for work. Both are beyond my budget."

Coop searched the report for personal effects. "She was found wearing a Movado watch, one diamond ring, and a diamond pendant on a gold chain. That's all."

"I guess the creep didn't notice those items, but the missing jewelry is all high dollar."

Camille bit into a still warm cookie, oozing chocolate and said, "I would think it if was a burglary, he would have taken the jewelry she was wearing."

Coop nodded as he scanned the photos for the umpteenth time. "I'm going to guess the assailant is a man, based on the method used to kill Callie. So, either he was there for something else and the jewelry was an opportunistic find or he was interrupted or spooked before he could get to other items, like electronics."

"If he was on foot, maybe he could only take the small items and was in a hurry," said AB.

"Could be, but with her so tense about whatever item she had discovered, I'm inclined to think he had another focus and helped himself to the jewelry as a bonus." Coop shook his head. "Burglars usually stake out a house and go in when it's vacant.

Her car was outside and her television would have been on and the light from it visible. He knew she was home."

"I'll ask if her family has any photos or descriptions of the jewelry and get them to Ben so he can put them in the system for pawn shops and the like," said AB, clearing the table and heading to her desk. Gus remained near the plate of cookies, content to rest under the table.

Camille left for her hair appointment and Coop suggested they use his conference table to analyze Callie's GPS data. They concentrated on her activities the day of the murder and worked backwards. The data contained coordinates, which AB plugged into the computer to find addresses. Coop made a list on his large white board with times and places. They spent the afternoon logging the information from her car for the last ten days.

It was well after dark and the time had passed to close the office. They hadn't yet finished with the set of coordinates. Coop gathered the data and snapped a photo of the white board with his phone. Gus loaded into the Jeep and AB followed them to Aunt Camille's house.

Camille invited AB to join them for supper, anticipating they would be working late on the case. When they arrived, Coop excused himself to update Callie's mother on the progress before they gathered at the table.

Mrs. Henderson had prepared a delicious smelling pot roast with roasted veggies. The two women were waiting for Coop to join them and Camille was doing her best to cajole AB to stay another night when he returned. "Callie's mom is…efficient. She's more than capable of containing her emotions. She did say she was glad we were both coming to the reception for Callie. I told her we were in the midst of tracking Callie's movements and conducting interviews."

AB nodded as she served herself and passed the platter to Coop. "From what I remember Mrs. Baxter was always cool and business like. It's been a long time since I've been around her, but when I visited, she never appeared relaxed. Always dressed for business, high-end and classy, but never exuded warmth or fun."

Coop helped himself to a warm biscuit and heaped some of the leftover applesauce on his plate. "Yeah, that's the feeling I get when I talk to her. She said her assistant is emailing photos of Callie's jewelry. It was insured, so they have the records." He added butter to his biscuit and said, "She also gave me Ollie's name, so we can check him out."

"From what Callie said, he's a waste of gravity," said AB.

Coop steered the conversation to other topics. "Your hair looks pretty, Aunt Camille. How were the girls today?"

She smiled and moved her hand to the side of her head to give her wisps of white a gentle pat. Her hair had thinned as she aged and she went to the salon every other day to get it styled and fluffed to cover her pink scalp. "They were fine. Of course, we discussed poor Callie. They had never met her, but can't believe such a thing took place in such a safe neighborhood. Some of the single girls are concerned."

"I don't think it was a random attack," said Coop. "Tell them not to worry." He tried again to change the topic. "Did AB tell you she's going to the Bahamas with her family for Christmas?"

"The Bahamas?" Aunt Camille frowned and said, "That doesn't sound very Christmassy."

"It's a change from the traditional, that's for sure. I'm looking forward to it," said AB.

"I've got so much to do to get ready for Christmas. I'm not sure where the time has gone this year. Coop and I are spending Christmas here and I've invited a few friends." Mrs. Henderson appeared to clear the table and brought out some of the leftover peach cobbler, warmed and paired with scoops of vanilla ice cream.

"I'm sure you'll make it a wonderful Christmas." AB eyed her helping of dessert. "Oh, my goodness. I'll never be able to wear a swimsuit if I keep this up."

After finishing their cobbler, Coop and AB holed up in his home office and dissected Callie's activities, as dictated by her GPS. They worked to complete the entire list of coordinates and attempted to identify each address along with a reason for Callie to be at each location. Coop used the computer at his desk and AB used a laptop from her corner of the couch. After hours of tedious work, Coop looked up and saw AB had fallen asleep. Gus was snoozing at the other end of the couch.

With gentle hands, Coop displaced the laptop from under her hands and covered her with a cashmere blanket. He tiptoed out of the office and closed the door connecting his bedroom suite to the office. He dropped into bed, feeling the soreness in his neck and shoulders from hunching over a computer for hours. His eyes stung from squinting at the screen. He closed them, trusting the exhaustion would result in a few precious hours of sleep.

5

Tuesday afternoon Ben arrived at Coop's office and the threesome sat around the conference table and summed up what they knew about Callie's activities. Coop ran through the addresses they had researched from the GPS. "We think we can account for all of them with the exception of her visit to the Hilton late Friday afternoon."

Ben frowned. "She didn't mention anything, AB?"

She shook her head. "No. She was a few minutes late getting to the event at the library, but blamed it on her hair."

Ben scribbled in his notebook. "We'll need to double check with her boss and find out if she had any reason to be at the Hilton for work." He flipped back to a page and said, "So, the ex-boyfriend, Oliver Talbot, works for a financial firm in Virginia and has no record. His parents are wealthy, not in the same league as the Baxters, but close. I contacted his boss and Ollie arrived in Nashville on Saturday. He's attending a conference and staying near Vanderbilt. The hotel is about two miles from Callie's house. Jimmy and Kate are going to check it out."

"What did Mr. King have to say?" asked Coop.

"No problems with Callie at work. Said she was a great

lawyer, talented, responsible. We asked about his indiscretions with the assistant and he waffled a bit, but admitted to it. Says it was a moment of weakness, not an ongoing affair. Kate talked to the assistant and she caved right away, crying about not telling her husband."

"Do you think either of them would have had Callie killed?" asked AB.

Ben pursed his lips. "I don't think so, but I still want to dig a bit deeper into it."

"She didn't have any problems with anyone at the party at Vanderbilt, right?" asked Coop, giving AB a quizzical look.

She shook her head. "Not that I can think of, except for Trixie. She's always been a rival of Callie's. She was her usual charming self and had to rub it into Callie that she married Chandler and has a wonderful life. Callie dated Chandler in college." She shook her head. "It's probably nothing, but she said she wanted to make sure Callie wasn't there to seduce Chandler." She sighed and added, "She was never out of my sight except on the scavenger hunt. Despite Trixie, Callie enjoyed the evening and was more relaxed at the end of the night."

"We're analyzing the tote bag we found at her place. There was nothing visible and the contents didn't reveal any surprises. We don't expect results until next week."

"I still don't think you'll find any drugs. I'm confident she had conquered her addiction." AB wiped an errant tear from her cheek.

Coop put his hand atop hers. "It's just something we need to check, especially with Ollie in the picture." He turned his attention to Ben. "Any way I can tag along on the interview with Ollie? I'd like to get a read on him myself."

"Sure, I'll let Kate know to give you a call." He tapped a text into his phone.

He scanned his messages on the phone and stood. "We put the jewelry out to all the local pawn shops, but so far haven't had anyone call with information. I gotta run. I've got a meeting on one of my other cases—the poor guy shot while running."

"I'll see you Friday for breakfast. We've got a flight later in the morning, but that'll be a good time to catch up on the latest."

Ben nodded. "Unless something pops before then."

"I'm going to pay a visit to the Hilton and try to learn about Callie's stop there," said Coop, walking Ben to the door.

Kate arranged to meet Coop at Ollie's hotel, where she planned to surprise him as soon as the last session of the day ended. They perched on a bench outside the conference center until Mr. Talbot appeared.

Kate and Coop rose and she intercepted Ollie with her badge displayed. "Oliver Talbot, Nashville Police. We need a word with you." Kate's voice was loud and authoritative.

"Uh, sure. What's this about?" His eyes darted from them to the throng of men and women spilling from the doors of the conference center.

"We need to talk with you about Callie Baxter."

"Oh, man. She turned me into the cops for calling her? What a bitch."

Kate's eyes widened. She guided Ollie to a sitting area, away from the noise. The three sat and Kate asked, "When did you last contact Callie?"

"I've been texting and calling her off and on since I got to Nashville. She was supposed to stop by and meet me here."

"When did you arrive in Nashville?" asked Coop.

Ollie shrugged. "Uh, I guess it was around three o'clock on Saturday."

"What did you do that night?" asked Coop.

"I walked around, drove downtown, and visited a few bars. Not much, really."

"What time did you return to your room for the night?

Ollie glared at Coop. "Why? What's this about?"

"Just answer the question," said Kate.

Ollie looked from Coop to Kate, both of whom bore down on him with an unyielding gaze.

"Um, I guess it would have been a little past midnight when I got back here. I'm not sure of the exact time."

Kate pulled several sheets of paper from a folder. "According to the hotel you checked in Saturday afternoon at 3:48 and the last time your card key was used to enter your room was 3:33 in the morning on Sunday."

Ollie ran his hands through his hair and fidgeted in his chair. His eyes flicked across the hallway. "Oh, yeah, I ran out for some beer. I forgot about that."

Kate continued her stare. "Where did you go to buy beer?"

"Uh, some convenience store down the street."

"Do you have a receipt?"

His eyes widened. "Uh, no. I, uh, paid cash."

"What time was this?" asked Kate.

"I guess around three."

"Let's take a walk and you can show us the store." Kate slid her papers back in the folder and stood.

"Um, right now?"

"Yeah, right now." She motioned for him to lead the way.

He gripped his leather case and trudged to the lobby. "It looks like I'll need a coat."

"I'll walk you to your room to get it," offered Coop.

While the two men were gone, Kate checked with the security office and requested their security tapes for early Sunday morning. They agreed to copy the data to a DVD for her and have it ready within the hour.

Ollie returned, his face filled with dread. Coop walked behind him and said, "We're ready."

Ollie led them outside the main doors and turned left. They

walked a bit more than a block and Kate pointed to the lit sign of the convenience store on the corner. "Is this it?"

Ollie looked around and said, "Yeah, I think so."

Kate looked at her watch. "So, it took us three minutes to walk here. You say you were here around three o'clock. How come it took you thirty minutes to get back to the hotel?"

She saw his eyes flash in the light from the store. "I, uh, don't know. I guess I just took my time."

"Describe the clerk on duty."

"What? I don't remember."

"Man or woman?" asked Kate.

"Uh, man."

"What else?"

"I didn't pay attention. Just bought the beer and left."

"Okay, let's go back to the hotel."

They trudged back in silence. Kate motioned Ollie to an empty chair in the lobby. She opened her notebook and recapped his story. "Anything else you want to add or anything we need to change?"

He shook his head. "What's this have to do with Callie?"

"Callie Baxter was murdered early Sunday morning. We're interviewing anyone associated with her."

Ollie's head slumped into his hands. "Murdered? How?"

"She was strangled in her home."

"Had you ever been to her home, Ollie?" asked Coop.

Ollie shook his head back and forth. "No, I didn't know where she lived. I just had her phone number." His voice cracked. "I wanted to get back together with her. I was hoping to do that on this trip."

"Had she expressed an interest in getting back together with you?" asked Kate.

"No...I wanted to talk to her and ask her to give me one more chance." Tears ran down his face. "I can't believe she's dead."

"We'll be in touch, Ollie. Don't leave town," said Kate.

They left him in the lobby, holding one of Kate's cards. Coop left her to pick up the DVD and she promised to call him in the morning once she had a chance to view it.

When Coop exited through the lobby doors, Ollie was still in the chair, holding his head in his hands.

Coop picked up some donuts and stopped by Ben's office the next morning. Ben was in a meeting, but he found Kate at her desk. "Hey, Coop. I was just going to call you." She motioned to a chair and took a pastry, smiling at Coop's t-shirt. Today's read *I'm not arguing, just explaining why I'm right.*

"What's the latest?"

"Well, the video shows our friend Ollie leaving the hotel around seven in the evening. He takes his car and returns at 3:25 in the morning. We saw that on the garage camera. No footage of him leaving through the lobby doors at all."

"Any video at the convenience store?"

She tore off another piece of donut. "Nope. Cameras don't work. Since they don't sell beer after midnight, I figured it was all a lie, but wanted to determine how far Ollie would go with the story. He's up to something because I also have a message to call a Benton Hamlin. He's an attorney representing our good buddy Ollie."

Coop smiled. "Now why would Ollie need an attorney?"

"'Cause he's guilty of something." She shrugged and offered a weak smile. "No offense, of course."

"None taken."

"I'm going to call the attorney and set up a meeting. I need to resolve Ollie's inconsistencies and him to make sure Ollie doesn't leave town."

"Let me know how it goes. I'm going to take another swipe

at Mr. King and the assistant, just in case there's more to their story. AB and I leave Friday for the memorial."

Kate nodded as she took the last bite. "Yeah, Ben said you guys were going. I'll let you know what I learn." Her desk phone rang and she gave Coop a quick wave.

He used his cell to check in with AB and headed downtown. He presented his card to the receptionist and asked to see Mr. King, explaining he was investigating the death of Callie. She nodded and said, "Of course. Let me ring him. Poor Callie. We all liked her so much."

She murmured into her headset and then turned her attention back to Coop. "Mr. King's assistant, Audrey, will be right with you and take you back to his office."

Coop nodded his thanks and before he could sit down, an attractive redhead appeared. "Mr. Harrington, right this way."

As he followed the alluring scent of her perfume and her shapely figure down the hall, it didn't take much to discover what may have tempted Mr. King. Audrey was stunning. Her short skirt emphasized her long, toned legs and Coop had to concentrate to keep his eyes from drifting to admire the view. She stopped at a set of double doors and opened one, motioning Coop to go through first.

"Mr. King, I have Mr. Harrington for you," she announced.

"Thank you, Audrey, please bring us some refreshments," said the handsome man Coop recognized from the legal circles in Nashville.

Coop extended his hand, "Thanks for meeting with me, Mr. King."

"Please, call me Brandon," he said, shaking Coop's hand. "I understand you're looking into Callie's death."

"Yes, I've been retained by her family."

"They're wonderful people. We're all just devastated about the whole thing. Do you have any leads?"

"A few, but still looking into her movements and who may have had a motive."

Brandon held up his hands. "I know we're on the radar, because of the impropriety Callie witnessed." He shook his head. "Both Audrey and I were wrong and feel horrible about it. I can assure you neither of us would be involved in Callie's death. It was a moment of weakness and it's over."

"Does your wife know about it?"

"No, like I said, it's not an on-going issue." He was interrupted when Audrey returned with a tray of coffee and tea, along with cookies.

She bent over to place them on the table and Coop was treated to a perfect view of her lacey bra and the cleavage spilling out of her blouse. He knew he should avert his eyes, but couldn't bring himself to do it. She was a beautiful woman and dressed to entice the opposite sex.

She offered him a cup of coffee and he squeaked out his thanks, mesmerized by her décolletage and the allure of her sheer black blouse. She handed him the saucer with a quick wink and a sultry smile. She turned her attention to Brandon and passed him a saucer. "Let me know if you need me." She walked away, while both men gazed in admiration.

The door clicked shut and Coop turned his attention to the forbidden cup of coffee in his hand. "I can understand why you were tempted. She's quite appealing."

Brandon smiled as he sipped his coffee. "Yes, she's worked here for four years and I finally surrendered to the desire. I know it was wrong. We'd been working a lot of late nights on a project and the willpower to resist gave way. I've tried to suggest she wear less revealing clothes, but it's a touchy subject and I obviously haven't gotten through to her. I'm not proud of it and neither is she. I suggested I try and find her a spot at another firm. I'm in the process of working a deal to get her on at an all-woman firm."

"Is she angry?"

"Not at all. She's married to a great guy and doesn't want to ruin it. I know she looks like a player, but she's not. That time Callie walked in on us, was the only time she'd responded in such a way. She's flirtatious, but harmless. I made the first move and she responded in kind. It's a mutual attraction and we both agree it's best if we don't work together." He took another sip of coffee and Coop remained quiet, letting him confess his sins.

"Just so you know, we hadn't…uh, you know, completed the act. When Callie walked in, we were both on the couch. We didn't notice her come in until she gasped. It took us a few minutes to, you know, disengage and get dressed and by then Callie had left. She stumbled on her way out of the room and ran out of here like the place was on fire."

"Did you discuss it with Callie after that night?"

"No. I was ashamed and didn't want to bring it up and from her actions, she was equally embarrassed." He paused and added, "In retrospect, I should have talked to her and cleared the air."

"She was afraid you'd fire her."

Shock traveled across Brandon's face. "I would never fire her. She did nothing wrong. I don't even think she uttered a word about it to anyone here at the office. Neither of us heard any gossip about it."

"I'm sure she didn't say anything. She only told her sponsor at AA. It caused her stress and worry, so she talked about it to help her resist drinking to deal with it."

His broad shoulders sagged. "I'm sorry to have caused Callie any concern," he said, his eyes downcast. "I'm ashamed of my behavior. I love my wife and should have had the strength to resist the attraction. It was unprofessional."

"Has Audrey threatened you about the incident?"

Brandon frowned. "No, of course not. She feels terrible about it."

Coop nodded and finished his coffee. "Did Callie have any issues or problems with anyone at work or clients?"

"Not at all. She was well-liked and did a good job. She kept to herself and was quiet. Not involved in any office gossip or politics."

"Would she have any reason to be at the Hilton last Friday?"

Brandon squinted and looked at his planner on the desk. "Chief Mason asked me about the Hilton yesterday." He shook his head, "Not that I can think of. We don't have any clients there and most of what Callie did was at her desk. She ran to the courthouse and a few other law offices, but the Hilton isn't a place we would do business or have clients staying right now."

Coop stood and extended his hand. "Thanks for your time and the coffee." He made his way to the door and stopped. "I'm going to have to interview Audrey as well. I hope you understand."

"Yes, of course. Feel free to use my office. I'm due at a meeting in the conference room in a few minutes."

Coop stepped through the door and approached Audrey's desk, where the scent of her perfume permeated the space and tickled his nose. "I've got a few questions for you and Mr. King said we could use his office."

She blushed and pressed some buttons on her phone before vacating her desk. Mr. King was coming out of his office as they entered. "I'll be in the conference room."

Coop took a deep breath as he followed Audrey into the office and willed his mind and eyes to stay on topic. He sat as far away from her as possible and asked her many of the same questions he asked Mr. King.

She gave him the same story about the night Callie found them on the couch. Through tears she told him how sorry she was. "It was just the one time. We were both exhausted and let our hormones get the best of us."

"Did you tell your husband about the incident?"

The color left her face. "No. Brandon and I agreed it was a slip and it would never happen again. We didn't want to worry either of our spouses." She went on to volunteer the information Mr. King had shared about finding her another position. "It's a better job with a raise, so I think it will work out well for me." She wiped her eyes with a tissue. "I've learned my lesson. I'm also so sorry about Callie. She was nothing but professional and didn't run around the office and talk about what she saw."

"Do you know of any reason Callie would have visited the Hilton after work on Friday? Was she running papers for the office or anything?"

Audrey shook her head and her thick curls bounced across her shoulders. "No, I checked the client log and delivery log for anything related to the Hilton and found nothing. It must have been personal."

Coop stood and thanked her for her time. Not trusting himself to get any closer to Audrey than necessary, he left a card on the table between them and asked her to contact him if she remembered anything of significance.

"Thank you, Mr. Harrington. It's been a pleasure." She reached for the card giving him one more generous glimpse of cleavage.

Coop shook his head and smirked as he made his way to the lobby. Audrey was a natural flirt and a magnet for men. Brandon King would be well served to get her out of his practice as soon as possible.

6

Coop used the valet at the Hilton to park the Jeep. His stomach growled reminding him he had missed lunch. He walked to Broadway for a burger at one of his favorite spots before tackling the hotel. He called Kate while he was finishing his fries and asked if she could pave the way with security for him. He wanted to get a look at any footage they had from the time of Callie's visit on Friday.

After making his notes related to his visit with Brandon King, he walked back to the Hilton and made his way to the security office. Kate made good on her promise. The supervisor was expecting Coop.

He offered Coop a chair and showed him how to work the software so he could scroll through the video from Friday afternoon. Thinking Callie was conserving money, Coop concentrated on the self-parking area, but struck out. He moved to the valet lanes and witnessed her car pull up at 4:48. She talked with the valet for several minutes, gesturing with her hands and retrieving an envelope from her tote bag. The valet nodded and pointed. She pulled her car forward and left it in a spot outside the entrance. He saw her put the envelope back in her bag and hurry into the lobby. He continued to watch the video and saw her return to the car at 5:03, tip the valet, and drive away.

He stopped the video and asked the supervisor if he could get a copy of it and also asked to view the cameras inside the lobby area, so he could pick up Callie's movements once she entered the hotel. The supervisor clicked a few screens and showed him the group of cameras installed in the lobby area.

Coop scrolled through several screens until he spotted Callie and watched her go through the lobby and take a side door where she exited back outdoors. She went past the Hilton property and kept going down the sidewalk. Then at 5:01 she came back from the same direction and used the side door to enter the Hilton. She took the same route and exited through the lobby doors and back to the valet where she picked up her car. Coop requested the footage be added to his DVD of the valet area and thanked the man for his time.

Coop wandered out to the valet stand and saw the man he recognized from the video footage. He approached and asked the valet if he remembered Callie parking her car to deliver an envelope. Coop described Callie's BMW and showed the man a picture of her.

The valet's eyes sparked with recognition. "Oh, yes. Pretty lady. She said she had to drop something off and would be right out."

"Did you get a look at the envelope she had in her bag?"

He shook his head. "No, sir. I didn't pay any attention. She came back in a few minutes and gave me a tip. It was no big deal. We're not supposed to, but we had room and she seemed like a nice girl. Just in a hurry."

Coop gave him a card and asked him to call if he remembered anything else.

By the time he got back to the office it was close to five. Gus greeted him at the back door and he found AB shutting down her computer. "Did you learn anything new today?"

Coop shook his head as he petted Gus. "Not much. I talked to Mr. King and his attractive assistant, Audrey." He wiggled his eyebrows. "She's got a fabulous figure and is quite the flirt."

She rolled her eyes. "You are such a…*boy*. So, beyond enjoying the physical attributes of Audrey, what did you gain from your visit?"

"My gut tells me they had nothing to do with Callie's death." He put the DVD from the Hilton on the coffee table and sat on the couch. "They were both forthcoming and had the same story. I guess they could have cooked it up, but I believe them. They both said Callie being at the Hilton had nothing to do with her work."

"Hmm," she said. "I wonder what she was doing there."

"She used the valet to park her car for about fifteen minutes." He picked up the DVD. "I watched the video footage. It shows her going through the Hilton and back out down the street and then she returns a few minutes later and goes back inside and out through the lobby. She showed the valet an envelope from her tote bag, which wasn't found in the bag when the police inventoried it."

"So, what was in the envelope and where did it go?"

"I'll get the DVD to Ben and request his techs enhance it, but I don't have much hope."

"She said whatever was bothering her was something she came across at work. Maybe it was whatever was in the envelope. We need to scour all the cases she was working on for Mr. King. Maybe it has nothing to do with the affair, but something she discovered in the course of her work."

"I'm happy to go back to the office and interrogate Audrey… and Mr. King, in depth."

She slapped the back of his head. "Enough already. Maybe I need to go and get a look at this woman who has such power over the weaker sex."

~

Thursday morning AB secured them an appointment with Mr. King, who was willing to let them examine all of Callie's work products and files. Audrey escorted them to Callie's cubicle. As they walked behind her, Coop elbowed AB and raised his eyebrows. "See what I mean," he whispered, taking in today's cream-colored short skirt and another sheer blouse. AB rolled her eyes and gave him a scowl.

They spent the morning at Callie's desk going through file after file. As they scoured the files, AB took notes of the names of the clients and the case descriptions. Callie was working on several cases, none of them involving serious amounts of money or controversial subjects. Most of her work was mundane, even boring. None of the clients were important people and most of her work involved research.

Coop knew Ben's team had searched her workstation, but he and AB took another look through all her drawers and storage areas. They found nothing of significance and with a bit of sadness AB said, "Poor Callie, she didn't even have any personal things here. No photos or anything."

"Maybe she was hoping this would be temporary and she would move on to something better," suggested Coop.

She shrugged and closed the last drawer she had searched. "We've got to figure this out, Coop."

They made their way back to Audrey's desk to let her know they were finished and Coop asked to speak with Mr. King. He was available and invited both of them to sit down. "Thanks for letting us look through Callie's work. We didn't discover anything resembling a possible motive. I'm wondering if Callie ever met with clients herself or had occasion to meet with other lawyers at their offices or anywhere else in the course of her work?"

"Well, she visited other law offices, but only to pick up

paperwork. We could do our best to pull together a list for you. She didn't meet with our clients offsite and when she was involved in meetings here, she wasn't alone. The other place she visited would be the courthouse, again dropping off or picking up documents.

"Do you have a record of documents she would have been charged with delivering or retrieving from the courthouse or other offices?"

Mr. King frowned. "Not a formal list. Let me check with Audrey and find out if we can piece anything together."

"We'd appreciate it. We'll be out of town this weekend, but I'll check back with you Monday for an update."

Friday morning Coop met Ben in their usual booth at Peg's Pancakes. Ben's bloodshot eyes and haggard face touted his dedication to his job. "You look like hell," said Coop.

"That's how I feel." He gulped his coffee and Myrtle appeared to warm his cup.

She shook her head at the sight of him. "Oh, my heavens. Y'all need some rest. This job is gonna be the death of you."

Ben gave a slight smile. "It's just busy right now, Myrtle. I'll be okay once I get these cases solved."

"They say bad things always happen in three's, so maybe it'll quiet down now." She plucked the pencil from behind her ear. "What'll it be?" She scratched their orders on her pad and hurried to the kitchen.

"I'm happy to help, if there's something I can do. Gratis, of course," said Coop.

"I may take you up on your offer. I've been staring at video footage for hours and getting nowhere. We did find a black SUV. It's a match to the one that hit the kid. It was abandoned and partially torched, left in a rundown industrial area north of town. Stolen from Georgia a few days before the accident."

Myrtle arrived with their plates and set them down. "Y'all eat up," she said, refilling their cups.

Ben shook his head as he chewed. "I've got bupkis on the guy shot in the park. He runs a route around the park area each morning. We know the type of gun, but there's no match in ballistics. One shot to the chest and one to the head, no brass left at the scene. Professional." Ben took a bite of his omelet. "No witnesses. A couple of cameras in the area by the parking lots and buildings, but no vehicles recorded. We've got a few runners on camera but they're all bundled up and we haven't been able to identify any of them. All the tips from the phone have been nothing but pranks or weirdos."

"Callie's case lends itself to an experienced killer and the guy in the park sounds like a professional hit. Maybe the messenger is the work of a pro. It's hard to imagine a local had an accident and decided to torch his car. Any connection between the owner in Georgia and anybody in Nashville?"

Ben shook his head and he shoved a biscuit in his mouth. "No, nothing. We've checked the owners out and they're clean. We're working on prints in the vehicle now. We might get lucky and get a match." He paused and gulped his coffee. "Last night we located a guy on the video. He darted out of an alley and rummaged through some of the papers the messenger was carrying. It didn't look like he took anything, but we're trying to identify him and not having much luck. Our guys had only secured the immediate area of the accident, so the bag and a lot of the papers were outside the perimeter. The bag got run over and moved down the block from subsequent vehicular and pedestrian traffic. The guy from the alley was on foot and wearing a hoodie. Can't see his face. We're trying to trace him with other cameras, but haven't had any luck. We lost him after he took another alley and can't locate him on any other cameras. It's tedious work, but has to be fleshed out."

"Do you think the hoodie guy was just curious or searching for something?"

Ben's head bobbed up and down. "That's the question of the hour. I've got Kate and Jimmy working with the messenger service to try and piece together all the items he was carrying and attempt to narrow down what the guy in the hoodie may have wanted. He could have just been a guy who happened upon a bunch of papers and the bag and was curious. A homeless guy would have taken the bag. It was the end of the day and Billy's satchels were full. It's a nightmare."

Coop brought Ben up to date on his latest visit to Mr. King's office. "I'll check back on Monday and get a list of offices Callie visited. She must have encountered whatever it was through an outside office. We didn't find anything in her files that even sparked our interest." Coop slid his empty plate to the edge of the table. "Any word from the techs on enhancing the video of Callie's envelope she showed the valet at the Hilton?"

"No luck yet. From what they say, the angle is bad and they can't get anything from the front of the envelope, just the back and there isn't any writing they can detect." Ben's eyes widened. "I almost forgot, Kate said to tell you she talked to Ollie and his lawyer. Once she confronted him with the video evidence of his car, he admitted to staying out and scoring some cocaine Saturday night. She's going to pin down where he says he was, but thinks the guy is telling the truth. He was afraid he'd be in trouble for the drugs, but when faced with the bigger problem of murder, he saw the light."

"What a tool. We knew he was lying when we talked to him at the hotel."

Myrtle appeared with the check. "Are y'all getting an order for AB today?"

"No, I've got to get to her place and pick her up. We're on a flight this morning and I need to get a move on. Next Friday, though." Coop smiled and pulled a wad of bills from his wallet. "You have a nice weekend, Myrtle."

As Mrs. Baxter's assistant had promised, a driver was waiting for them at Dulles. With practiced expertise, he stowed their bags and navigated the traffic, making the drive to the privileged enclave of McLean in less than thirty minutes. The driver turned into the development, touched a button on the console and they sailed past huge gates, connected to a gatehouse that could have been featured in *Architectural Digest*. They made their way through the exquisite homes lining the wide streets and turned into a driveway, where another impressive gate blocked the entrance. The driver hit another button and the gate opened, allowing them access to the stunning brick and stone home of the Baxter family.

As soon as the car stopped, they were met by a man in an elegant suit, who introduced himself as Mr. Belmont. "Welcome. Mr. and Mrs. Baxter are off property at the moment, but have requested you join them for drinks this evening at six o'clock in the family room. I'll show you to your suites now."

A young man appeared and carried their bags, while they followed Mr. Belmont. Coop's eyes widened as they entered the white marble foyer. They were led up an ornate staircase spilling out of a rotunda. They glimpsed the huge yard through the wall of windows across the back of the house and Mr. Belmont stopped at a room on the right overlooking the vast lawn. "Mr. Harrington, this is your suite." He gestured to the next door at the end of the hall. "Ms. Davenport will be next door."

Mr. Belmont opened the door and Coop stepped through behind him. Somehow his bag was already in his room. Mr.

Belmont gave him a quick tour and said, "Mirabelle will serve both of you and take care of all your housekeeping needs. If you require anything, feel free to ask her. The cook has prepared some light snacks for you. Once you're settled feel free to avail yourselves of the theatre or the pool. There's also a small library and a racquetball court in the lower level. Please make yourselves comfortable."

He led AB to her room where Mirabelle was busy unpacking her suitcase. "Ma'am," she said and went about her duties. Once she stowed the bags in the closet, she added, "Refreshments are in the library downstairs. If you require the assistance of a staff member, pick up any telephone and ring zero." She gave a slight bow and left AB in her lavish suite.

AB plopped on the bed and rested her head against the mountain of pillows, taking in the large television mounted to the wall and the elaborate pink and gold décor of the room. She recognized Callie's childhood room, but it had been redecorated and updated since she had stayed in it with Callie.

A tear leaked out of the corner of her eye and she wiped it away as a soft knock sounded. She opened the door to Coop. "How ya doing?"

She nodded, "Okay, I guess." She motioned him inside. "This was Callie's room. Just brings back memories."

His eyes took in the large room. "I'm sure it does. Do you feel like going downstairs and getting something to eat? We could take a walk around outside first."

"Yeah, I could go for some fresh air." She grabbed her jacket and they made their way back to the staircase.

After a tour of the property, AB and Coop settled in the library, in awe of the floor to ceiling bookcases filled with every imaginable topic, and snacked on the buffet prepared for them. "I could live here," said AB, selecting a leather-bound copy of *To Kill a Mockingbird*.

Mirabelle appeared as soon as they had finished eating. "Mr. and Mrs. Baxter will meet you in the family room for drinks at six o'clock." She gave them the once over and added, "After you change clothes, of course. They appreciate promptness as they have a gathering tonight for Miss Callie at her brother's home. Cook will serve you supper in the dining room at seven-thirty. I'll show you the way."

With the fire roaring in the cozy room, AB would have preferred to relax with a book, but after Mirabelle's announcement staying put wasn't an option. Like well trained dogs, Coop and AB trailed the commandeering maid up the stairs to the main level and to the family room. "The dining room is just down the main hall on the other side of the staircase," Mirabelle said, pointing her finger in the right direction.

"Great, we'll make sure we're ready by six. Thanks for the snacks," said AB.

As they made their way to their rooms, Coop leaned in close to her ear. "I didn't bring many clothes. Just my suit for tomorrow."

"Aren't you glad I didn't let you wear one of your t-shirts here?"

"I have one in my suitcase. Maybe I'll wear it for drinks?" Coop gave her an impish grin.

"You'll just have to wear your suit jacket and hope for the best." She opened her door. "I'm going to try to take a nap. I'll pick you up a little before six."

Coop flipped on the television and rested against the pillows, while he scanned his email on his phone. He saw one from Ben reporting Kate had checked out Ollie's whereabouts and so far, he was telling the truth. Ben was also able to confirm the alibi Mr. King and Audrey gave. Both were at home, verified by their spouses and neighbors. He was in the process of checking all the other employees at King's firm.

Coop grabbed a legal pad from his bag to catalog possible suspects and motives. He scribbled down the names of Callie's brothers and left the motive blank, hoping to learn more this weekend. Ollie had been their best bet, but he was looking less guilty, unless he hired someone. Coop made a note to check on Ollie's financials.

He dug out his laptop and turned his attention to Callie's cell phone data. He had intended to investigate the calls before they left, but ran out of time. He first eliminated calls between Callie and her office and calls to AB. He highlighted those numbers with a Virginia area code and noticed a call to Callie's phone on Sunday, after her death. He saw the same number again on Monday morning. He marked both of them and followed with a different color for Ollie's calls. He identified the cell phones of Mr. and Mrs. Baxter, along with the house phone, which left one number to research.

The only texts on Callie's phone were from Ollie and AB. He was curious about the unknown Virginia number. He dialed zero and asked for Mr. Belmont. He was connected to the man who appeared to be much more than a butler. He inquired about the number and Mr. Belmont identified it as the cell phone of Callie's sister-in-law, Winnie.

"Was Callie close to Winnie?"

There was a long silence before Belmont spoke. "No, I wouldn't say they were at all close."

"Any idea why she would call Callie?"

"None whatsoever, sir."

Coop asked, "When was the last time Callie was here to visit?"

"Hmm, it would have been for Thanksgiving. That was her only visit back here since she moved to Nashville."

"Who was Callie closest to in the family?"

"Her daddy. She was the apple of his eye, even when she got into trouble. She was the baby of the family and was never close to her brothers. She spent lots of time with Cook as a youngster. She was always in the kitchen underfoot."

Coop thanked him and added more notes to his pad. He then made a quick call to Mirabelle and asked her to press a long sleeve black t-shirt he had found in his bag. If he wore the suit jacket over it, nobody would see the gold Vanderbilt lettering on the sleeve and it would solve his problem.

He was just putting his jacket on when AB knocked. "Come on in."

"Look at you. You solved your wardrobe dilemma." She eyed his ensemble and tilted her head. "You look handsome, Coop."

He offered her an arm and they made their way to the family room, arriving with five minutes to spare. Mr. Belmont was waiting at the bar cart and offered them a drink. Coop opted for a beer and AB took Mr. Belmont's suggestion and had a gin fizz. As they made their way to the sofa nearest the fireplace, Mr. and Mrs. Baxter arrived.

"Annabelle and Mr. Harrington, it's a pleasure to have you in our home," said Arden. Carter stepped forward and shook Coop's hand and embraced AB in a hug.

Tears filled AB's eyes as she continued to hold Carter's hand in hers. "I am so sorry about Callie. I just can't believe it."

The older man's eyes turned to liquid as he nodded and squeezed her hand. "Thank you for coming, Annabelle."

Mr. Belmont handed them drinks and they took a seat in the chairs opposite the sofa. "I'm sorry we're leaving you on your own tonight, but we have a family gathering at David's home tonight," said Arden.

"We understand," said Coop. "Would you like to discuss our investigation or wait?"

Arden looked at her husband and he nodded. "Yes, go ahead, please."

Coop summarized what they had discovered and the steps they had taken with regard to Ollie and to Callie's workplace. He also touched on the mystery item Callie had discovered through work that had upset her. "I saw on Callie's cell phone she had been in contact with both of you. Did either of you know if there was something bothering her?"

They shook their heads. "No, not that we knew of. We had been talking to her about holiday plans and such, nothing more," said her mother. "So, you don't think robbery was the motive?"

Coop shook his head. "I'm inclined to think it had something to do with the item she mentioned to AB. I'm afraid we don't have anything concrete, just trying to piece together her activities and figure out what it was she discovered."

Carter spoke in a soft tone. "I understand you uncovered a bit of a dalliance on Brandon's part, but I can assure you he's a fine man and would never hurt Callie. He called and told me himself."

"I tend to agree with you, Mr. Baxter," said Coop. "It was just an avenue we had to investigate. Both Mr. King and his assistant have alibis and they've been verified." With a shaky hand, Carter guided his drink to his lips.

"Which brings me to another uncomfortable path I must take." Coop paused and took a drink from his glass. "Were there any issues with Callie and the family or close friends here in Virginia?"

Carter opened his mouth to speak, but Arden interrupted. "No, not with the family. Callie had her share of problems and trouble, but was putting them behind her. That's why she was in Nashville. To start over. The one problem person we knew of was Ollie."

"Did Callie have a good relationship with her brothers and their wives and families?"

Arden's eyes shifted to her husband and she continued. "Of

course. They didn't see much of Callie. Different circles you know. We all had a marvelous Thanksgiving together here at the house."

"That's the last time we saw her," said Carter.

Arden glanced at her watch. "We need to get going, dear." She stood. "Tomorrow Mr. Belmont will arrange a car to take you to the reception at noon. Once again, please excuse our departure tonight. It was a pleasure to meet you, Mr. Harrington. Always lovely to see you, Annabelle."

"If either of you think of anything, no matter how small, please give me a call," said Coop.

Carter rose and shook Coop's hand again. "Thank you for all you're doing. If we can do anything more, let me know." He followed Arden out the door.

7

Mr. Belmont ushered Coop and AB to the dining room where a lavish meal awaited. After they were served, the staff left them with a bell to ring should they need anything.

"Arden definitely runs the show around here," whispered Coop.

She nodded. "Oh, yeah. Always has, always will. She's a force."

"Belmont told me Callie was close to Cook. Do you remember her?"

"Yeah, I can't believe she's still here. She was old when I was in college."

"Let's pay her a visit tonight while they're away."

They finished the meal and opted to have dessert in the library. They requested Cook meet them so they could express their thanks.

After a few minutes, a plump older woman wearing a white apron came through the door. "You asked to see me?"

Coop stood. "Yes, I'm sorry I don't know your name, but I'm Cooper Harrington and this is Annabelle."

"Oh, yes, I remember Miss Annabelle from when she visited with Miss Callie. I'm Eunice Hillman."

Coop invited her to sit with AB on the sofa. "Your meal was delicious. We wanted to thank you and also ask you about Callie."

Eunice plucked a hankie from her apron pocket and dabbed her eyes. "Miss Callie was such a special girl. I just cannot believe she's gone."

Coop explained he was a private detective and had been retained to work on Callie's murder. "We're just trying to get a feel for Callie's relationship with her family and friends here in Virginia. We understand she was here at Thanksgiving and wondered if everyone got along. Any problems?"

The cook's eyes stared at the ground. "I don't speak out of turn about the Baxters. They've been nothin' but good to me."

"We're just looking for the truth to help find out what happened to Callie," said AB.

The old woman nodded and looked at AB. "Callie's troubles caused some embarrassment for the family. They're important people and with John's upcoming appointment by the governor this coming year and David a judge, they didn't want anything to taint the Baxter name. I think that's part of the reason Miss Callie moved to Nashville. It was best for them. She also broke her daddy's heart, so I think it was easier for him not to have her around here. She just stayed in the guest house most of the time she was here."

"Was she close to John or David or their wives?" asked Coop.

"No, not at all. Winnie, John's wife, was furious with her. Worried her troubles would impact John's chances of appointment by the governor. I think they wanted to distance themselves from Callie."

"Did Callie have friends visit while she lived here?" asked AB.

The woman shook her head. "No, Miss Annabelle, not a soul came to visit the poor girl."

Coop passed her a business card. "If you remember anything that might help us, please give me a call."

She took the card and slipped it into her pocket. "Miss Annabelle, I hope you find out who killed poor Miss Callie. She was a sweet child and didn't deserve this." She wiped her eyes again and closed the door behind her.

Dreary skies greeted AB on the morning of Callie's service. By the time she and Coop had eaten breakfast and were ready for their drive to the country club, the threatening clouds were producing a steady drizzle. Mr. Belmont supplied umbrellas and made sure they were ensconced in the limousine without getting wet.

They arrived at the Woodhaven Country Club and made their way to the ballroom. The tasteful room was teeming with people, most of whom looked to be the age of Callie's parents. Coop and AB smiled at strangers and busied themselves at the buffet stations. They chose seats near the large table reserved for family and nibbled at their food while they watched and listened.

Much of the chatter centered on John Baxter's upcoming appointment. As receptions went, it resembled a political activity more than it did a memorial service. There were the appropriate murmurs of condolence here and there, but John and Winnie were the center of attention.

Coop spotted Brandon King and his wife searching for a table. He guided his wife through the clusters of people and chose the chairs next to Coop. "This is my wife, Tiffany." Coop and AB greeted her and introduced themselves as college classmates of Callie.

The foursome made small talk until they were joined by two other couples. The newcomers exchanged polite smiles, but kept to themselves. Coop offered to take AB's plate with his and after depositing them on a tray, took to meandering through the room.

He was soon joined by AB and together they feigned talking to each other while lingering on the outer edges of various groups and eavesdropping. They stopped at the family table where they were introduced to Callie's brothers and their wives and children. After introductions Arden added, "Mr. Harrington and Annabelle will be joining us for dinner this evening at the house."

"Your parents have been gracious enough to let us stay at the house. We look forward to visiting more with you tonight," said AB, as she shook John's hand.

Winnie held her glass of champagne and nodded at both of them while her eyes looked past them and scanned the room. Her eyes locked onto a tall man and she turned to her husband. "John, there's the governor. We must go and say hello." She tugged on his arm and he sighed.

"Pleasure to meet you two. We'll see you back at the house," he said as Winnie pulled him away.

Coop and AB circled through the room a few more times, picked up a few more tidbits, ate dessert, and then called Mr. Belmont for the car. Coop asked the driver a few questions about the Baxters, but soon found out he was hired for the day and didn't know them well.

Mr. Belmont met them in the driveway and once again escorted them to the house, under a protective umbrella. "Drinks will be in the library at seven tonight, followed by dinner in the dining room. Should you need anything, just let us know." He left them at the foot of the staircase and they made their own way upstairs.

After changing clothes, Coop met AB in her room. Rain pattered against the windows and she shivered inside her sweatshirt. He lit the fire and AB called down for something warm to drink. Coop brought his laptop and notepad and as soon as Mirabelle delivered the drinks and shut the door behind her, they got to work. He made sure to turn on the television to mask their conversation, should anyone be in the hallway.

"Winnie is a piece of work, huh?" AB raised her eyebrows and took a sip from her cup.

"Let's compare notes on what we overheard." He flipped a page and scribbled. "I gather the son, Kevin, is actually John's stepson and is Winnie's son from a previous relationship. Sounds like Kevin has some problems of his own related to drugs and anger issues. The little girl, Chloe, is their child together." He jotted on the notepad.

AB nodded her head. "That jives with what I heard. I didn't catch anything negative about John, but plenty of innuendo about Winnie. The term gold digger was used. I get the feeling she was a nonentity prior to meeting John." She moved to warm her hands by the fire. "It sounds like she spends money like a drunken sailor on shore leave."

"Yeah and I picked up on something about rehab for alcohol, disguised as recovery from a medical procedure." He tapped some keys on his laptop. "According to records, Winnie and John have been married for fifteen years. Kevin is nineteen and is a student at a private college. I can't locate any records of Winnie being married before."

Her eyes went wide. "Maybe Winnie has some secrets of her own. I didn't hear about her rehab, but I got the distinct impression she isn't held in high regard. People think Kevin is a spoiled brat and gets away with murder." She shook her head. "She's a hypocrite. It's a known fact she was worried Callie would damage John's appointment, but it sounds like she and her son could prove just as detrimental."

"In my experience, women like Winnie have to throw rocks at others to detract from their own deficiencies." He finished writing and added, "I thought she was pretentious and rude."

"I gather John and Winnie made the move to Richmond right after the election in November. He must be confident the governor will be appointing him. I overheard Winnie crowing about their new house in a posh neighborhood."

Coop nodded and continued to jot on his notepad. "Yeah, from what I heard Arden still has a family home in Richmond, but that wasn't good enough for Winnie. Sounded like Carter wanted John to wait to be appointed and use the family home, if necessary. Winnie insisted they buy an extravagant home in a new neighborhood."

"Did you pick up on the whispers about Callie having a nervous breakdown?"

Coop nodded as he wrote. "Yeah, I did hear a few people mention it."

"From what I gather, that's what everyone thinks happened to Callie when she left the law firm and lived at the guest house. A plausible excuse her parents gave their friends to keep people from speculating about why she wasn't working."

"I was surprised there wasn't more said about Callie. Most people were talking about John's upcoming appointment. The governor being there was the focus."

"The whole deal was weird. Not much mention of Callie, but Winnie acted like the belle of the ball. If I didn't know better, I would have thought we were at a political fundraiser, not a memorial. Winnie is what I'd call a highfalutin phony."

Coop lips wriggled into a slow smile. "The question is— do you think she'd hire someone to kill Callie?"

She shrugged. "I guess it would depend on how much she felt threatened. People do psycho things when they think their world is ending. Let's poke into their financials."

Coop nodded. "The other brother, David, and his wife, were quiet and reserved. I couldn't get much of a read on them. He downplayed the upcoming chance at being selected for the high court. I didn't run into anyone who was connected to Callie, beyond Mr. and Mrs. King. No friends from growing up in Virginia. Nothing. Don't you think that's weird?"

"I did meet one woman on my way to the restroom. She was leaving and I introduced myself as a friend of Callie's. She said she knew her long ago in high school, but hadn't seen her for years. Her name is Ginny Fremont and she still lives in the area. I explained we were investigating Callie's death and she gave me her contact info."

"Let's try to coordinate a meeting with her tomorrow before we fly home." While AB was on the phone arranging a time, he busied himself on the laptop. When she rejoined him, he was scrawling on his notepad.

"We're set for tomorrow. She's willing to meet us at a coffee shop on the way to the airport and offered to drop us at Dulles."

"We can just get a taxi."

"I told her she didn't need to go to any trouble. We can decide tomorrow. She said she's happy to help."

He nodded. "So, I dug into Winifred Elizabeth Edwards and found out she was born and raised in a rural area near Appalachia, Virginia. Coal country. It's a poverty ridden area of the state. Birth records show no father listed on Kevin's birth certificate. When any mention of Kevin is made in the news, they say his father died when he was an infant. Looks like Winnie's parents are deceased. She left her hometown when she married John in 2000. I wonder how they met? Appalachia is a long way from McLean."

"We could ask tonight. Try to work it into the conversation."

"David and his wife, Dorothea, have a more conventional relationship. She's known as Dot and they've been married thirty some years and have two grown children. We met them today at the service. David is a respected judge and is certain to be the next justice appointed to the Supreme Court of Virginia. From all I found, he and Dot maintain a low profile. They're involved in several philanthropic organizations, but nothing controversial. No hints of impropriety."

Coop's phone beeped with a text. He read it and said, "Ben says they got a match to a print off the black SUV that hit the messenger. Turns out it belongs to a wanted felon out of Georgia. They're looking for him now and suspect he was driving during the hit and run."

"At least he's making progress on one case. I hope they catch the jerk." She glanced at her watch. "I guess we better get ready to go downstairs soon."

Coop gathered his notepad and laptop and left to dress. He met AB at the stairs and they made their way to the library together, redressed in their memorial attire, since neither of them anticipated the number of times they would be expected to change outfits.

She raised her brows and he gave her a conspiratorial wink as they rounded the corner and entered the cozy room. Arden and Carter greeted them and Mr. Belmont fetched drinks for the pair. "The boys will be here soon," said Carter.

"Everyone is worn out from the day's events," said Arden. "They wanted to rest for a bit before our dinner."

"It was a lovely memorial. Thanks again for your hospitality," said AB, taking her drink from the tray.

"I know you're both overwhelmed," said Coop, taking the frosty glass of beer Mr. Belmont offered.

Tears floated in Carter's eyes as he nodded and removed a handkerchief. "I never thought I'd have to bury my little girl." He wiped his eyes and Arden patted his shoulder.

"I'm sure it's the worst thing a parent will ever experience. We're sorry for your loss and pain," Coop said.

They were interrupted by the arrival of the two brothers and their wives. Mr. Belmont appeared within moments, carrying drinks for the foursome. The two women gathered by the fire, while the others stood together across the room. Still chilled,

AB made her way to the sitting area in front of the hearth and said, "Are your children joining us tonight, Dot?"

"I'm afraid not. They decided to return home after the reception today. With the holidays coming, they'll be back soon."

"And what about Kevin and Chloe, Winnie?"

Winnie took a sip of her drink and said, "Oh, he's got studying to do for exams next week. Chloe's in the guest house with the nanny."

"Did you both grow up here in McLean?" asked AB.

Dot was the first to respond and explained her family had been in the area for generations. If David gets the upcoming judgeship, he'll spend more time in Richmond. Arden has a home there and he'll use it during the week and come home on the weekends. She glanced across the room and said, "Poor Carter. I hope he survives this. Losing Callie has taken a toll on him."

"He really needs to pull himself together. For John's sake," said Winnie, rolling her eyes.

Dot's eyes widened. "I can't imagine anything worse than losing a child. Callie was such a daddy's girl. I don't understand how Carter mourning his daughter is going to impact John's appointment, Winnie." Dot stared at her sister-in-law without blinking.

Winnie huffed and snapped her fingers, motioning to her empty glass. Mr. Belmont appeared with a fresh drink and she took a few sips. "Callie's lifestyle was bound to lead to trouble like this. I'm not sure why anyone is surprised."

"Why would you say that? Callie had been doing well in Nashville," said AB.

"Once a druggie always a druggie. That's what I say. I'm sure she got in with the wrong crowd and paid the price."

"I don't think so, Winnie. I've known Callie a long time and I know she wasn't on drugs. She went to meetings all the time and was making progress. She was determined to change her life," said AB, feeling the color rise in her cheeks.

Dot nodded. "I agree with Annabelle. I think Callie was heading in the right direction. She was doing well at Thanksgiving."

"You're so quick to defend her, Dot. With David looking to be the next justice, I would think you, of all people, would understand the harm a scandal like Callie's could cause. She could ruin both of her brothers."

Dot's eyes narrowed. "There's been no mention of a scandal and I find your comments to be most distasteful. We've just memorialized the poor girl." She took a sip of her drink and added, "I know Callie was thankful to have you for a friend, Annabelle. She spoke so highly of you."

As tears stung her eyes, AB fought to control her voice. "Thanks, Dot. I'm going to miss her." She regained her composure after a sip of her cool drink and pressed forward. "So, did you grow up here as well, Winnie?"

She shook her head. "No, I grew up a long way from here, closer to the border of Kentucky. We live in Richmond now. I insisted we move last month so we're ready for John's new job there."

AB nodded. "So, how did you and John meet?"

Winnie's eyes sparkled and she said, "It was love at first sight. John was in town for his law firm and I was a waitress in the only diner in town. He was there for weeks on end and we just clicked." She took another gulp from her drink.

"Sounds quite romantic," said AB.

"Oh, it was. He swept me right off my feet."

"Do you get to visit your family much?"

"I don't have anyone left. My mama and daddy died before I left. I just had Kevin."

"Oh," AB feigned surprise. "I assumed Kevin was John's child. I didn't realize you were married before."

"Kevin's daddy died when he was a baby," said Winnie as she downed the rest of her drink.

"I'm so sorry. I'm sure it was difficult for you, raising a child alone."

Winnie snapped her fingers again, signaling for a third drink. Mr. Belmont obliged and placed another glass in her hand. "Well, it was a long time ago."

"Callie's phone records show you called her cell on Sunday and Monday. What were you phoning her for?"

Winnie's eyes narrowed and she took a long drink from her glass. "I'm sure it was about holiday preparations. I honestly don't remember. It's all been such a shock." She brought her hand to her throat.

Arden interrupted the conversation by announcing dinner was ready and asked the group to follow her to the dining room. She pointed out seats for Coop and AB, next to Dot and David.

They enjoyed an elaborate meal and AB noticed when Winnie asked for another drink John gave her a small shake of his head. She huffed and rolled her eyes at him. John handed Mr. Belmont her empty glass and said, "Just water for the duration." By Coop's count, she had consumed six drinks since she arrived.

As they were eating dessert, Carter tapped his glass. "I just wanted to thank Mr. Harrington and Annabelle for their help. I told them we are all focused on finding out who killed our poor Callie and are happy to help. Do you have any questions for us?"

Coop looked around the table and said, "Do any of you have any theories about who killed Callie or why she was killed?"

"From the little I heard, I assumed it was a burglary gone wrong," said David.

"We think it was more than that. She didn't live in a high crime area and the attack had professional elements, not those of a typical burglar. We've been retracing Callie's steps in the weeks leading up to her murder to piece together any motive that may have existed."

"She was a drug addict. I'm sure she was back…in the life and met up with the wrong…people," said Winnie, slurring her words. The slash of her mouth uglier, fed by the flow of alcohol.

The entire table looked at her with surprise and contempt. John took her arm and brought her to her feet. "That's quite enough, Winnie. We need to get you back to the guest house." He turned to the others while Mr. Belmont escorted Winnie out of the room.

"I'm sorry Mother, Father. She's had too much to drink."

Dot shook her head in disgust. "She was saying the same thing when she first arrived, John. She is beyond inappropriate."

"I apologize. I'm sorry for the outburst. For the record, I don't believe Callie was back involved with drugs. I know she was determined to put all of that behind her."

Carter's hands were shaking as he gripped his coffee cup. "Son, I don't want to hear any more about Callie from Winnie. You need to talk to her."

"I understand, Father. I'll speak with her. I'm sorry, Mr. Harrington. Annabelle, thank you for making the trip to remember Callie. I know she'd be glad you were here." He shook David's hand and then Coop's, before depositing a kiss on his mother's cheek and squeezing Carter's shoulder. "I'll talk to you tomorrow."

After his exit, a hush filled the room. Coop and AB turned their attention to dessert. After several minutes, Coop broke the silence. "We've looked into Callie's ex-boyfriend, Ollie. From what we've discovered, I don't believe Callie was involved in drugs or alcohol. She attended her meetings faithfully. Does she have ties to any other old friends, in addition to Ollie?"

Arden looked around the table and spoke. "After Callie's departure from the law firm, she kept to herself, here at the estate. Once she was with Ollie, she abandoned her old friends and then when her life took a turn for the worse, she was truly alone."

David nodded along with Dot. He said, "That's one reason we suggested Callie go back to Nashville. She had happy memories there from Vanderbilt and could have a fresh start."

"We were so glad to know she had reconnected with you, Annabelle," said Carter, his voice weak. "I thought she was on the road to a better life."

"I think she was, Mr. Baxter," said AB. "I know she was a bit lonely, but she was starting to feel more secure. We got together after work and had a great time at the fundraiser. She was happy when we left the library Friday night." Tears threated to spill from her eyes and she wiped at them with her napkin.

"If you think of anything that could be important, please give me a call," said Coop, standing and helping AB to her feet. "Thank you again for your hospitality. I'll be in touch as soon as we know more, Mrs. Baxter."

The family said their goodbyes and Coop and AB headed upstairs for some much needed rest.

8

AB woke with a sore throat and congestion. She drank two pots of tea at breakfast trying to stave off the head cold. She swiped a box of tissues from her room and stuffed it in her carry-on bag. Dampness hung in the air as Mr. Belmont wished them safe travels.

The driver left them at a local coffee shop not far from the airport. They spent less than an hour listening to Ginny reminisce. She insisted she drop them at the airport and they waved goodbye when she pulled away from the curb.

"What a colossal waste of time," said Coop, grabbing their bags.

"Yeah, I think she just wanted to talk to someone about Callie."

They waded their way through the check-in and security lines and found seats at their gate. "So, all we learned is Arden thought Ginny wasn't good enough to be Callie's friend and forced them apart as high school ended."

She nodded and blew her nose. "It's sad. Ginny would have been a far better person to have in her life than the likes of Ollie. She was a scholarship kid at a prestigious school and I'm sure

Arden was looking for Callie to network with a different type of girl."

"I got the feeling Ginny was accepted because Callie was her friend. I think she paved the way for her at the school. Callie was a sweet girl," said Coop, as he picked up the bags to get in line to board.

AB's eyes were red and watery. She blew her nose again. "Are you going to be okay?" asked Coop.

"It'll be a miserable flight. I hate having a cold and flying." After maneuvering through the aisle, they took their seats and waited for the plane to fill.

She turned off her phone and tucked it in her purse. "I just looked up the school Callie and Ginny attended. In today's dollars it runs over sixty thousand a year. It's gorgeous, with stables, tennis, outdoor recreation, dorms, and a chapel. Beyond ritzy."

"From what Ginny said, it was a great school for making connections that would be important later in life. Ginny was able to secure a scholarship for college and instead of a career like Callie, she opted for a husband. She appears to have a happy life," he said as they wedged into their seats for the short flight home.

"It's a shame Callie didn't stay in touch with her. She's a sweet lady. A bit odd, but harmless."

"And she wasn't able to connect Callie with anyone else. Sounds like Callie moved on once she went to Vanderbilt."

"I think I was her closest friend there. Callie was likeable, but reserved and didn't get close to many people."

"I guess we better check out Trixie, since she still was holding a grudge when she saw her at the fundraiser. Anybody else come to mind from the event?"

She shook her head. "Trixie was the only one who was hostile. She's always been a nasty menace, so nothing new."

Coop smirked. "I remember her. One of those girls who was always nice to guys, but not so much to other girls."

"Trix the Bitch is what we called her. It fits." She blew her nose again and took a sip from the cup of tea she had requested. She shut her eyes and her head drifted onto Coop's shoulder.

By the time the flight attendants served drinks and snacks and picked up all the trash it was time to land. The jolt of the wheels hitting the runway woke AB from her nap. "Sorry, I'm zonked," she said, withdrawing her head from his shoulder.

He smiled and retrieved his phone. When it came on, he saw a message from Aunt Camille. "You're supposed to come to the house for supper. Orders from headquarters," he said. "You need to eat and rest."

"I need a proper nap first, but supper sounds wonderful to me. I'm too tired to cook."

He dropped her at her house and drove home, where he was hailed with hugs and licks upon his entry through the door. "We've missed y'all," said Camille, as Gus wedged himself between Coop's legs.

"I can tell," he said, as the dog's tail walloped him. "I'm going to unload my bags and rest for a few minutes before supper. And, before you ask, AB will be here tonight. She caught a nasty cold on our trip."

"Oh, dear. We'll fix her up with some of my homemade chicken soup." Camille grinned and kissed his cheek before bustling to the kitchen, humming to herself.

Coop unpacked and settled in to peruse his notepad while he petted Gus with one hand. He made a quick list for Monday, including Trixie, Winnie, and checking in with Brandon King. Gus took off like a lightning bolt when he heard AB arrive and Coop followed.

Camille made sure Coop's plate was full before she said, "I hate to ask you this, Coop, but one of the girls at the salon has a problem."

Coop fought against his inclination to roll his eyes. The girls at the salon had more than their fair share of problems. "I'm pretty busy, Aunt Camille."

She nodded her head and took a sip from her glass. "I know, dear. But Lola Belle is my old friend and her niece, Daisy, is in an awful fix." Camille rambled at a nervous pace explaining Daisy had custody of her daughter and her ex-husband had been calling and threatening to take the girl from Daisy. "Lola Belle is fit to be tied. Daisy is livin' in constant fear from the harassment and threats. It's taking a toll on the little one."

"Sounds like Daisy needs to talk to the police. She could also get a restraining order if the situation is serious."

"Oh, Coop, I knew you'd know just what to do. I told Lola Belle you could sort this out. You can figure out all the legal mumbo jumbo." She beamed and passed him a platter.

"Now, wait…I didn't say I could solve all this." He let out a sigh. "I'm too tired to put up a fight. Have Daisy call the office for an appointment and I'll meet with her and discuss the situation to determine if I can help her."

AB grinned as she forked another bite into her mouth and watched Aunt Camille dote on her nephew. "I was so hopin' you would agree. I had Mrs. Henderson make one of your favorite desserts." She gave AB a quick wink and then asked about their trip to Virginia.

They spent the rest of the evening enjoying the delicious chocolate praline cake Camille unveiled, while they brought her up to date on all they learned in Virginia. After she listened to their description of the family affair, she said, "Winnie sounds downright vile. I wouldn't put it past her to be the murderer."

Coop got up early and met AB at the gym before work. He was surprised to see her. "Are you feeling better this morning?"

She nodded as she programmed her treadmill. "Yeah, I think Camille's soup is a miracle cure. I had two bowls and slept like a baby." Coop suggested they cut their routine short, to give AB's system a chance to recover from her cold.

This was the last full week at the office before they would close for the holidays and Coop was feeling the pressure to get Callie's case solved. He left AB to run financial records on Winnie and Trixie while he made a stop at King's office. Gus elected to stay with AB and parked himself under her desk.

After an easy drive downtown, Coop was escorted to the ever-charming Audrey's office. She provided him a folder of information outlining the visits Callie had made to various law offices and courtrooms over the past month. "If you need anything else, y'all just let me know. Friday's my last day and then I'll be starting at the new firm the first of the year."

Coop held the list further away so his eyes could focus on it. He snatched the folder back to him when she looked up, realizing he was embarrassed to show his age in front of a woman who exuded youth and desire. She was dressed in red today and as with all his past encounters, Coop found it hard to resist glancing at her blouse.

"I'm glad to hear the new job worked out for you. I'll review this right away and give you a call if we need anything else."

"If you can't reach me, feel free to ask for Brandon. He's happy to help in any way possible."

Coop thanked her, was tempted by, but declined, her offer of coffee, and hurried to his Jeep. He set out for Trixie's house, having received a text from AB confirming she had arranged an appointment. He knew Chandler and Trixie lived in the Woodlawn area, between his office and the home he shared with Aunt Camille. He found the house, a grand Colonial Revival with a private drive.

A maid answered the door and led him to a formal living room with an impressive array of windows showcasing a huge backyard with a pool. She placed a tray of coffee on the table and poured him a cup. He hadn't had time for more than a few sips from his one cup of real coffee this morning, so decided to break his new health rule and indulge in the elixir he craved. He held the warm cup and savored the rich aroma before taking a sip.

He held back a moan of delight and took another swallow before Trixie made her entrance. "Why, Cooper, it's wonderful to see you." He stood as she moved close to him and planted an air kiss on each side of his face. "I haven't set eyes on you in ages."

"Nice to see you, Trixie. I think AB told you I'm working on Callie's case."

"Oh, yes. What a tragedy. Chandler and I were stunned and shocked to learn of Callie's horrible murder. I assumed the police were investigatin'."

"Callie's family hired me to look into it. I understand you were at the fundraiser and saw Callie there. Is that right?"

"Yes, there were over a hundred of us there Friday night."

"Did you have any contact with Callie after the event?"

She shook her head as she picked up a silver bell from the tray and rang it. "No, I'm afraid we weren't in the same social circles. I didn't even know she was back in Nashville."

The maid appeared with a plate of warm cookies and poured Trixie a cup of coffee. She offered Coop a cookie and he declined, remembering the torture of his morning at the gym. He consulted his notepad. "I talked to some of the guests from the fundraiser and I understand you made a point of bringing up Chandler with Callie. You were described as agitated and perturbed."

"That's quite the exaggeration, Coop. It's just girl talk someone took the wrong way, I'm sure."

"What did you say to Callie?"

"Oh, heavens, I'm not sure I can remember the details. I

know I asked her what she was doin' in Nashville and told her I had married Chandler and he worked for Daddy. That's the extent of our conversation."

"So, you didn't say," he flipped a page and stared at a blank sheet, "she should stay out of your lives and question her intentions related to Chandler?"

Her cheeks reddened and she took a slow sip from her cup. "I don't think it was as dramatic as all that. I was just surprised to find her there."

"Where were you between one and five in the morning on the Sunday Callie was murdered?"

She huffed and said, "Why, here, of course. I can't believe you think I'd do somethin' so horrendous."

"I suppose Chandler can vouch for you? You didn't leave the house at any time early Sunday morning?"

"Yes. I mean, yes, he can vouch for me. I don't ever leave the house in the middle of the night." Her genteel voice was losing its charm, replaced by sharp responses.

"Do you know who may have wanted to harm Callie?"

"No," she snapped. "As I said, I just learned she was in Nashville. I don't know anythin' about her life apart from our college days."

"Did you observe or overhear anything at the fundraiser that would shine any light on the matter?"

She shook her head. "Nothin' comes to mind."

He placed his cup on the tray. "Well, if you think of anything related to her death, please give me a call." He stood and handed her a card. "Thanks for the coffee."

She walked him to the door and he turned and asked, "What did you think of Callie's dress?"

A look of surprise flashed in her eyes. "It was fine. She and I chose to dress like Audrey Hepburn."

"I know. I saw the photos. I thought Callie looked magnificent. Maybe even better than she did in college." He continued through the door. "Thanks again."

She took a deep breath, but couldn't disguise the fury on her face, now devoid of her normal facade of sweetness. Without a word she slammed the door.

He chuckled to himself as he climbed in the Jeep. He drove the short distance to the office and was met by Gus at the back door. He found AB in the kitchen. She leaned in close and whispered, "Lola Belle is here with Daisy. Unannounced."

He sucked in a breath. "Go ahead and show them into my office. I'll be right there." He grumbled and muttered to Gus as he poured a glass of sweet tea to ready himself for the impromptu meeting.

Coop shook hands with both women before slipping behind his desk. AB had already provided them with refreshments. Lola Belle gripped her niece's hand and said, "Camille told us you could help and we're ever so grateful." Daisy nodded and Lola Belle continued, "Daisy is concerned that Trent, her ex, is going to resort to doing something drastic. He's been threatening to take their daughter."

Coop asked several questions and explained he could contact Trent and try to reason with him as a first step. "If that doesn't work, we can go before a judge for a restraining order."

Daisy bobbed her head up and down. "That's what I want. I want him to stay away from us."

"It's best to have some type of evidence when we go before the judge. Do you have any voicemails with his threats?"

Daisy fumbled in her purse and retrieved her cell phone. She played him three messages and Coop wrote down the dates and times. "Good. Keep a log of any contact he makes with you. I'll get the paperwork completed and get us a court date."

Daisy excused herself to visit the ladies' room and Lola Belle took out her checkbook. She paid for the visit and fees associated with the court appearance for the restraining order.

"Thanks so much for meeting with us so quickly, Cooper. Your aunt holds you in such regard and now I know why."

He ushered her to the reception area where Daisy was waiting. AB collected their contact information and explained she would be in touch as soon as they had a court date. Coop returned to his office and let AB finish the paperwork.

She joined him after they left. "How are you feeling?" he asked.

"Much better, thanks. The sore throat is gone and so is my stuffy nose." She made her way to the conference table. "I'll submit the paperwork and coordinate with Daisy and Lola Belle." She placed a stack of papers and files on the table. "Shall we get back to Callie's case?" she asked.

He nodded and she showed him the financial reports she had run on Winnie and Trixie. Ben had emailed their cell phone histories. He checked the financials and saw no cash withdrawals from either account. He saw the highlighted purchases on Winnie's statements. "Looks like some huge expenses for rehab."

"And from what we witnessed, she needs another session."

"And some large deposits to the son's account. So, he's still in trouble, at least financially. I wonder if her husband knows all this?"

She shrugged. "It's hard to say. They look to have a complicated marriage. I think I'll take a look at the son's account, just in case Winnie is more devious than we think. I don't detect any glaring indicators of a payoff or criminal activity."

"Nothing looks out of whack."

"Except Trixie and Winnie both spend a boatload of money. Good thing they have lots of it."

He continued to scan the reports. "But it's all traceable and no wires or cash. Credit cards show enormous amounts of activity. Looks like they pay all their bills and have good credit."

"I'd just like their reward points from their credit cards. I could live on them alone," said AB, wrinkling her nose.

"They're both miserable excuses for human beings. You, my friend, are wealthier than either of those snobs will ever be." He then shared the slight jab he inflicted on Trixie. She rolled with laughter when he described her face.

After composing herself she asked, "Do you think Trixie was involved?"

He shook his head. "Nah. I think she's a mean junior high girl who's insecure and offensive, but I don't think she's a murderer."

He reviewed the cell phone records AB had researched, but didn't notice anything strange. "No calls to unidentified or prepaid numbers. Nothing stands out in these."

"Just the call from Winnie to Callie, but no pattern of calls."

"Once you get the financials on Kevin, I'll consider taking a swing at Winnie," said Coop. "I need some lunch and then I'll tackle the list from Brandon King."

"Aunt Camille stopped by with a delivery on her way to the salon this morning. Leftovers are in the fridge and she made some cookies."

A smile filled Coop's face and he wiggled his brows. "She makes me crazy sometimes, but I love that woman," he said, as he made a beeline for the kitchen with Gus at his heels.

Coop took a handful of cookies back to his office and constructed a timeline on his white board. He added to the GPS data which included Callie's AA meetings, shopping, eateries, and several trips to the parking garage close to the courthouse. He concentrated his analysis on the list from the law office during the last week of Callie's life. Hattie Mae had said Callie was upset about a work situation on Saturday morning when they met for coffee. The week before Callie divulged the affair between Brandon and Audrey, but this issue was new, so he assumed whatever Callie encountered happened between those two Saturdays. She told AB about it on Friday night and based on how upset she was, he couldn't imagine her waiting longer than a week.

He logged Callie's visits to the law offices and courts under each day on the timeline. He elected to begin with the law offices and set out to visit the four Callie had been to during her last week at work. Gus sat in the front seat of the Jeep while Coop drove downtown.

Coop asked the same questions at each stop and gathered notes from each office manager. After the last stop, he climbed into the Jeep and exhaled a heavy breath. He gave Gus a pat on the head. "That's what you call a bust, old boy." It was cold and dark, minutes before five o'clock, so he headed for home, intent on beating the rush hour traffic.

9

Tuesday morning brought a light dusting of snow over the city. Gus was overjoyed and romped through the yard before he could be herded into the Jeep. Once they arrived at the office, Gus took several more laps around the yard before being coerced inside with the promise of a treat.

Gus let Coop and AB towel dry his paws and brush out the tiny snowballs attached to his feathers, before lounging near the fireplace in Coop's office. Coop filled the largest mug in the cupboard with his favorite caffeinated coffee and reviewed his notes from last night. He had gleaned little valuable information, only that Callie was always polite, didn't linger or chat much, and her tasks involved picking up or delivering files pertaining to mundane cases. No strange events took place in any of the law offices during Callie's visits.

He knew he'd be spending the majority of the day at the Justice AA Birch Building, doing his best to charm court clerks into giving him information about Callie's visits. King's firm represented a variety of clients, both civil and criminal, which meant Callie had visited a dozen different courts in the week prior to her death. Coop scribbled a few notes in his notebook.

As he was finishing, AB hurried into his office. "I ran Kevin's financials and they show several large cash withdrawals."

Coop eyed the report. "Dammit. I hate asking this stuff on the phone, but I also don't want to fly all the way up there to do it."

"Do you think we'd get a straight answer out of John? I don't trust Winnie and I think Kevin might be like mama."

"Hmm. I need to think about it. I'd like to get Ben's take on all this." He returned to his desk and sent Ben a text.

"Do you have Kevin's phone records?"

"Not yet. Ben's supposed to send them over."

Coop reviewed Winnie's financials against Kevin's and saw the cash withdrawals coincided with the transfers she made to his account. He ran a longer history on both of them and determined this had been going on for a long period of time, not just in the time surrounding Callie's murder. He reviewed Kevin's credit cards and tapped some keys on his computer. "Ah, looks like Kevin might have an addiction to gambling. All these charges in Maryland are for a horse track."

"Maybe he gambles on more than horses, huh?"

Coop nodded. "If the rumors about drugs are true and he's a gambler, the cash makes more sense." Coop sat back in his chair, deep in thought.

Coop's phone pinged. He read the screen and said, "Ben says do whatever I think best." He eased back in the chair and closed his eyes.

"I can hear the hamster running on the wheel in your head. What are you thinking?" asked AB.

"I'm considering contacting Carter and asking him to video conference with me. I'll question him about Kevin and Winnie. John may try to protect them, no matter what he knows. Carter is focused on Callie and the one who's most distraught over her death."

"Dot would be the other option for getting at the truth. I

don't think there's any love lost between those two sisters-in-law."

"I like it. You contact Dot and quiz her about Kevin and Winnie and I'll set something up with Carter."

She returned to her desk and dug through all the contact information they had gathered from their visit to Virginia. She left Dot a message on her cell phone asking her to call concerning Callie's case.

Coop was able to reach Carter's assistant, who set up a video chat for the afternoon. "Mr. Baxter told me if you got in contact to make sure and do whatever possible to help with the investigation. He'll be available in an hour and I'll make sure he's set up," said the efficient woman.

After getting the information to connect the video call, he made a quick list of bullet points to bring up with Carter and then took Gus outside for one more opportunity to enjoy the snow, which was melting and would be gone soon. When he and the dog came back in, AB was on the phone with Dot.

He hustled Gus into his office to dry by the fire and got his computer ready to connect to Carter. As soon as he clicked on the connection, Carter appeared on the screen. "Mr. Baxter, hello. Thanks so much for squeezing me in on such short notice."

"Of course, Mr. Harrington. I hope you have some news for me."

"Instead of news, I have some rather difficult questions for you. I don't want to offend you, but need to ask some things about Winnie and Kevin."

Carter's face fell. "I understand. Go ahead."

"Part of the investigation involves looking at any contacts Callie had in the weeks prior and there was a call from Winnie. After our visit with your family, it's apparent Winnie has some strong feelings about Callie. I ran a financial history and uncovered some irregularities involving large amounts of money transferred from Winnie to Kevin. I also found several cash withdrawals coinciding with those transfers. Do you know anything about them?

"Kevin isn't John's son, as you might have heard. Winnie indulges the boy and has never made him suffer a consequence for his reckless behavior. I guess some may say the same about me with Callie. Her mother and I bailed her out of her situation, but I'd like to think she was on the right road. Kevin, on the other hand, is a real problem. He's been involved with drugs and gambling."

"Does John know?"

The old man nodded. "Oh, yes. Winnie believes she keeps everything from him, but John is shrewd and smart. He knows about the money and Kevin's problems. Winnie has her own problems. It's quite a mess. It's laughable that Winnie is so concerned about Callie tarnishing John's reputation when Winnie and Kevin are the real threat. We've managed to keep most of his antics away from the public eye, but people talk and he's been in trouble for years, since he was a youngster."

"Sir, I'm sorry to even ask, but do you think Winnie or Kevin could be involved in a conspiracy to kill Callie?"

Carter's chest heaved as he sighed and he retrieved a handkerchief to wipe his eyes. "I would hope not, but honestly don't know. Kevin runs with a rough crowd. I can't believe they would consider harming Callie, but I can't be one hundred percent sure. Terrible, isn't it?"

"No, sir, just honest. I'm inclined to think the activity I saw was related to drugs and gambling debts, but was hesitant to ask Winnie or Kevin. I only met Winnie, but I don't have faith she would be truthful, not when it comes to her son."

"Let me discuss it with John and get back to you. We don't have any secrets and he may know the details about the transactions. Maybe he'll be embarrassed enough to actually put his foot down with that woman once and for all."

"Would you rather I contact him? I don't want to make it more difficult for you."

He shook his head, "No, no, it'll be beneficial for us to talk. You can be the excuse, but we need to talk about this anyway. The governor does plan to appoint John and he needs to understand what a detriment his wife and step-son can be once he's in the political arena. He's just put Winnie in another treatment facility today, in fact."

"I'll wait to hear from you, sir. Thank you."

Carter promised to be in touch the next day and disconnected the call. As soon as he did, AB came through the door. "I was just waiting for you to be done."

"Carter confirmed drugs and gambling and Winnie funneling money to the kid. The husband knows, but Carter is going to talk to him and get more information." Coop shook his head and said, "What a sad family."

She plopped in a chair by the fireplace and said, "Dot was full of information. She said Kevin has been in rehab, like his mother, more than once. They all know Winnie protects the kid and bails him out with money for whatever trouble he gets in and they know about the drugs and gambling. None of the family care for Winnie or Kevin. They all express concerns about the family money and property. Sounds like the parents have set up a trust excluding her and Kevin, which makes Winnie even more obnoxious. Dot and David don't socialize with John and Winnie. Sounds like they love and respect John, but can't stand the wife. Dot also thinks Chloe is a brat and will grow up to be just like her conniving mother."

"Did you ask her if she thought Winnie or Kevin could be involved in Callie's murder?"

"I did. She said she didn't think so, but couldn't be sure. She said the woman is unpredictable and obsessed with John getting the appointment. Dot said Winnie would go to any length."

"That meshes with what Carter said. He can't be sure she

wouldn't do something drastic. He's going to talk to John and said his son is aware of all the issues with Winnie and Kevin. Sounds like it will give him an excuse to have a serious discussion with his son. Winnie is in another rehab facility as of today. He'll get back to me tomorrow, but I'm tempted to ask Ben to allow the Virginia authorities to question Kevin. I think it would be wise to catch him off guard, without his mama there to talk for him."

AB reached to retrieve the ringing phone. She made a note and thanked the caller. "That was Judge Mallot's court. He can hear Daisy's request tomorrow morning. I'll get in touch with her and make sure she knows where to report in the morning."

She turned back when she reached the door. "Also, Brandon King faxed over a list of documents Callie was charged with delivering or picking up that week before her death. I gave them a once over and nothing looks suspicious to me."

He glanced at the clock and saw it was too late in the day to traverse the courthouse. He punched Ben's name on his phone and gave him the latest update. After they discussed the situation at length, Ben agreed rattling Kevin's cage would be a wise move. They made a plan and Ben promised to contact Carter Baxter as soon as he got word the police in Virginia were interviewing Kevin. Coop didn't want Carter to think he didn't trust him and didn't want him to feel betrayed. They made a plan to meet at Coop's office after work on Wednesday to review the outcome.

"I'll be at the courthouse first thing in the morning. I can't imagine I'll learn much, but need to check Callie's movements on the off-chance she encountered something there. I was banking on learning more at the law offices, but it was a bust. I think whatever she had in the envelope is the key to this thing."

"Good luck. I hope you get something soon. I'll bring dinner for you and AB tomorrow night. Maybe between the three of us, we'll hit on something."

"I want to get this wrapped up this week. AB leaves on her trip this weekend and we're supposed to be closed the next two weeks."

"I hear ya. I've got two other deaths to solve, not to mention the usual Christmas uptick in stolen goods and scams to deal with. I'd like to be able to enjoy some time with family during the holidays, but it's not looking good."

After dragging himself to the gym Wednesday morning, Coop left Gus with AB while he made the trek downtown. He stopped and bought a giant cup of coffee before his mission, knowing he would need the fortification to face the ominous gatekeepers of the court system.

Since he was already on the court schedule in less than an hour, and he knew the clerk, Martha, through his aunt, he elected to visit Judge Mallott's court first. Martha had worked at the courthouse for over thirty years and been the clerk before Judge Mallott took the bench. He was shown into her large office overlooking the river. "Coop, what brings you by this fine mornin'?"

"I'm working on a case, investigating the murder of a lawyer, Calista Baxter, from Brandon King's office."

"Oh, yes, I read about her. Horrible, just horrible. What can I do to help you?"

"I'm retracing Callie's steps the week before her death, trying to figure out a motive. She visited this office three times the week she was killed and I was hoping to find out if anyone remembers anything that could prove helpful."

"I'm afraid I didn't know her. Let's go up front and check the log and y'all can talk to the girls at the front counter. They'll be more help."

He followed Martha and she introduced him to the two

women at the reception area. While he asked them about Callie, Martha retrieved the document log they kept, noting all the documents received or transmitted by the office. She flipped back to the week in question and scanned the column for Callie's name.

The women remembered Callie and were saddened to learn of her death, but as with the law offices he visited, they only recalled Callie as polite and businesslike. Neither remembered anything of significance.

Martha returned with a copy of the document list for Coop. "Here y'all go. This shows she dropped off files and picked up others during the week. We saw her Monday, Tuesday, and Wednesday. They were all routine files and cases, nothin' looks questionable to me."

"Do all the courts maintain a document list like this?"

"I would hope to shout. I've trained most of the clerks in this buildin' and explained it was an absolute necessity."

Coop grinned. "Great, that'll be a huge help. I've got one more favor to ask." He showed her his list of courts and asked her to pave the way for him with the other clerks. She penned the name of the clerk who would help next to each court on his list. "Sweetie, all you need say is Martha sent you. If you have any trouble, you just call me."

Little did he know Aunt Camille's friend wielded the real power in the courthouse. She sent him on his way, his step lighter with a handful of her business cards, on which she'd scribbled her direct line. He equated them to a stack of get out of jail free cards.

He had a few minutes to spare and found Lola Belle and Daisy waiting outside the courtroom. There was no sign of Trent. Coop sat with Daisy at the table and faced Judge Mallott. The judge went through the formalities and requested proof Trent had been notified of the hearing. The clerk confirmed notification and the judge proceeded. Based on the evidence Coop presented and the perceived danger to the child, the judge granted a temporary restraining order and set another court date in thirty days.

Once the judge ruled, Coop ushered the women out the door and explained the provisions of the order. "Daisy, you still need to keep a log and record any of his calls. Don't answer the phone, let it record him. If he continues to harass you or violate the order, call the police right away, okay?"

She nodded her head and Lola Belle answered, "Thank you, Cooper. We will do whatever you say."

"Be sure and notify her pre-school or babysitter and give them a copy of the order," he reminded them as they made their way to the elevator.

He set out on his rounds through the building and only had to pull the Martha card once, when the woman she had recommended was out ill and he was forced to talk with another. When he explained who he was and let the clerks know Martha had recommended them, it was like hearing a key click in a lock. Each of them copied her document lists for him, with a smile.

He had reached his last stop of the day when he arrived at Judge Hunt's court. Sadie was at the front desk and shoved her reading glasses down her nose when he approached the counter. "How may I help you?" she said, in an apathetic tone.

He consulted his list and asked for Hildie, invoking Martha's name. Sadie punched a button on the phone and summoned Hildie. A brunette in a polished skirt and jacket appeared from the back and invited him to step into a conference room. He explained who he was and the case he was investigating before asking about Callie.

"I don't work the front counter often, so I'm afraid I don't know her. Of course, I read about it and the courthouse has been all abuzz with talk of the horrible murder. Mr. King is a frequent attorney in our court. Let me get our log and I'll do my best to help you."

She returned with Sadie in tow and explained Sadie was the person who would know about Callie's visits firsthand. She consulted the log and nodded. "Yes, I remember she came in several times to drop off and pick up files." She looked at the pages in the log. "Oh, my, she was here right after poor Billy, the night he was killed."

Sadie ran her finger down the list of documents. "These are all marked up and colored because we were trying to verify which documents had been recovered from Billy's bag." She sighed. "Judge Hunt was fit to be tied when we discovered Billy had been the victim. He stayed late with us and went through the log. He directed us to recreate all the documents and we called a different delivery service to get them out."

"Judge Hunt is meticulous about our operations and wanted to make sure there were no delays related to losing files in the accident or waiting for them to be released by the police. We all loved Billy. It was such a tragedy, but we had to focus on the work," said Hildie.

"That's why you'll notice all the same documents listed again. We logged the second shipment with the other company," said Sadie. "We got them out right away."

"So, do any of the documents Callie dropped off or retrieved during the week have any significance or importance?" asked Coop.

Both women scanned the list. Hildie shook her head from side to side as she read each line. "These are all routine files, nothing notable." She snapped the rings on the file and took out the pages to copy. "I'll send you with a copy so you can peruse it. If you have any questions, just give me a call."

He left with the list, Hildie's card, and a smile from Sadie. He finished his next two stops without any earthshattering developments. It was well after lunch and he was starving. He stopped for a quick snack and called AB to check for any messages.

"Mr. Baxter just called for you. He'll be available the rest of the afternoon."

"I'm heading back in a few minutes. I'll call him as soon as I get there." Coop scarfed down the gourmet grilled cheese sandwich he bought from the food truck outside the courthouse and hurried to his Jeep.

10

When he got back, he gave AB the copies of the logs and asked her to go through them and combine them into one readable list. He retrieved a glass of sweet tea and closed the door to his office.

As he took his chair, the intercom buzzed. AB's voice filled the room. "Uh, Coop, your mother is on the line for you. She insists on talking to you right now. Says it's an emergency."

He mumbled his thanks and took a long slow sip of tea. After a deep breath he picked up the phone. "Cooper Harrington," he said, in his all business voice.

"Didn't your girl tell you it was your mother?" The voice he hadn't heard in years gave him an instant headache.

"I'm busy. What's the emergency?"

"I'm in the neighborhood and wanted to see you." The last time she had visited Nashville, Coop had been a freshman in college.

"I'm in the middle of a tough case. It's not a great time for a surprise visit."

"Ah, Cooper, come on, I'm your mom."

"What's the story? I haven't heard from you for years. You never come to visit, so what's up?"

"It's Christmas, Cooper." Her voice was thick with tears, phony or real, he couldn't tell.

"I'm booked today. Give me your number and I'll call you when I'm free."

"You don't have time for your own mother at Christmas?" she whined.

He rolled his eyes and resisted the overwhelming urge to scream. Taking in a breath and letting it out he said, "It's the best I can do right now."

She recited a number and he scribbled it on a sticky notepad and replaced the receiver telling her he'd get in touch later.

As soon as he hung up the phone, AB came through the door and gave him a questioning look. "What was the emergency? Is everything okay?"

Coop put his hands behind his head as he leaned back against the chair. "No emergency, just another lie. She's in the neighborhood and wants to meet me."

AB gritted her teeth and winced. "Uh oh. What did you say?"

"Told her I was busy right now, which I am."

She nodded. "Maybe you should call your brother and find out if he knows anything?"

"Yeah, I was thinking the same thing. Right now, I need to work on the case. I'll deal with her later." He leaned forward and fingered the note AB had given him with Carter Baxter's number. As he picked up the phone, she left and clicked the door closed behind her.

Carter came on the line moments after Coop called. "Sorry I missed your call, Mr. Baxter."

"No problem. I just wanted to report back. Your colleague, Chief Mason, called me earlier today and said the police were interviewing Kevin. I hope it serves as a wake-up call for the young man. Of course, Kevin demanded to call his step-father. I was so proud of John when he told Kevin to answer their questions truthfully and didn't help Kevin conceal his wrongdoings."

"I haven't talked with Chief Mason. I just got in from some other interviews."

"John and I had a heart-to-heart last night. I feel so bad for him. He has a miserable home life, but because of this appointment, he feels stuck. He thinks if he gets divorced, the governor may elect to move on to someone not involved in such drama. Politicians are always thinking about voters and their next election, so I understand."

Coop let the man ramble on about his family situation, while he sipped his tea. "As it sits now, Winnie is in rehab, again. She'll be there for at least the next month, which is the timeframe of the appointment process. I explained to John he may want to withdraw from consideration, as Winnie being in rehab has negative connotations, just like a divorce would." Carter exhaled a heavy breath. "I think John may finally be ready to cut loose of Winnie and Kevin and make a new path in life. I told him there's always another job. He's a talented attorney and could work anywhere, but his happiness in life is more important."

"Excellent advice, sir. Back to Kevin, did you get any information that would shed light on his possible involvement with Callie's death?"

"Oh, yes, I'm sorry. It's been a trying few days. John doesn't believe they are involved in any conspiracy to kill poor Callie. John said Kevin used the cash to buy drugs and pay gambling debts. He said this isn't the first time, but I think it might be the last. Winnie thinks John has no clue about the money she spends, but he's very much aware of it. This has forced him to examine the hard facts. He has spent hundreds of thousands of dollars on Winnie and Kevin, trying to help them and it's a vicious circle. I hope he's done with her."

"I appreciate the call, Mr. Baxter. I'm sorry for your difficulties. I hope things work out for John and I'll contact Chief

Mason to get further information. I trust you'll update Mrs. Baxter and I'll be in touch if I learn anything new."

Coop disconnected and rubbed his temples. "Makes my dysfunctional family look somewhat normal." He moved over to the sofa and extended a hand to pet Gus while he contemplated the case. He sat back and shut his eyes.

Coop was fast asleep when AB came in with the new list. She tiptoed out of the office and shut the door, letting him rest.

She waited until five-thirty to wake him, knowing Ben would be there soon. With a gentle hand she nudged him awake. He blinked several times and said, "Sorry, my insomnia has been relentless this past week."

"Your mom called again. I told her you were out of the office on a case."

He blew out a breath. "Thanks, AB."

Gus raised his head and stretched before closing his eyes again. "Too bad you can't sleep like your dog. He has no trouble. I'm sure you're worrying too much...about Callie's case."

"Ben will be here soon." Coop stood and studied the white-board. He heard the backdoor and Gus bolted from the chair to investigate. Ben arrived with bags of takeout, followed by Gus with his nose in the air, and AB carrying cold drinks.

Coop took Gus to the kitchen and filled his bowl with kibble. Like a vacuum, Gus inhaled his dinner and followed Coop to his office, where Gus gave AB his best begging face and was rewarded with a bite of tortilla. Ben had unearthed a selection of food from a popular Mexican restaurant not far from Coop's office. They heaped their plates full and then gathered around the table and white board.

Ben produced a DVD from a file and said, "Here's a copy of the interview Virginia did with Kevin. It's entertaining. He called his step-dad who came and did more to help us than he did the kid. In the end the kid broke down, even cried. His money went to drugs and gambling, as Mr. Baxter suspected.

Once he figured out he was a suspect in the murder of his aunt, he wised up and came clean. They're going to follow up on the drugs and illegal gambling, but I'm confident he didn't have any involvement in Callie's death."

Coop finished a taco and asked, "You don't think Winnie used him as the middleman to contract a hit?"

Ben shook his head. "I don't think so. Watch the video, but I'm in agreement with the detectives in Virginia, I think he's telling the truth." Between bites, he continued, "Kate dug through Ollie's financials and found nothing to link him to any kind of murder for hire scheme. He's a dirt bag druggie, but she followed every trail and came up empty."

"Damn, I was hoping he was the one. It would serve him right for being such a complete asshat," said AB.

"Kate did tip off the Virginia authorities to his involvement in drugs. She's convinced he sells as well as uses. She said they vowed to make him a priority."

She rolled her eyes. "So, if it isn't Ollie and you think Winnie and Kevin are in the clear, we're back to square one. Winnie would have been another perfect candidate for the murderer. She's easy to hate."

"Maybe with Winnie in rehab for the month, John will give serious consideration to a divorce. Carter made it sound like John might pass on the governor's appointment and concentrate on fixing his life," said Coop.

"He could do much better than Winnie," said AB. "From what Dot said, Winnie won't get much in a divorce situation. She may be a gold digger, but when you marry into a dynasty of lawyers, you gotta figure they're going to protect themselves."

"Kate and Jimmy cleared all the employees from King's firm. So that's a dead end, but we can cross it off the list." Ben finished off the chips and salsa and said, "A bit of good news today. We found our wanted felon, who turned out to be the hit and run driver."

"Was it an accident?" asked Coop.

Ben nodded. "At this point it looks like it. The guy knew he was wanted and didn't stop because he didn't want to go to jail." He took a gulp from his drink. "So, now the scumbag is looking at a much greater problem. The DA is considering vehicular homicide."

"What about the guy from the video who was going through Billy's bag? Did you ever figure it out?" asked Coop.

Ben shook his head. "We could never find him again on any video. It's not a great picture. We did recover all the documents Billy was supposed to have in his bag. They were a mess from the rain and traffic, but Kate and Jimmy were able to piece them together and they matched the company's transmittal list from the labels scanned from each item. Billy makes three stops a day at the courthouse. It works a lot like regular delivery services. The customer puts in the shipping information online and prints a label for the item and the messenger scans those labels before he leaves each stop. So, once the messenger picks up the item, it's in the system. The company was a great help in identifying the items and matching them to their data."

They finished their meal and AB gave them each a copy of the list from the court logs. "There's one oddity I discovered on the list of documents from Judge Hunt's court. Your notes said they recreated the documents lost in the hit and run with Billy. There's one discrepancy in a document with the name H. Featherstone and a delivery address downtown on 5th Avenue. It appears in the second batch, but not the first."

"His was the only court staff who took the time to duplicate documents the same night. The others chose to wait it out and work with the delivery company and the police." Coop's forehead wrinkled as he looked at AB's list and then reviewed the original list from the court. He punched the keys on his laptop. "So, this address on 5th is a mailing service store."

"It's just a block from the Hilton and in the direction Callie was walking," said Ben.

"That's a bit of a coincidence," said Coop.

"And we don't believe in coincidences," said Ben.

"Exactly."

"The document doesn't have a case number associated with it. It just says Hunt in the space for the case number," said AB. "I looked through all the logs for any similar notations and found a few from other courts. My guess is when a judge is sending something for personal use, it's noted with his name. Then the judge is charged for the fee when the court receives the billing from the messenger company. Some of the other logs had things sent to accountants and even relatives where the judge's name was listed, so that's why I assume it's personal."

"I'll call Martha and ask her if your theory is correct," said Coop. He pulled the card from his pocket and tried her direct line, even though it was past closing time.

He perked up when she answered. He asked and nodded as he listened and then disconnected. "Martha says you are spot on. Judges are authorized to use the service for personal items as long as they note their name and pay their monthly charges."

"We need to find out what Judge Hunt was sending to someone named Featherstone at the mail service store." said Ben. He went up to the white board and used a red marker to circle the visit to Judge Hunt's courtroom on Thursday and drew an arrow connecting it to the entry of Callie's trip to the Hilton down 5th Avenue on Friday. He added a note about the delivery for the address on 5th from Judge Hunt.

"We need to research Judge Hunt before we put him on the defensive. I think AB and I can stay tonight and dig into his background. Will that work?," he asked AB.

AB nodded her head. "Yeah, no problem." She knew he was determined to distract himself from the situation with his mother and would use work to avoid her.

Ben used his cell to call and get his team moving on the necessary paperwork and technology to trace Mr. Featherstone. He tasked Kate and Jimmy with finding any video footage of Callie's walk down 5th Avenue. He ended the call with, "Get over to Billy's family and let them know before the press gets wind of it."

"I'm glad you found the driver who killed Billy," said AB. "At least you'll get one of these cases off your plate."

"Yeah," Ben let out a sigh as he stood and donned his jacket. "We added another one today, but it's solved. Domestic turned into a homicide. The jogger is still unsolved and we're getting nowhere on it. I'm hoping this mailbox place leads to something on Callie's case. We've been working around the clock and we're all tired. I'm going to take tonight off and try to get some sleep."

"We'll touch base in the morning and let you know what we find out about the judge," said Coop, giving him a tap on the back.

"We should have something on Featherstone by then. I'll talk to you later," said Ben, as he gave AB a quick hug before leaving.

Coop put in a call to Aunt Camille to let her know he'd be working late. Gus sacked out in his chair by the fireplace and Coop got to work. Before Ben drove away, AB was at her desk digging into the life of Judge Reese Hunt. She scoured the Internet while Coop concentrated on running the judge through the databases they used for backgrounds.

After an hour, Coop went to the kitchen to make some decaf coffee while his printer spewed forth pages of information about Judge Hunt. He filled the kettle for tea for AB and pondered the case while he waited. His brain was foggy, his thoughts slow, and he knew he was no sharper than a butter knife. He was exhausted from going without sleep over the past several nights and his sluggish synapses were little help.

He poured a large mug of coffee and fixed AB her favorite

tea. "How's it going?" he asked, as he set her mug near her screen. He took a seat on the sofa near her desk.

"Lots of information. He's been in the news often, so several hits on him. I'm going through and trying to print out the important ones. He grew up here in Nashville and went to Vanderbilt. He's mentioned as a strong candidate for a spot on the Tennessee Criminal Court of Appeals. The governor is supposed to select the judge in January."

He listened, but felt himself drifting off, sinking into the squishy leather of the cushions. She turned from her screen and saw him, with his eyes closed, mug still in his hand. "Coop, you need to get home or go sleep in your office. You're dead on your feet."

No response. She removed the mug, lifted his legs and positioned him on the sofa, and covered him with a throw. She shook her head and retrieved the printed pages from his office and added them to her stack.

She worked for the next few hours, reading the pages and transferring relevant information to their standard background profile sheet. It helped to have a checklist of information they collected, so they didn't overlook anything. It was after midnight when she had the basic data completed. She yawned and saw Coop was still sleeping.

She wrote a quick note on a sticky pad and stuck it to Coop's mug. After checking on Gus, who was passed out in the office, she made sure the front door was locked and tiptoed out through the back door.

A slight noise woke Coop and he was alert to someone near him. He could feel breath on his cheek. Defensive techniques ran through his mind. He feigned sleep and then sprang from the sofa to surprise the intruder. The pink light of dawn was beginning to come through the front window of the office and his eyes adjusted to the figure next to the sofa. He exhaled a loud breath and said, "Gus, what the hell?"

A soft rumble came from the dog. Coop collapsed on the sofa, his heart pounding in his chest. He gave Gus a pet and scratched him behind the ears. "You scared me, buddy." Gus rested his head on Coop's thigh and sighed. Once Coop's pulse slowed, he got up and poured dogfood in the bowl and let Gus out the back door. As soon as Gus visited his favorite bush, he bolted back inside and devoured breakfast.

Coop turned on the lights on his way back to the reception area and spied the fluorescent orange note. *Background sheet is on your desk. I'll be in by 9. Sweet Dreams, AB.*

He rebuilt the fire in his office, set the timer on the coffee maker to brew, and loaded Gus in the Jeep to hurry home for a shower. He didn't want to wake Aunt Camille and left her a note in the kitchen, explaining he had slept at the office and would be there all day. He and Gus were back at the office before eight, refreshed and ready for the day, Coop wearing a t-shirt imprinted with *Before you give me your best shot, I recommend you read my return policy.*

The rich scent of roasted coffee filled the office and Coop filled his Vanderbilt mug to the rim. He reviewed AB's work and summarized Hunt's background on the whiteboard.

Coop noticed his dog's ear perk, announcing the arrival of AB. Gus rushed to the back door to greet her. The dog's nose was in the air, inches away from the box of decadent pastries she juggled. She made her way to Coop's office and slid the box onto the table. "I stopped at the fancy bakery and brought us some fortification."

Coop opened the box and the comforting aroma of warm sugar and cinnamon drifted through the air. "Smells great and I'm starving." He plucked a still warm giant sticky bun, oozing caramel.

"What time did you wake up?" she asked.

"Not until this morning. I ran home and showered and got back here about an hour ago. I've been staring at my summary notes. Keep hoping I'll notice something that would lead to a break in this case."

"Just for fun, I tried to find something on the surname Featherstone and found a golfer and a guy in England. I don't think either is our Mr. Featherstone," she said, selecting a pastry. "Hope Ben comes up with something."

He reviewed the information they had gathered. "So, Judge Hunt is older than us, but went to Vanderbilt. He graduated high school from a fancy private academy in 1980. His parents had money, but they weren't uber rich. He's respected, fair, no family troubles picked up by the press, and from what I saw looks like a shoo-in for the seat on the appeals court."

"His financials show cash withdrawals, but nothing over a few thousand each time, and no recent change in the pattern. Not sure why he needs cash so often, but it's been the same pattern over the last several years. He makes good money and his wife works as an architect. They have a healthy savings and investments. They pay their bills and their mortgage is paid off, so they're more than comfortable."

"Kids are in college, so just the two of them at home. Anything hinky with the kids?"

"I didn't dig into them, but nothing on the surface," she said, forking the last bite of her croissant into her mouth.

"Dig a little more, just to make sure we don't miss something." By the time they heard the front door open, Gus had already sprung from his chair and slid through the office to greet Ben.

Ben took a chair and helped himself to a braided concoction covered in powdered sugar and nuts. He eyed the white board and added, "Mr. Featherstone is a dead end, so far. He's not a resident of Tennessee. We checked airline manifests, rental car agencies, hotel stays in the city. Zip, nada, nothing. Kate and Jimmy went by the mailbox place when they opened this morning and got nowhere. They have cameras inside, but they haven't worked for years. Nobody there remembers Mr. Featherstone and the owner says he won't release information without a warrant. So, Kate's writing it up now and we hope to have it today. They're tracking down video from businesses, but haven't had any luck yet."

Ben concentrated on the whiteboard and frowned. "Judge Hunt went to Mount Camden Academy?"

Coop nodded. "Yep. Class of 1980, why?"

"That's where my dead jogger went to high school. Same graduating class."

11

Coop shook his head back and forth several times, like Gus does when he gets out of the pool. "So now we've got a fine thread connecting your dead jogger to Judge Hunt? This is insane."

"I don't have the file with me, but I remember the school, because it's exclusive and my guy is an auto parts manager and lives in a modest neighborhood. It didn't fit. Turns out he was a scholarship kid and an excellent athlete."

AB flipped through her notes. "I don't have much on Judge Hunt's time in high school. I'll get on it and ascertain if there's a true link between the two."

Coop nodded. "We better check for connections in any of Hunt's cases. We'll need all the background you have on the jogger, Ben."

Ben was tapping keys on his phone before Coop finished his sentence. "You'll have an email in a few minutes with our file on Avery Logan." He stood and helped himself to another breakfast treat. "I've gotta run. I'll be in touch with whatever we learn from the mailbox place on Featherstone."

AB grabbed a napkin and used it to dust the white trail of

powdered sugar from Ben's suit jacket. He let out a sigh, "Thanks, AB."

"Once we comb through more of this stuff, I want to talk to Judge Hunt. Might be easier if I did it as a PI, instead of involving you at this point. If there's nothing there, you won't be risking the department's relationship," said Coop.

"Agreed," said Ben. "If we end up with something on him, we'll need to make sure our ducks are in a row. I'll have to involve the DA in it." He shoved the rest of his pastry in his mouth, jutting his neck over a plate to catch any errant crumbs.

"Yeah, that's why I want to talk to him on my own. Approach it as the family wanting answers and me just following Callie's steps." Coop added, "I can act dumber than I look."

Ben and AB both looked at each other and laughed. "Oh, yeah. I can vouch for that," she said.

"I think you need a new shirt with that phrase printed on it," Ben said, hurrying to the door before Coop could retort.

Coop dug Hildie's card out of his file and put in a call to arrange an appointment to meet with Judge Hunt. She told him to stop by late in the afternoon. The judge could meet with him after the last case of the day.

Coop spent the next several hours poring over the information AB had gathered on Judge Hunt's time at Mount Camden. After culling all she could online, she took a trip to the school and left Coop to dissect the file on the jogger, Avery Logan.

While he was immersed in reading, Ben called to let him know they didn't get much on Featherstone. The mailbox store didn't require anything beyond a form requesting a name, address, phone number, and email contact. His first name is Henry and he paid cash for the mailbox for six months and rented it in November. The address he gave was bogus and turned out to be an empty lot. The email was a free one and no longer active. The phone number was also a presumed dead end, as it ended up being the main number at the State of Tennessee.

"We're going to run down personnel at the State of Tennessee, just to make sure they've never employed Henry Featherstone, but my gut tells me it's just a fake number. I think the email is useless, since he didn't have to tell the truth to create one of those free email accounts."

"Was there anything in his mailbox?"

"Nothing, empty."

"What about putting some surveillance on the store to catch anybody accessing the box?"

"It's a worthy idea. I just don't have the manpower for a long shot. I might be able to get a traffic camera positioned to cover the area. That's the best I can do."

"Do you think you could get a warrant to put a camera in the store, right on the box?"

"I don't think we have enough. The owners promised to contact us if anyone came in to access the box during business hours."

"I could put Ross and Madison on it at night. I know it's a long shot, but it's all we have right now."

"It's up to you. If I can't get a traffic camera moved, I could try to get a temporary camera set up in a phony utility construction area."

"I've got an appointment with Judge Hunt at four-thirty, so I'll do my best to get any information out of him related to our Mr. Featherstone."

"Tread with care," said Ben.

~

He no sooner disconnected from Ben, when the phone rang. He heard the panicked voice of Lola Belle. "Cooper, Trent has kidnapped the little one from her nursery school."

"Have you called the police?"

"Yes, yes. Daisy called right away and they're sending a car to the school." He scribbled down the address of the school and told her he was on his way.

He locked the office and sent AB a text before loading Gus in the Jeep and rushing to the school. When he arrived, he found two uniformed officers on the scene, an inconsolable Daisy, Lola Belle, and the manager of the nursery school.

Coop introduced himself to the officers and provided them a copy of the recent restraining order. They assured Coop they had already transmitted Trent's information and had the entire state looking for the missing toddler.

After a few words with the panic-stricken manager, Coop gleaned the basic facts. Trent had come to the school and approached a young volunteer, asking to collect his daughter. The volunteer was the only person in the office at the time and didn't know about the restraining order. She collected the toddler and her things and handed her over to her father.

The volunteer was hysterical and the manager had phoned an ambulance for her. Coop wasn't able to gather any additional facts from the distraught young girl and suspected he wouldn't until she calmed down.

He bypassed Daisy, who was resting on a sofa, still sobbing out of control. Lola Belle stood outside the establishment, her gloved hands clutched. Coop inquired about Trent's habits, friends, and relatives in the area. Lola Belle answered his questions, pointing to Trent's mother as his closest relative in Nashville. "I've given the police the same information, so I'm hopin' y'all will catch up with him soon." She glanced to the doorway of the school. "I'm not sure Daisy is strong enough to survive much of this."

"Do you think Trent would hurt the child?" he asked.

Lola Belle shook her head. "I don't think so. He's fuming mad at Daisy. He's doing this to hurt her or get back at her. He's never shown much interest in the baby, until the divorce."

Coop promised to be in touch and made his way down the sidewalk. He put in a call to AB and gave her an update. "Get Madison and Reed to start checking out Trent's workplace and friends. I'm going to stop by his mother's house and interview her. She might be able to point us to where Trent would go. He took her two hours ago, so he could be long gone by now."

Coop and Gus made their way to the mother's address, a rundown apartment building. Coop knocked on the door and it was opened by a harsh looking woman with deep wrinkles puckered around her mouth. A cigarette hung from her lips, smoke trailing out of her nose. "I ain't got no money, so no point in trying to sell me nothin'," she said.

Coop explained he was a private detective and was working for Daisy, helping her locate her daughter. He described Trent's actions at the nursery school. "Have you seen or talked to Trent or your granddaughter today?"

She took a long drag from the cigarette. "Nah, I haven't heard from him today. She is his daughter. I'm not sure how y'all think this is a kidnappin'."

"We're just trying to make sure the child is safe and get Trent to speak with the police to get this matter straightened out. Do you have any idea where he may have gone? Does he have any favorite places he likes to go?"

She shook her head, covered in tight gray curls. "His apartment and work are all I know of. He likes to go fishin', but this ain't fishin' weather."

He quizzed her more about Trent's fishing spots and possible fishing buddies and gave her his card before leaving. He connected his phone to AB before pulling away. "We need to target any of his friends who fish. His mother said fishing is his hobby. One of them might know of a place Trent might go."

"Okay, I'll let Ross know. I've been trying to work with the police to track his cell phone, but it's off."

"Trent will be in a panic himself and want to stay under the radar. The police will blanket the area looking for the car and they'll get a location on his phone if he turns it on. I'm trying to figure out where he would go to hide out. If Ross gets anything, tell him to let me know."

He and Gus drove back to the office, keeping an eye out for Trent's Subaru on the way. They bounded through the backdoor and found AB at her desk. He asked, "Anything from Ross and Madison?"

She shook her head. "Not yet. The two of them split up and are interviewing anyone in Trent's life. They'll keep us posted."

"How'd you do on Callie's case today?"

"I've got copies of Mount Camden's yearbooks and the contact info for the headmaster and the dean for the period when they both attended."

"Anybody there remember either of them?"

She shook her head. "No, nobody's been there that long, so we're stuck with trying to find the retired staff."

Coop culled the pages of the yearbooks and found both young men pictured in several group photos related to sports and clubs, but nothing stood out linking the two of them. AB took the tedious task of combing through Judge Hunt's cases, using their online database. She searched for Avery Logan as a party to any of the cases before the judge and came up empty.

Coop answered the chirp of his cell phone and after a few short sentences disconnected. "That was Ross. He found a childhood friend who was a fishing buddy of Trent's in high school. The friend's family used to have a cabin near J. Percy Priest Lake."

"You don't have time to run all the way out there. You've got to be at the courthouse soon."

He nodded as he punched buttons on his phone and connected with Ben. He gave Ben the information Ross had found and asked him to forward it to the detectives running the abduction case. "I'll touch base after I'm done at the courthouse."

He hurried to the armoire and grabbed a shirt. "I've gotta get moving," said Coop. "Why don't you plan to come to supper tonight? You could keep Aunt Camille calm. I'm sure she's in a dither with all this. We can get caught up on whatever I learn from Judge Hunt."

"Sure, sounds terrific. Shall I call Aunt Camille?"

He nodded as he layered a respectable button-down shirt on over his t-shirt. "Thought I better tone down the snark if I'm meeting a judge."

"I'm so proud of you, Coop. Sometimes you're like a real grownup." She laughed as she picked up the phone and let Camille know there would be one more at the table tonight.

"Go ahead and get Ross and Madison set up to do surveillance after hours on the mailbox store. We're going to attempt to catch any activity on the box. Schedule me for some shifts too." Coop waved a goodbye and petted Gus on the head. "You stay with AB and she'll take you home." Gus thumped his tail against the wooden floor.

After fighting for a parking spot, Coop quickened his pace through the courthouse and arrived at the judge's office with not a minute to spare. Hildie was at the front counter. "Mr. Harrington, come on back. Judge Hunt is ready for you."

She showed him into a large space, with windows overlooking the river. Judge Hunt moved from behind his desk and shook hands with Coop. "Mr. Harrington, come on in and have a seat." He requested beverages from Hildie and motioned Coop to the seating area.

"I appreciate you seeing me on such short notice, Judge Hunt. I'm not sure if Hildie explained, but I've been hired by Calista Baxter's family to look into her murder. I've been retracing her steps, which led me here. She visited your office several times during the course of her work at Brandon King's office."

The judge nodded. "Yes, Hildie told me the reason for your visit. I'm happy to help in any way, but I didn't know Calista on a personal level."

"I didn't think you would have, but I'm a stickler about thoroughness. I've reviewed the cases she'd been working on and didn't notice anything suspect, but wanted to run them by you."

"Of course," he said, taking a cup of coffee from the tray Hildie held.

Coop helped himself to water and rattled off the names associated with the files Callie had picked up from the court.

Judge Hunt listened with a brow furrowed in thought. He shook his head after Coop read each name. "Those are all rather boring cases, run of the mill. Nothing I can think would precipitate a murder."

Coop sighed. "We've been hitting a brick wall with this one." He took a long swig from his glass of water. "I reviewed all of the files on the log that went in and out of your office the week of her murder. There's just one thing that puzzles me."

The judge's eyebrows rose, "What's that?"

"The last time Callie was here was the evening Billy, the bike messenger, was hit by a car and killed. Hildie said you had the staff work late to recreate all the documents and send them out with another service."

"That's right. I didn't want to take any chances with delays during the investigation or lost documents."

"I understand. I did notice you had a personal document going to a Mr. Featherstone downtown. It was on the second list, but not on the first list. Do you recall what you were sending him?"

Judge Hunt's forehead gathered and creased. "Featherstone...let me check my files." He returned to his desk and looked through a leather appointment diary. "Ah, yes. I was sending him a response to speak at a community group."

"Do you know him?"

"No, I understood he was the coordinator for the event. Let me have Hildie pull the file." He picked up his phone and requested the information.

Minutes later, Hildie came in and handed him a file. He perused it and brought it over to Coop. "Here's the information I sent and the original request. Henry Featherstone. He's with the Nashville Coalition for Informed Citizens." He handed Coop the file.

"Would you mind if I copied this?"

"Not at all," he picked up the phone and Hildie appeared and took the file.

"Had you spoken at other events for this group in the past?"

"No, this was a new one for me. I remember we checked the website and it looked like a grassroots type of organization. I've been doing a lot of speeches and appearances over the past few months. I'm being considered for a seat on the Tennessee Criminal Court of Appeals and it always helps to connect with the community."

"This one was scheduled for the East Park Community Center in January. Is that a common venue for these types of events?"

The judge nodded. "Yes, they tend to be in free or low-cost locations around the city. Different groups want to know more about how the judicial system works and ask questions. I paid for the delivery myself. I want to avoid the perception of using taxpayer money to further my own career." Hildie returned with the file and copies. "Is there a reason you're so interested in this group and Mr. Featherstone? I'm not sure I understand how it's related to the poor woman's death."

"Just an anomaly at this point, but I haven't been able to locate Mr. Featherstone. He doesn't appear to exist and the address you sent your response to is a mailbox store."

The judge frowned in disbelief. "What? That doesn't make any sense."

"Do you know why the document wasn't listed on the original list and only the second list with the alternate delivery service?"

The judge shook his head. "No. I would suspect it was a clerical oversight. The intern must have missed logging it."

"So, how did the staff know to include it in the second list?"

"We reviewed all our work products for the day and it was one of the documents created, so it was included in the second list. I don't remember it being a concern at the time. We were in a hurry."

Coop stood with his file copies. "Well, this will help me sort it out. I appreciate your time."

"If we can help further, just let me know." The judge shook Coop's hand and walked him to the door.

Coop was met by Hildie in the hallway and escorted back to the front counter. The office was closed, so she used her key to unlock the door and let him out. "Have a good evening," she said.

He made a detour to the precinct to check on the status of the tip he had passed to Ben. He found Ben at his desk on the phone. After Ben disconnected, he ran his hand over his balding head. "What a couple of days this has been."

"Any good news on the missing toddler? Did the cabin tip pay off?"

"The guy's parents sold the cabin years ago and he doesn't remember who bought it. He's out there now with a team trying to lead them to it. He hasn't been there since he was a kid, so it's slow."

"No other sightings of Trent, huh?"

Ben shook his head. "Not as far as I know. They were happy to get the information on the cabin. They're going through camera footage now trying to spot his car heading in that direction."

"It could be a long shot, but it'd be a great hiding spot. Especially this time of year." Coop checked his watch. "I need to get a move on, but I'll meet you in the morning and we can catch up."

Ben stood. "I need to get going myself. I'll see you tomorrow, Coop. They've got word to get in touch with you if they locate Trent and the girl."

Coop's mind spun with possible theories related to Callie's case on his drive home, but as soon as he opened the door and the aroma of roasting meat met his nose, his stomach became his focus. Gus met him at the door and trailed him through the house. Coop followed his nose to the kitchen where he found AB and his aunt working. Surprised to hear his mother's voice for the second time in as many days, he turned to see her sitting at the counter.

"What are you doing here?" He took in his mother's graying dyed blond hair and the deep wrinkles etched in her face, courtesy of years of smoking. Her eyes were hard, as he remembered them. The aging process had not been graceful or kind to her.

"Is that any way to greet your mother, Cooper?" She slid off her chair and approached him with her arms out.

He smelled the foul odor of smoke wafting from her. He moved out of her direct path and said, "I told you yesterday, I'm in the middle of a tough case and would call you when I had time."

"Your aunt was kind enough to invite me to stay for supper." Her stringy hair hung in her face and she brushed it away.

Coop gave Aunt Camille a look from the side of his eye. She fumbled with a spoon and dropped it on the floor. The tension was as thick as honey on a cold morning.

AB asked Coop's mother, Marlene, to help take some food to the table. She gave Coop a quick wink and loaded his mother's arms with bowls while she directed her to the dining room.

"How could you invite her to stay?" whispered Coop.

Aunt Camille's hands fluttered across the countertop. "She showed up at the door a few hours ago and said she had talked to you. She said you told her to stop by the house. I didn't know what to do."

"She's such a manipulator. I meant to call my brother and forgot." He pulled his cell phone from his pocket and tapped out a text to his brother, Jack. He lingered in the kitchen awaiting a reply.

Aunt Camille bustled back into the kitchen, leaving AB to babysit Coop's mother. His aunt spooned mashed potatoes into a bowl. "I'm sorry, Coop," she whispered. "I was shocked and didn't know what to do. I didn't want to bother y'all. One meal won't hurt us."

"What does she want?"

Her wispy hair fluttered as she shook her head. Her cheeks reddened and her hands shook as she manipulated the spoon in the pot. "She hasn't really said, but sounds like she's found herself without a home and estranged from her latest beau."

"Of course, she has. She's not staying here." He twisted his head to look into her eyes. "Got it?"

She nodded and took the empty pot to the sink. "Supper's almost ready," she hollered. She handed him a bowl of heaping mashed potatoes and asked him to take it to the dining room. "Mrs. Henderson made a fabulous meal for us. I'm just puttin' the finishin' touches on it."

Coop followed Camille into the dining room and placed the last of the food on the table. His mother tried to entice them to discuss their current case, but Coop deterred the topic with a harsh gaze at Camille and AB. "It's a difficult case. One that demands confidentiality. In fact, AB and I will be working on it through the night."

Marlene then asked, "What are you doing for Christmas?"

Before Camille could say anything, Coop answered. "Aunt Camille and I have been invited to join AB's family in the Bahamas. We leave in just a few days."

Marlene sputtered as she struggled to swallow. "The Bahamas. That sounds wonderful."

AB intervened and described the trip, highlighting all the activities at the resort. Marlene said, "That's a bit disappointing. I was so hoping to spend Christmas with family."

"I guess that's the risk you take when you surprise folks with a visit, expecting them to drop everything for you." Coop eyed his mother over the rim of his glass as he took a swallow of tea. "Why are you here?"

"Like I said, just wanted to visit. I've missed you."

Coop heard his phone emit a soft beep. He glanced at the screen and saw Jack had replied saying he hadn't talked with their mother and didn't know what was going on.

"So, where are you living now?" asked Coop.

"I was in Florida, but am...in between houses," said his mother. "I thought I'd pay you a visit and figure it all out."

"So, how'd you get here from Florida?"

Marlene looked down at her plate. "The bus."

"Where are you heading next?" asked Camille.

"I'm not sure, but I called an old friend in Vermont. I'm hoping to get up there. My plan was to spend Christmas here and then make the trip north. With you being gone for Christmas, I'm not sure..."

"I guess you better call your friend and find out if you can come early," said Coop, scooping up the last bite from his plate.

His mother nodded and used her fork to push the food around on her plate. "I suppose I better make a call."

"Have you talked to Jack lately?" asked Coop.

"No, not in a long time." Her eyes sparkled and she added, "Maybe I should take a trip to visit him?"

"Dad's spending Christmas with Jack and his family," said Coop.

"Oh, yeah, that makes sense."

"Where are you staying?" asked Coop.

"Well, I, uh, hadn't finalized any plans. I called you yesterday from one of the bus stops. I didn't get here until this morning."

Coop shook his head with disgust. "So, you just thought you'd show up here after what, twenty years or so, and think I'd just welcome you back with open arms?"

Marlene winced at the sharpness of Coop's tone. "I, uh, really hadn't thought it through." Camille and AB made a point of studying the pattern on their own plates.

"No, no, you never think it through. When you walked out on Dad, did you think that through? When you didn't give a rat's ass about your sons or even Jack's kids, did you think that through?" He flung his napkin on the table and stormed out of the room.

Camille let out a sigh. "Well, I've got some dessert ready. Would anybody care for pie?"

AB sprang from her chair to help clear the table. Camille returned with a coconut cream pie and dessert plates. Coop reappeared and placed a slip of paper in front of his mother. "I booked you into a hotel and called you a cab. It'll be here in five minutes." He thrust his hand into his pocket and extracted his wallet. He seized several bills and flung them atop the paper.

With a bewildered look, Marlene took the paper and stuffed

the money in her pocket. She stood and said, "Okay then, I'll catch up with you tomorrow sometime."

"I won't be around. Like I said, I'm working." Coop stood across the room, his usual warm eyes hard as granite.

Marlene thanked Camille for the meal and said her good-byes as the cab honked outside. Camille walked her to the door and wished her a pleasant evening.

"Oh, my heavens," she said, returning to the dining room. She gave Coop a disapproving look. "She's still your momma."

"On paper, but she gave up her rights long ago." He took his chair and patted his aunt's hand. "You've always been more of a mother to me than she'll ever be. Mothers don't abandon their families and only show up when they need something. She's not a mother, she's a mooch." Resentment and anger filled his voice.

Camille smiled and gripped Coop's hand. "You need to forgive her, for your own sake." She saw the hurt young soul she had welcomed in her home so long ago, in the man next to her. "That's all I'm going to say on the matter. I love you Coop. I couldn't love you more if you were my own son."

He heard AB sniff and saw her swipe her eye. Camille cut the pie and passed the plates around the table. "Did you find Daisy's daughter yet?" she asked, pressing her fork into the fluffy custard.

Grateful to leave the topic of his mother behind, he filled them in on the lead about the fishing cabin. "How's Lola Belle holding up?"

Camille pursed her lips. "She's mighty upset. She's a strong woman though. Daisy has always been a dramatic child and she's draining poor Lola Belle. She enlisted the help of their doctor this afternoon and he gave Daisy something to sleep." She wiped her mouth with a napkin and added, "I do hope they find the child soon."

"I'll get a call with an update. If anything happens, I'll let you know." Coop gave her hand a squeeze and then changed the topic to his conversation with Judge Hunt. "Now we'll need to check out this citizen organization and the event. Something just doesn't add up." He slipped his first bite into his mouth and turned to AB. "Did you have any luck today?"

"I left voicemails for the dean and headmaster who served at Mount Camden in the late seventies. Hunt and Logan were both athletic and on the school teams together, but I didn't uncover anything suggesting a closer link. They were both part of a school sponsored study program in Europe their junior year."

"Mount Camden is a well-respected school. It's been around for well over a hundred years. Most of my friends sent their children there and they went on to the most prestigious colleges and careers," said Camille. "I know Judge Hunt's family. They're wonderful upstandin' people. Been in Nashville forever."

"She's right about the school," said AB. "All their students are college bound and have some of the highest test scores around. Most are accepted by top tier schools. Judge Hunt went to Vanderbilt and Mr. Logan was accepted to Auburn University, but never attended. I'm not sure why, but hope to learn more from talking to the headmaster."

"After we're done here let's dig into the Nashville Coalition for Informed Citizens. I've never heard of them. Have you, Aunt Camille?"

She shook her head. "No, I don't recognize it." She took a sip of sweet tea. "I could ask the girls at book club tomorrow if they've heard of the group."

Coop choked on the last bite of his pie. He coughed and said, "No, Aunt Camille. We need to keep this quiet, so don't mention anything." The dejected look on her face made him realize his tone was harsher than he intended. He cleared his throat, "I'm sorry, it's a sensitive case and I can't risk any information getting out." He sighed and added, "With AB leaving Saturday, we're running out of time to get Callie's murder solved."

"About my trip..." said AB. "I called my parents today and

told them I was going to postpone my flight and meet them a few days later. I want to see this through for Callie."

"No," he said. "You're going on your trip. I can handle the case."

Camille gathered the dessert plates and returned with a pot of tea. AB reached and placed her hand atop Coop's. "I need to do this, Coop. For Callie. It's a two-week vacation and if I miss a few days it's not a big deal. Callie deserves my help."

He looked into her eyes and saw the determination behind the hint of tears threatening to form. He turned his hand over and gripped hers in a tight squeeze. "Okay, AB. I have one condition."

Aunt Camille poured AB a cup. "What would that be?" asked AB.

"I pay for the ticket change."

She smiled as a single tear slid down her cheek. "Deal."

Coop smiled at his aunt. "AB's going to delay her flight a few days and stay on to help on Callie's case. Isn't that great?"

Camille eyes twinkled. "Wonderful news. I guess that means our trip will be delayed, right?" She gave Coop a wink.

"Sorry I made up the story about all of us going. I wanted to squelch any ideas she had about worming into our Christmas. I couldn't miss Christmas with you, Aunt Camille. It's one of my favorite times of the year here."

She sunk into her chair and gripped her cup. "It's just not the same since...Uncle John." She plucked a hankie out of her sleeve and dabbed her eyes. "I'm sorry y'all, this time of year makes me miss him all the more."

Coop stood and went to his aunt's side. He knelt and embraced her in a strong hug. "I know. I miss him too." He kissed the top of her head and looked across the table to witness tears streaming down AB's face.

Coop took in the scene of the two most important women in his life crying. He swallowed against the lump in his throat.

"How about we take a ride and look at Christmas lights tonight?"

Aunt Camille's head bobbed and he saw the trace of a smile start to form on AB's face. "Coop and I can clear these dishes while you get ready," said AB, gathering items from the table.

Camille took Coop's hand and excused herself to freshen up while they made quick work of tidying the kitchen. Coop summoned Gus. The foursome loaded into Camille's SUV with Coop at the wheel.

Camille pressed some buttons on the dash and Christmas tunes filled the air. Coop rested his hand atop Camille's while Gus snuggled with AB in the backseat and they made their way through the festive streets of Belle Meade.

12

After hot chocolate and a plate of cookies when they returned home, Coop and AB shuttered themselves in his office. Coop sent Callie's mother an email update and then they reviewed the background information on Avery Logan. "Married, no criminal record, same job for the last twenty some years. Three kids, still owes on a mortgage, good credit, kids all in private school, oldest one is eighteen and left for college this year, wife is a secretary. Nothing looks suspect," he said.

With Judge Hunt being a public figure, the query returned hundreds of pages of information. Coop elected to concentrate his research on Logan's online profile. It was easier to search for any mention of Logan and try to connect him to Judge Hunt. He also sent Ben a quick text asking him to find out why Logan didn't attend Auburn University after Mount Camden.

AB was left with searching the court cases. She had already looked for Avery Logan as a party to any of the cases before Judge Hunt or cases where Hunt was the attorney, before he was a judge. She decided to expand her search and check other courts. For the next few hours, only the soft tapping of keyboard keys and muffled snores from Gus filled the room.

"I've got something," said AB, looking from her screen to Coop. "Logan's oldest son has a case pending in front of Judge Woodburn. Looks like he got arrested for drunk driving around Halloween. The cops found drugs during the arrest. His case comes up in January."

"The kid goes to the University of Tennessee in Knoxville," said Coop, referring to the file Ben had provided. "Must have been home for a weekend visit."

"There's nothing to indicate anything to do with Judge Hunt. Looks like a normal case."

"Who's the attorney?"

She clicked the mouse and said, "Uh, oh. It's Brandon King."

Coop's eyebrows rose atop his computer screen. "Well, that's interesting. I wonder if Callie had anything to do with the case. I'll call on Brandon tomorrow and find out what he can tell us."

Coop answered his ringing phone. He thanked the caller and turned to AB, smiling. "That was the precinct. They located the cabin and Trent's car. They just breached the place and took Trent into custody. The little girl is unharmed, but scared."

"Yay, some good news. You better go tell your aunt." She yawned and said, "It's after one in the morning. I need to call it a night."

"Camille has the guest bedroom ready if you want to stay. Get some sleep and we'll follow up in the morning."

She tilted her head and pursed her lips. "Okay, I'll take you up on it. I'm beat." Gus opened one eye as she disengaged herself from the couch, but made no effort to move from his spot. "We need to hit the gym in the morning. Does six work for you?"

He rolled his eyes. "Yeah, yeah, six it is."

~

Friday morning, Coop met AB in the foyer as she was heading to her car and followed her to the gym. After the workout and a quick shower, he met Ben at Peg's Pancakes. Ben was already in their booth cradling a cup of coffee.

"Mornin' boys," said Myrtle as she filled Coop's cup. She plucked her pencil from behind her ear and scratched their order on her pad.

"I'm glad the kidnapping had a happy ending. The guys said to thank you for your work on getting the lead on the cabin."

"Yeah, I talked to Daisy's aunt last night when I got the word. She was relieved to know the little girl was safe." Coop blew breath out of his cheeks. "It's been an eventful week."

Ben stirred sugar into his coffee. "So, how'd it go with Judge Hunt?"

Coop savored a long sip of the rich brew before answering. "He gave me some background on Mr. Featherstone." While they waited for breakfast Coop filled him in on the citizen group and the speaking engagement. "AB's going to call them this morning and find out more."

"We've been in contact with the State of Tennessee and they've never had an employee named Featherstone. Another dead end."

Myrtle delivered breakfast and warmed their coffees. "I've got an order of banana pecan pancakes with AB's name on it as soon as y'all are ready," she said with a wink and bustled to the next booth.

"We've got it worked out to cover the mailbox place at night. At least for a short time," said Coop.

"I've got it set up to install a makeshift construction area on the sidewalk outside the store so we can hide a camera. Might not happen until the middle of the week."

Coop nodded. "One other thing we uncovered last night," he said, taking a bite of his waffle. "Logan's oldest son got nabbed for drunk driving and his case is up before Judge Woodburn. Looks like he got caught with drugs in the car when he was pulled over. Small amount of weed. His attorney is Brandon King."

Ben's eyes widened. "Another strange coincidence."

"I'm going to talk to him today and explore that angle."

"I'll talk to the wife and inquire about the kid's case.

"I didn't want to tip him off if he's involved, so I didn't ask Judge Hunt if he was a friend of Avery Logan's. The wife might know if they were still close."

Ben nodded. "I'll delve into it with her."

Coop asked, "Any progress in Logan's murder?"

Ben shook his head. "Nothing. We're taking a deeper look at his financials. All his kids were in private school and now the oldest is in college, but it doesn't look like they make enough money to cover all of their expenses. I'm going to quiz the wife today."

Coop caught Mrytle's eye and gave her a nod. By the time they finished, she appeared with a box for AB, the check, and treat bags full of her famous chocolate bourbon truffles. "Y'all have a Merry Christmas and enjoy."

Both men gave her a hug and she swiped a finger under her eye as she waved goodbye.

In between bites of pancakes, AB updated Coop. "I talked to the former headmaster for Mount Camden. He said he remembers Hunt and Logan and said they were close friends. His recollection about Logan not attending college had to do with a knee injury. His football days were over and football was his main reason for going to Auburn. He said the two were from different backgrounds, but got along well, with Hunt taking Logan under his wing."

Coop punched in a text to ask Ben if Judge Hunt had attended Logan's funeral. Ben always covered funerals of unsolved murder victims. Seconds later his phone chirped and he shook his head.

"Ben says no to the judge being at the funeral."

AB slipped the last bite of pancake to Gus and closed the lid on her takeout box. "Odd with them being close and both still living in Nashville. I wonder if they had a falling out or grew apart? I'd like to think I would attend the funeral of a childhood friend."

"Ben hopes the wife can shed some light on Logan's relationship with the judge and the kid's drunk driving and drug case. We'll have to wait for his report." He stood and added, "I'm going to give Brandon a call. Will you look into the Nashville Coalition for Informed Citizens?"

With any hope of more pancakes gone, Gus followed Coop into his office and curled up in front of the fire. Coop put in a call to Brandon King and was told he was in court, so he left a message. He hung up and leaned back in his chair, perusing the white board.

He looked down at his t-shirt, lettered with *Sorry I'm late—I didn't want to come,* and plucked a long-sleeved dress shirt from the armoire. He covered up the slogan and headed for the back door. "I'm going to run to the courthouse," he hollered as he left.

He slipped into the court room where Brandon was representing a man accused of drunk driving and watched the end of the proceedings. The judge gave the client the lightest sentence he could and Brandon packed his briefcase and turned around with a smile on his face. Coop stood and Brandon extended his hand.

"Mr. Harrington, what brings you to court on this fine Friday?"

"I need a minute of your time."

"Sure," he glanced at his watch. "I've got a few minutes. Shall we grab a coffee?"

Coop treated at the coffee cart and they found a quiet bench.

"While working on Callie's case, I ran across another recent case and your name popped up as the attorney for Brad Logan."

The lawyer's eyes sparked with recognition. "Yeah, yeah, a kid on a DUI with weed in his car. First time, college kid, right?"

"That's the one. Did you know his father, Avery Logan?"

"Only when he came in with the kid. He's the jogger who was murdered, right?"

"He was. I just wondered if there was any connection with the kid's case and Callie's work?"

Brandon took a gulp from his cup and shook his head. "No, she didn't work on it. It's not up until January, so I haven't done much yet. I've got another associate assigned to it and I'll get involved after the holiday. I'm going to try to get a delay due to the tragedy."

"Anything strike you as odd about it or Avery Logan?"

"Not that I recall. He was pissed. The kid's basically a decent kid. Never been in any trouble. Has a scholarship to college. Went to a private school. The dad was concerned about money and my fees." He tilted the cup and finished his coffee. "Not unusual. Most parents are upset when their kids get in trouble and flinch at the money they'll have to pay."

"Did the mom come to the meeting?"

Brandon shook his head. "No, just the kid and the dad. The kid was nervous and worried about his scholarship." He stood and tossed his cup in the trash. "I've gotta run, but nothing springs to mind related to Callie."

Coop thanked him and ordered four more coffees before taking the elevator to Judge Hunt's office. He saw Sadie at the front counter and waited while she finished a phone call. She looked up and said, "How may I help you?"

"Good morning, Sadie. You may remember me, I'm Cooper Harrington. I was hoping to speak with Hildie. Is she in?" He placed the tray on the counter and offered her a coffee.

"No, thank you," she said and poked a button on the phone.

"I'll see if she's available." She relayed the request and said, "You may go back." She hit a buzzer and unlocked a door to permit his entry.

He followed the corridor and saw Hildie waiting outside her office. "Mr. Harrington, what can I do for you?"

He held the coffees in front of him. "It's Coop, please. Care for a coffee?"

"Sure, thanks. Come on in." She motioned him to a chair in front of her desk.

"Sadie didn't want one. Maybe you can pass these to others in the office," he slid the cardboard tray across her desk.

"Thank you, I'm sure I can find a few interested addicts."

"I'm still working the same case and talked to Judge Hunt about an envelope he sent to Mr. Featherstone. It was on the second delivery list, after Billy was killed, but not the first list. It's a bit of a sticky wicket and I'm just trying to figure out how it got missed in the first list. Judge Hunt thought it was a clerical error, but I wanted to check with you and try to get a clearer picture."

"You think it's important to your case?" She set the paper cup, bearing a fresh pink lip print, on her desk.

"I do, Hildie."

"Wait here and let me take another look at the log." She carried the tray of coffees and made her way to the front counter. She was back in minutes and thumbed through the book. "You're right. It's an anomaly. We had an intern working who is no longer here and she prepared most of the outgoing correspondence for the delivery service. I'm thinking she must have missed preparing it in the first batch. We had several problems with her work and had to let her go just last week."

"Judge Hunt said it was found because staff searched all the documents prepared during the day before you processed the second shipment."

She nodded. "He did request us to review our documents for

the day to make sure we didn't miss anything. The intern I'm thinking of was tasked with preparing all the items for delivery." She shook her head. "I tried to talk him into letting us wait until the following day and work with the police to retrieve our documents, but he was adamant we stay and reship all the items."

Hildie turned to her computer and punched in several keys while watching the screen. "I was just checking to find out if the document had been processed in the messenger service system and just not logged in our book, but can't locate it. It's only in the second shipment with the different service company."

"What happens if you prepare a shipment and then something comes up and you want to pull it or wait to deliver it until a later time?"

"We can suspend the item in the online system and then reactivate it later. The item can also be deleted."

"Does the system retain the deleted records?"

Hildie frowned and took another sip from her cup. "I don't think so. Let me call our rep and find out." She searched through a file on her desk and dialed. While she chatted and asked questions, he checked his phone for messages.

He had a text from AB saying she had an update on the coalition group. She also reminded him to pick up the liquor for the office party they were hosting tonight. He tapped back a quick reply and pocketed the phone as Hildie hung up her call.

"Well, our system doesn't show the deleted records, but the delivery service can retrieve them. She said there was a record deleted in the afternoon. The item was for Mr. Featherstone at the same address as the second shipment. It was created in the morning, by the intern I mentioned. It should have gone out in the morning batch before noon, but it didn't. They show the item deleted just after three o'clock, the same day it was created."

"Who deleted it?"

"The same intern who prepared it earlier in the day." Her forehead crinkled. "I remember Judge Hunt was upset with her that day for something to do with an item she had prepared for the messenger service."

"Was it this shipment?"

"I can't be sure, but it makes sense. She had a string of problems with her work. She was easily distracted." Hildie paused in thought and looked at her desk calendar. "Anyway, now that I think about it, I'm sure this was the day. Judge Hunt was angrier than I'd ever seen him. He told her to go home early, because she wasn't here when we did the secondary shipment with the other service. She left right before Billy's accident."

"What's the intern's name?"

She pulled open a file drawer. "Lindsay Winter. She's a student at Vanderbilt. Pleasant girl, but didn't appreciate the seriousness of our work. She lacked attention to detail and had trouble retaining information." She scribbled on a sticky note. "Here's her contact info." She sighed as she refiled the folder. "I wish you could tell me how this is related to Calista's murder."

"It's a lead at this point. One I need to follow. I'm not sure how it connects yet."

"Well, Martha sings your praises and if she vouches for you, I'm happy to help. From what she said you always solve the toughest cases. And Judge Hunt told us to help in any way we could. We're all in shock about Billy and Calista. It's horrible."

Coop stood. "I appreciate the help and the vote of confidence. We're having a small Christmas party at the office tonight. You ought to stop by after work. Martha will be there." He watched the shy smile spread across her face. Unlike the suggestive clothing and mannerisms of Brandon's assistant, Hildie was all class and a subtle beauty.

"Maybe I'll see you there." She followed him to the lobby where he gave her a quick wave.

He took the stairs and found a quiet alcove to make a call. He dialed Lindsay's number and explained he was investigating the death of an attorney. "I'd like to ask you a few questions related to some work in Judge Hunt's court."

She was doing some last minute Christmas shopping and they agreed to meet for lunch in Green Hills. Coop secured a quiet table at a popular eclectic grill and left Lindsay's name with the hostess. He was soon joined by a fresh-faced brunette with a sprinkling of freckles across her cheeks.

Coop stood and extended his hand, "Thanks for meeting me, Lindsay."

"Sure thing," she said, placing her coat on the back of her chair. The waitress appeared and recited the specials. Coop took a swig of sweet tea and said, "I wanted to ask you about a particular document you prepared for Judge Hunt." He saw a flash of fear in her eyes. "I talked with Hildie this morning and she told me about the document. It was sent out on the day of Billy's accident. He was the bike messenger killed in the hit and run."

The girl's eyes widened. "Oh, yes, that was horrible. He was a super nice guy. So, what document are you interested in?"

"It's one Judge Hunt sent to a group called the Nashville Coalition for Informed Citizens. The organizer was a Mr. Featherstone."

She nodded. "Oh, boy, do I remember that one. I sort of think it's the reason I got fired."

Coop's brows furrowed. "Really? How so?"

"Well, Hildie had talked to me about mistakes I'd been making and told me Judge Hunt wasn't happy with my performance. She was gentle, but told me I was in jeopardy of losing my placement. Anyway, I prepared the document for the judge and put it in the system, like always."

They were interrupted with the arrival of their meal. After the waitress left Lindsay continued, "After I got back from lunch, Judge Hunt called me into his office and wanted to know what happened to that specific delivery. He said he had received a call wondering where the document was. It should have been delivered by noon since it was part of the morning shipment."

She chewed a bite from her plate and sipped her drink. "I remembered typing the document and getting the envelope back after Judge Hunt approved it. Anyway, I checked and I had done a shipment label. The label had never been scanned into the system, so I must have set it down or something and misplaced it. I told him what I found out and he went ballistic. He asked me to prepare another copy of the document and get it out in the afternoon shipment."

She paused and took another drink. "You won't believe this, but somehow I messed it up again. I got it ready and put the envelope on his desk, like he asked me. Turns out more stuff got piled on top of it and it missed Billy's afternoon pickup. He found it right after Billy left." She let out a sigh. "He was crazy mad and when I tried to help find it on his desk, he told me to just get out and leave." She paused and ran her finger along her glass. "I told Hildie I didn't feel well and left. I was too embarrassed to tell her what I'd done. They let me finish the term, but let me go last week. Now I'll have to find a new internship for the rest of the year." She shrugged her shoulders and gulped a drink from her glass.

"Did Judge Hunt discuss it any further with you when you returned the next day?"

"No. He never said another word to me. I kept screwing up stupid things and Hildie talked to me about my failure to improve my performance. She stuck me in the file room for the rest of the term and had me doing menial stuff. But at least they let me stay. Otherwise, I'd have to start all over."

"So, you deleted the first entry that never got scanned and you never found the original item?"

She nodded her head. "Yeah, I was waiting for him to get the envelope back to me before I prepared a new shipment label. I got busy with other things. I should have checked with him when I didn't get it back." She took a few more bites and asked, "Why is it so important to a murder investigation?"

Coop smiled as he sipped his tea. "I'm still figuring it out, but it's a weirdism I need to explain."

13

Gus greeted Coop as he came through the back door toting boxes of wine and liquor. He stowed the bottles in the kitchen and followed Gus to AB's desk. She was on the phone and Coop slipped a takeout container atop a pile of papers. He slumped on the couch and waited for her to finish. Gus deposited his head in Coop's lap and Coop obliged by rubbing the dog's ears. He looked around the office at AB's tasteful decorations. The place looked festive, but not overdone.

Lola Belle came through the front door and approached AB's desk. Coop stood and said, "Hi, Lola Belle. What brings you by? Everything okay?"

She touched her gloved fingertip to her mouth. "Oh, Cooper, I didn't notice you there. Yes, yes, all is fine. I just wanted to stop by and pay you for the extra time and tell you how grateful we are for your help. The police told us you were the one who gave them the lead on the cabin."

"We're just happy it all worked out. AB can help you with the bill." He gestured to her desk.

"Your aunt always tells the girls at the salon what a marvelous detective you are." She dropped her eyes and her cheeks reddened. "I just took it as her braggin' about you a bit, like any good aunt would do. But you are very talented and I shall now sing your praises as loudly as Camille." She darted to him and embraced him in a hug. "Thank you again."

"You're more than welcome, Lola Belle. You have a Merry Christmas." He left her at AB's desk and he and Gus retired to the kitchen.

When he heard the front door close, he ventured out of his hiding spot. AB was holding a check in her hand and lifted her brows when she saw him. "Lola Belle gave us a generous bonus." She flashed the check in front of his face.

"Wow, that was considerate of her." He resumed his position on the couch. "Sorry to leave her with you, but I just can't take all her sappy sweetness."

She answered the phone as she stamped the check for deposit. She hung up and let out a loud sigh. "All the food will be delivered by four. I think we're set." She turned her attention to her takeout lunch. "Thanks, this looks great."

"I appreciate your help this week. I know how much work you've put into this party." He continued to pet Gus. "What do you have on the coalition?"

She picked up her notepad. "I called the community center and found out Henry Featherstone was the person who made the request to use the event space. The address they have on file is the mailbox store. They did have a cell phone number for him, so I gave it to Ben to try and trace. I checked the website and the only contact information is an email address. The January event with Judge Hunt appears to be the only scheduled meeting on their calendar. The website is sparse."

"Maybe we should email and try to get more information. I'll set up a phony account and send something and try to elicit a response."

"Madison and Reed are set up to start surveillance tonight.

I've got you taking a shift tomorrow and Sunday to give each of them a day off."

"Ben thought they'd have a camera in play next week, so we'll play it by ear."

"We need to come up with a way to force Mr. Featherstone to the mailbox," she said, finishing the last bite of lunch.

"Maybe we could use the community center as a way to lure him to the box. Come up with some excuse and send him a document requiring a signature."

"That might work. Ben should have some influence with them, since the center is part of the city."

"I'll talk to Ben and pass on our idea." Coop displaced the dog's head and stood. "Go ahead and take off if you need to get changed for the party. I'll stay here and have Aunt Camille bring me a change of clothes."

She smiled and said, "Let me clean my desk and then I'm out of here."

After she left Coop concocted a ruse with Ben's help. The cell phone number Featherstone gave the community center was still active. It was a burner, so no ownership records, but it was functioning. Ben had staff running down the numbers it had called.

He disconnected from Ben and welcomed the caterer at the back door. She and her crew hauled in boxes and plastic containers by the dozens. He left them in command of the kitchen and coaxed Gus away from the action with a treat. He closed his office door and put in a call to Callie's parents.

Arden was out, but Carter took his call and Coop gave him a generic update, letting him know they had a new lead and were doing some surveillance to follow up on a possible link to Callie's murder. He didn't mention names and Carter didn't ask any questions.

Ben hollered out to Coop as he came through the kitchen and snaked his way through the caterers. "In my office," yelled

Coop. Gus dashed from his napping spot in time to greet Ben as he opened the door. "Don't let him out. He's looking for food."

Ben blocked the dog with his knee and shut the door behind him. He put two cold drinks he had swiped from the kitchen on Coop's desk and opened one. "I've got some updates." He took a long swig from the can.

"Me too." Coop popped the top on his drink. "You first."

"Our techs manipulated the phones so it would appear Kate was calling from the community center and she called Featherstone's cell. She left a message saying they had a new form that goes into effect for events after January first. She told him they had sent it to his physical address, as it required an original signature. She asked him to return it before the holidays, if at all possible. She also had the office manager send him an email with the same information. Any calls that come in from him will be redirected to our office. Same with any response to the email."

"Did the voicemail say it was Featherstone?"

Ben shook his head. "No, generic message. We messengered a phony form to the mailbox and it's there now. The camera won't be installed until late Tuesday. If he goes to the box, I think he'll go after hours, so we'll have to rely on your surveillance."

"Sounds good. Ross and Madison are set and I'm taking a shift each day this weekend."

"I talked to Mrs. Logan today. She's distraught over her husband's death. It sounds like he handled all the finances. The more questions I asked, the more upset she became. I did find out all three kids received scholarships for private school and the oldest is on a scholarship at the university. I took a closer look around their place while I was there. New cars, fancy boat and jet skis, big RV, lots of toys. The house is modest, but all the toys are top of the line. I didn't find any loans for the vehicles or other stuff."

"Hard to reconcile the scholarships with the extravagant stuff, huh?"

Ben nodded as he took another drink. "Exactly, unless they're not based on need. We're digging into the history on the toys. We'll figure it out. Kate and Jimmy are looking into the scholarships."

"Did the wife know Judge Hunt?"

"Nope. Said she didn't meet Avery until after college and he didn't associate with any college or high school buddies. Didn't attend reunions. Most of his friends are connected with the auto parts store or their hobbies."

"Life insurance?"

"Yeah, they both had policies on each other. They've had them since they had the first child and she's not a suspect."

"So, she'll be okay financially?"

"I think so. The life insurance should pay off their house and give her a substantial cushion to invest or save."

"The kid might lose his scholarship if he's convicted. I talked to Brandon today and he said the kid was worried about it. He met with Avery and the kid. Avery was mad and upset about how much it was going to cost him."

"Understandable. Most parents would have the same reaction."

"I visited with Hildie at Judge Hunt's today. She dug into the Featherstone delivery that wasn't on the first list." While they finished their drinks, he explained what he had discovered about the deleted entry and his lunch with the intern.

"So, we've got a delivery to Featherstone from Judge Hunt to a store that our victim may have visited, but we can't be sure. We've got a tenuous link between Hunt and our dead jogger. And we have Callie's boss as the attorney for the dead jogger's son. We know Callie had possession of something she discovered and we saw her with an envelope in her bag on Friday afternoon and the envelope was gone when we found her body. Where did it go?"

"She could have mailed it on the weekend. We tracked her to the mall and grocery stores, but she could have mailed it anywhere."

"Or her killer took it." Ben was interrupted by a knock on the door.

"Come in," said Coop.

The caterer stood in the doorway. "We've got all the refreshments set up and ready. I'm taking off, but the wait staff will be here and handle serving and replenishing."

"Sounds great. Leave the invoice and my assistant will get you paid." Coop stood and took the bill from her and walked it over to AB's desk.

"Yoo-hoo, Coop. I've got your clothes," Camille gawked at the trays laden with appetizers as she passed by the kitchen. "Oh, the food looks delightful." She made her way to the reception area and helped herself to a drink from one of the trays. "You better get changed." Her eyes darted toward the kitchen and she lowered her voice. "Your mother showed up just as I was leaving. I didn't know what to do, so I brought her with me. She's in the kitchen."

"Unbelievable." He let out a loud breath. "I don't have the patience to deal with her and don't want her at this party." He flung the garment bag across the couch and stormed to the kitchen.

He found his mother sampling appetizers, dressed in the same jeans and shirt she'd worn yesterday. He caught her eye and motioned her to the backdoor. "I stopped by to visit, but Camille was on her way here. I didn't know you were having a party."

"Yeah, it's for our clients. We do it every year." He paused and said, "I thought you were heading to Vermont."

"I talked to Ruben, my friend. He said he's busy until the day after Christmas, so I've got time to kill."

"Yeah, well you need to find somewhere other than here to kill it. We're swamped with this case. I've got surveillance work scheduled and I don't have time to babysit you. What city are you going to in Vermont?"

She hung her head and studied the ground. "It's a small town outside Burlington."

"Come on in and eat something and give me a few minutes." He strode back through the kitchen and retrieved his clothes, hurrying to his office.

While he changed, he explained the situation with his mother to Ben. Ben volunteered to visit with Marlene while Coop searched for flights and hotels. It took Coop ten minutes and a whopper of a blow to his credit card, but he found a flight and booked a room near the airport in Burlington for his mother.

Coop emerged from his office dressed in a dark suit and red tie. He spotted his mother, with a plate of snacks and a drink in her hand, still talking to Ben. She saw Coop and said, "You look so handsome. Your friend Ben has been keeping me company."

He murmured his thanks to Ben and turned to his mother, "Come on in my office. I've got some information for you." She followed him and he opened the door adding, "I need to keep Gus in here, so don't let him out."

He motioned her to a chair. "Wow, you've got a great office."

He remained standing and handed her a piece of paper. "Here's a confirmation for a flight and the hotel information for you in Vermont. I paid for you through Christmas night. The flight leaves in a few hours. I ordered a cab and it'll be here soon."

She eyed the information. "This must have cost a fortune."

"Consider it a Christmas gift."

"That's quite generous. Thank you." She looked at the paper

again. "I'm sorry, you know?" Coop pursed his lips and remained silent. "Anyway, I better get moving. Thanks for… everything." He stepped to the door and opened it for her.

As they emerged from his office, AB rounded the corner in a stunning red lace sheath dress. When Coop saw her his eyes widened and his mouth hung open. "Hey, guys," she said. "Looks like the caterer has things under control."

Camille said, "You look beautiful and festive in that dress. Doesn't she boys?"

Ben stood and gave AB a hug. "You look incredible, AB. Merry Christmas."

"It's a knock-out dress," said Marlene, smiling.

"Oh, hello, Marlene. I didn't know you were here," said AB, searching Coop's face for a clue.

She glanced at Coop, "I just stopped by to say goodbye. I'm leaving for Vermont tonight."

"How wonderful. I hope you have a Merry Christmas. It should be white, at least," said AB, with a nervous laugh.

Coop saw the cab pull up out front and retrieved Marlene's suitcase. She said her goodbyes as he carried it outside. She stepped in the back of the cab and he handed the man several bills. "Have a safe trip."

She smiled and said, "Merry Christmas, Cooper. Thank you again."

He nodded and tapped his palm on the roof of the cab, signaling the driver. He watched it until it turned the corner down the block. He let out a long breath and with it felt the heaviness in his shoulders subside. He ambled back to the porch, feeling both relief and sadness.

AB was waiting for him, hugging her arms to her body. "You okay?"

"Yeah, I'll be fine." He wrapped her in a strong hug. "You're shivering." He opened the door for her and said, "It's been a long day, let's enjoy our party."

As they entered, a waiter circled by with a tray of drinks and Coop reached for an Arnold Palmer. He took a few sips and said, "By the way, you are absolutely gorgeous, AB."

"Why thank you, Coop." She smiled and straightened his tie. "It's gonna be okay."

His head bobbed up and down. "Yeah…I know." He looked up and saw Madison come through the front door.

"Merry Christmas," she said. "I know I'm early. I've got the first shift tonight, but wanted to check out the party and steal some food." She laughed and gave Coop and AB a hug on her way to the kitchen.

The closer it got to five o'clock, more people came through the door. Beneath an undercurrent of Christmas instrumentals, laughter and conversation filled the house. Clients mixed with several officers and detectives, along with lawyers and court staff.

People drifted in and out mingling, eating, and sipping. Coop kept his eye on the door, trying to greet people as they arrived. It was nearing eight o'clock and the guests were dwindling when Hildie came through the front door. She was still dressed in her work clothes and she blew out a breath as she looked around the room.

Coop made his way to her and greeted her with a hug. "I'm so glad you stopped by, Hildie." He led her to the sofa and asked, "Would you like a drink?

"Would I? Yes, please." Coop caught the eye of one of the servers and he presented a tray of appetizers and took Hildie's drink order. She ate a mini quiche and said, "Sorry I'm so late. I just got out of work. Did I miss Martha?"

"I'm afraid so. She and my Aunt Camille visited while she was here, but she left about an hour ago."

"That figures. I had intentions of being here much earlier, but I had to finish up an emergency project for the judge." She leaned back against the couch and let out a sigh.

"Long day, huh?"

"Yeah. I'm officially on vacation now. Judge Hunt needed me to handle funding his foundation before I left." The server returned with her drink and she took a long sip. "Ah, that hits the spot after the afternoon I've had."

"It's good to know Judge Hunt is philanthropic, so all your hard work was for a noble cause."

"Oh, he's quite generous. He's funded his foundation for well over twenty years."

"That's a long commitment. Good for him. How long have you worked for him?"

"Basically, my entire career. I worked with him at his firm and he brought me with him when he took the bench. He's a decent man and an excellent judge."

"So, you'll go with him if he gets the appointment to the appeals position?"

She nodded as she swallowed another sip. "That's the plan. I think he's got a good shot at it and I'm ready for something new. That's why I'm taking two weeks off now. If he gets the appointment, I'll be busy with the transition."

"Sorry you had a rotten day, but glad you made time to come." Coop smiled and took a swallow of his drink.

"I normally have the scholarship recipients funded in early December, to avoid a rush like today." She raised her eyebrows and took another swallow. "Judge Hunt had decided to discontinue it for the upcoming year, but changed his mind today. So, I spent the afternoon, not only getting my desk cleared for vacation, but trying to track down people at the schools so I could wire the funds."

AB tapped Coop on the shoulder. "Leland's leaving. You may want to catch him and say goodbye."

Coop stood. "Thanks, yeah, I need to talk to him. This is Hildie from Judge Hunt's office. Hildie, this is my right hand, Annabelle. She's the real boss around here. I'll be right back."

Hildie offered her hand and AB shook it. "A pleasure to meet you and everyone calls me AB."

"What a gorgeous dress. I came straight from work," Hildie opened her hands in front of her. "So, this is what I'm stuck with. I would have never made it here if I went home and changed."

"Lots of people came from work. Don't worry about it. Coop and I like to dress up for the party, since we're hosting it."

"You've worked here a long time?"

AB nodded and smiled. "Ever since college. Coop and I both worked here for his uncle when we went to Vanderbilt. When Uncle John died, Coop took over the firm."

Aunt Camille meandered by and AB introduced her to Hildie. When Camille found out about Hildie's work at the courthouse she maneuvered onto the sofa and struck up a conversation about their mutual friend, Martha. AB left them to visit and with a handful of guests remaining, told the catering staff to start cleaning and packing.

After he wished the last guest goodbye, Coop freed Gus from the office and rejoined the conversation with Hildie. Aunt Camille was tipsy from too many cocktails and kept nodding off while the foursome chatted. AB raised her brows at Coop and said, "I'll drive her home. I only had one drink about four hours ago."

"Thanks, AB. I'll take her car home and leave the Jeep here overnight."

Hildie stood and said, "I don't want to keep you." She gathered her purse.

"No, sit down. I'm not in a hurry," said Coop. The caterers set a tray, filled with a few appetizers and desserts, on the coffee table. "You can help me eat some of these."

Camille wished them a good night and took AB's arm as she tottered out of the room and out the back door. "I'll see you in the morning," hollered AB as she shut the door.

Hildie finished her drink. "I should get going myself. I'm flying to Denver tomorrow afternoon for the holidays."

"Sounds like the perfect place for a white Christmas. Do you have family there?"

She nodded. "My sister and a brother. The whole clan is gathering there this year. That's why I was so frustrated today. I was hoping to sneak out a bit early, but with all the fuss for the foundation, my hopes for a quiet afternoon plummeted."

"I'm glad you took the time to stop by tonight. Maybe we can get together after the first of the year."

She smiled and retrieved a card and a pen from her purse. After writing on the back, she handed it to Coop. "Here's my cell and home phone. I'll be back to work in January. Give me a call if you'd like to meet up after work one night."

He flicked the card between his fingers and retrieved one of his own. He jotted all of his contact information on it and placed it in her hand. "I look forward to it." He held her coat and she slipped her arms through it. Gus raised his head, giving them a questioning look.

14

The unexpected visit from his mother didn't help Coop's insomnia. He rested his eyes, but never slept Friday night. Instead he relived the encounter, vacillating between anger and sadness. After the party he had texted Jack and asked if he could talk. Even though it was after midnight on the west coast, Jack called him back.

Coop told him about Marlene's visit and her latest sad story. Over the years Jack had also sent her money when she called him with one of her hopeless situations. They both agreed if money could actually fix it, it wouldn't be a problem. After a few laughs, Coop's mood lightened. Neither of them was skilled at talking about their feelings. Jack focused all of his energy on his wife and family. Coop didn't have the luxury of a domestic life and used work as his distraction from dealing with the emotional wounds inflicted at the hands of his mother.

Coop was happy to know his dad would be with Jack and his family throughout the holiday activities. Coop promised Jack he would make a trip to visit in person during the upcoming year. They wished each other a Merry Christmas and disconnected after over an hour of visiting. He stared at the phone, smiling as he replayed the best parts of the conversation with Jack, his spirits lifted.

~

Saturday morning Coop met AB at the office. He arrived with bags of takeout breakfast from Peg's. Ben joined them for pancakes and to review Callie's case. "No activity to report at the mailbox store yet. Ross is there now," said Coop.

"No reply to the email or voicemail Kate left for Featherstone," added Ben.

"We sent a phony request to the website email address and asked for more information on the group and upcoming events, but no response yet," said AB.

"Kate and Jimmy went back over the Logans' financials. No loans for any of the fancy toys at the house. They're all owned free and clear and it looks like they paid for them in full at the time of purchase. Either check or cash."

Coop eyebrows arched. "Wow, that's some serious money."

Ben nodded. "Yeah, they make cash deposits to the checking and savings accounts they have each month. They're all under five thousand, so no red flags get raised at the bank."

"Embezzlement?" asked AB.

"Kate and Jimmy are exploring the possibility, but the wife has no contact with money at her job. As the manager of the store, Mr. Logan would have access. We have a forensic accountant on it now, looking through the business records."

"Could be a motive for murder, if he was stealing," said Coop.

Ben shrugged. "He's worked for the same company for his entire career. They love him and have nothing but positive things to say about him. I think it's a slim chance. The owner said there's been nothing suspicious in the income for the store."

"What about the scholarships? Unusual to have all the kids awarded scholarships."

"Kate and Jimmy couldn't get anyone at the schools yesterday and now it's the Christmas break. They're going to try to reach people at home, but not sure how fast it will happen. The boys went to Camden Academy, like their dad."

"I'm going to search through newspapers for the time Hunt and Logan were in school together and look for a closer link than what the yearbooks at the school showed," said AB, gathering the takeout boxes from the table.

Ben checked his watch. "One other thing, the burner linked to Featherstone called and received calls only from other burner phones." He placed a copy of the phone data on the table. "Not much to go on."

Coop fingered the papers and said, "I've got the night shift tonight. I'll give you a call if we get anything."

"We're leaving tomorrow afternoon for Christmas. I'll be available by phone, but if I mess this trip up, I'm in the dog house. Permanently."

"Enjoy your time with family. We'll keep you posted and work with Kate and Jimmy if we get anything."

"I hate leaving this case, but Jen gave me the look when I mentioned I was swamped at work."

"I've been the recipient of her look. Be careful, man." Coop grinned and smacked Ben on the back. "Tell her Merry Christmas from me."

After Ben left AB exhausted her newspaper search online and decided to go to the library for further exploration. Coop concentrated on the burner phone data and plotted times of calls on the whiteboard. He searched in vain for any clues as to the identity of any of the burner numbers.

He phoned Kate and asked if she could have the techs try to narrow down the location of Featherstone's burner phone when he made calls. "I know it will take some time, but I think he's the link to this whole thing." She agreed to get them moving on the request.

"Are all the numbers associated with Featherstone's burner being tracked?"

"Yep. Ben submitted them as soon as he got the data from the burner. We've got them all being tracked and traced. Problem is they only come on for quick bursts, to make the call and then they turn them off. We suspect they remove the batteries. Makes it hard to do much."

When Coop headed home in the late afternoon, he called AB to check on her. "I'm still going through stuff at the library. It takes time. I'll check in with you when I'm done."

Coop took a quick nap before his shift. He left Gus at home with Camille and took his cooler, packed with provisions for his twelve-hour stakeout. He had a friend in the data cable business who let Coop use one of his vans for surveillance work. He parked his Jeep in the lot at the Hilton and walked to the van parked across the street from the mailbox store.

Madison was inside and opened the side door. "No action yet, huh?" he asked. They were both dressed in khaki pants and polo shirts topped off with jackets embroidered with the cable company name.

She yawned. "Not a thing. A few people went in today, but nobody approached Featherstone's box. I went ahead and took photos of everyone, just in case." She gestured to the camera with a long lens aimed at the store. "Ben snagged us a parking permit and it's on the dash. So far nobody has hassled us."

"Good work. Hopefully, it'll only be a couple more days of this."

She pointed to a stack of pillows and blankets. "You'll need those at night. It's cold. We rigged up a recording camera for when nature calls. We review it when we get back, but nothing so far." She showed him the second camera pointed at the same spot.

"Okay, got it. Get some rest and I'll talk to you tomorrow." Coop let her out and locked the door.

He settled into the chair for the duration. People wandered up and down the sidewalk, but not one of them entered or showed any interest in the mailboxes. His phone chirped with a text from AB letting him know she was home and would talk to him in the morning. Darkness settled in early this time of year, but the streetlamps illuminated the area, giving him a clear view of the entry point.

While he kept an eye out the window, the facts of the case tumbled through his mind. He pictured the white board and reexamined what they knew. He had a snack and set the camera before heading to the men's room at the Hilton.

He put on a baseball cap and looked out the tinted window, so dark it was like one-way glass, before jumping out of the van. He hurried to his destination, keeping a watchful eye on the door of the store until it disappeared from his line of sight. He was back on the street within minutes and climbed into the van. He checked the recorded footage, relieved to find no activity.

It was approaching midnight when his phone beeped. He narrowed his eyes as he read the message. It was from his security company. After AB had been attacked in the office a few months ago, he had upgraded to a system with a notification alert component. The system allowed him to monitor the live events taking place in the office. It activated cameras and recorded the activity while allowing him to view all the action from his phone.

He activated the recording camera in the van while he focused on his phone. He saw what appeared to be a man in a dark hoodie and dark pants walking through the office. He was at AB's desk, rifling through papers. Coop couldn't take his eyes off the screen as he watched the dark figure move to his own office.

He saw him searching the top of the conference table and

then watched as he eyed the white board and saw a flash of light. Hoodie man was taking a photo of the white board with his phone. Coop punched buttons on his phone and held it to his ear. "Ben, it's me. I just received a security notification from the motion detectors in the office. Someone is in there right now. He's wearing dark pants and a dark hoodie. I can't make out his face and he's wearing gloves." He nodded and said, "Okay, I'm at the mailbox store. Call me as soon as you can."

He poked another button and went back to viewing the screen. He kept glancing from it to the entrance of the store, trying to watch both. He saw the man and noticed his gloved hands going through the papers on top of his desk and opening drawers.

It took all of Coop's self-control to stay in the van and not take off for his office. He wanted to get his hands on this hoodie wearing jerk, preferably around his neck. Coop's heart pounded in his chest and his leg bounced as he watched the activity. He knew Ben would dispatch units and logic dictated they would arrive at the office before Coop could, but it did little to dampen his desire to bolt.

He watched the man make his way through the office, stop at the alarm panel, and creep out the backdoor. He followed him on the screen until he reached the edge of the property and fell out of range of the camera. Coop slid his fingers over the screen and called Ben to give him an update.

"Units are less than a minute away," he said, the siren blasting from his car. "I'm enroute, but at least ten minutes out."

"Look for him away from the house. He was heading west when he went out of range. He's about six feet, stocky build, black shoes."

"I'll call you back as soon as I know more," said Ben.

Coop called AB to let her know what was happening while he watched the store and waited for an update from Ben. After a lengthy discussion and AB's persistence, Coop agreed she could go to the office. "Wait for Ben and don't go snooping around the neighborhood. Wait in your car until you talk to the police. Don't go anywhere around there alone. We don't know what this jack wagon will do."

"I'll send the video files from the system over to Ben so they can get their techs to try and enhance it as much as possible. Plus, I want to check for missing items."

Coop let out a sigh. "All I saw him take was a picture of the white board. I didn't see him steal any paperwork." He kept his focus on the store. "Promise me you'll call me as soon as you get there."

"I promise. Do you want me to get Ross to relieve you early?"

"Nah, let him sleep. If we need him, we'll call him later."

Coop disconnected and returned to his vigil. A few minutes later Ben called. "We haven't found him yet. We're going block by block. This area is all residential, so no cameras until we get over several blocks. I don't hold out much hope. He could have stashed a car and driven away before we got here."

"Damnit. I can't wait to get my hands on this clown." He paused to let Ben address the radio chatter he detected in the background. "AB is on her way to the office. She insisted. I told her not to go in without the police."

"Got it. I'll let the officers on scene know. Talk to you later."

Coop eased his back against the chair and let out a breath. His brain filtered through possible suspects for the break-in. *Only the guilty party would be interested in what we know. We've shaken the right tree and somebody's worried. Has to be Featherstone.*

Coop mulled his conclusion over and continued to watch the store. He pulled an Arnold Palmer out of the cooler and drank half the bottle in one gulp. "Featherstone is connected to Judge Hunt. Sort of," he mumbled.

He checked the time and sighed, realizing he had four more hours to go. Time moved at the pace of an exhausted sloth.

Coop stood and stretched, longing for a walk to get rid of his pent up energy. He paced the length of the back of the van, which was less than two strides, and returned to the window. Hunched over, he checked the view and saw a man in a dark hoodie using a key to open the door.

He scrambled to his seat, turned on the backup recording camera and looked through the eyepiece. He clicked photo after photo, but could only see the back of his head. Dark pants, black athletic shoes, dark hoodie, gloves. "Unfreakinbelievable," he whispered as he continued to take shots. Coop watched the man approach the back wall and insert a key into Featherstone's box. He retrieved two envelopes and put them inside his hoodie. He turned, keeping his head down. Coop saw he wore a baseball cap under the hood and the brim shadowed his face.

Coop grabbed his phone and held it up so he could see the screen and the man and dialed Ben, all while clicking the button on the camera. "I've got a guy in a dark hoodie who just entered the mailbox store and picked up Featherstone's mail. It looks like the same guy I saw on the video in my office."

"What?" Ben asked and then Coop listened to his friend directing units to Coop's location. "I've got units rolling and I'm on the way. Are you sure?"

"As sure as I can be. Can't make out his face, but the build and clothes match." He's heading out the door. I'm going to follow him."

"Be careful, Coop. Don't let him see you."

Coop disconnected and pocketed the cell phone. He eased open the side door and took great care to minimize the noise when he closed it. He pulled his own baseball cap low and headed down the street, parallel to his suspect.

He watched the man, whose eyes never left the sidewalk, continue down the street in the direction of the Hilton. Coop kept hoodie man in his peripheral vision and meandered at a slow pace to stay behind him. The man came to an intersection, hesitated for a moment at the curb and crossed without waiting for the signal.

Coop quickened his steps and watched the man enter the Hilton property. The dark figure circled the perimeter and made his way to the self-parking lot. Coop followed, keeping his distance on a diagonal path.

The man, all but invisible in his dark clothing, maintained his pace, zigzagging through the parked cars. Coop saw the man's gloved hand move to the side of his head.

Coop slipped his phone out of his pocket and pressed Ben's icon. "Our guy is in the self-park lot at the Hilton on his phone right now."

"Got it. Units are about a minute away."

Hoodie man sprinted through the last rows of cars to the sidewalk. A dark sedan pulled up and the man opened the door with his gloved hand and jumped in the passenger seat.

Coop reached the sidewalk as the car was peeling away from the curb. He looked at the license plate. "Damn damn damn."

He reached for his phone. "He just got in a late model dark blue Toyota, four doors. No plates, dark windows. They're heading east on Broadway." He heard the crackle of radio traffic and Ben's voice transmitting the information Coop had provided.

"I'll call you with an update soon."

"I'm going back to get the van and collect the cameras. I'll be at the office if you need me," said Coop.

He jogged back to the surveillance van and broke down the equipment before hurrying to the lot to pick up the Jeep. He found the office ablaze with lights when he pulled behind it.

He smelled the fresh aroma of coffee when he opened the door. Two policemen were in the reception area with AB. "Coop, you're back already?"

"Yeah, the guy came to the mailbox. I think it was the same guy who broke into the office tonight."

"The guy disabled the alarm and reset it when he left," said one of the officers.

Coop shook his head, put down his large duffle bag, and slouched on the sofa. "We just upgraded this system to prevent tampering with the alarm."

AB retrieved the cameras from the bag and got to work transferring the data to her computer.

"We'll be fine here, guys. You can go," said Coop to the officers.

"Chief Mason told us to keep a car on your place until further notice. We'll be outside if you need us." Coop walked them to the door and made sure it was locked behind them.

He poured himself a cup of coffee and rejoined AB at her desk. She brought up the security footage from the office on one screen and filled the other with footage Coop took from the surveillance van.

They watched the screens until they went black. "What do you think, AB?"

She nodded. "I think it's the same guy in both videos."

"That's what I told Ben. The jerk is good at keeping his face hidden."

"I'll text Ross and Madison and tell them we're done with the surveillance, so they can have their Sunday back."

Coop replayed the videos again and watched hoodie man move through the office. The man's back was to the camera much of the time. He paused to get a better look at the man manipulating the alarm keypad. The intruder used an electronic device he carried in his pocket to bypass the alarm. Hoodie man walked through the kitchen and reached AB's desk, where he went through papers and perused the area. Coop watched the rest of the footage, checking to see if the man ever removed his gloves.

Hoodie man searched Coop's office and desk. Coop slowed the video when the man was in his office taking a photo. The flash from the phone was bright, but allowed Coop to get a better look at the guy's face. He saw only eyes and lips. The man was wearing a dark ski mask under the baseball cap and the hoodie. He wasn't taking any chances.

Coop slammed his hand on her desk. "This pisses me off." He stormed through the front door and paced the yard, muttering to himself. His cell rang and he saw it was Ben. "Did you get the guy?"

"No. We lost the car at the interchange. THP is patrolling the freeways as we speak."

"Crap. I thought he was going to get in a car in the parking lot. I should have anticipated a driver. Maybe you can get traffic camera footage to help."

"Kate's back at the office working on footage now. We're getting CCTV from the Hilton and anywhere else we can. We'll find it."

"At least we know we're on the right track. Quite a bit of cloak and dagger action to retrieve something from a mailbox. Not to mention the fact, AB and I just reviewed the footage from my office and the mailbox store side by side. It's the same guy."

"Send it over to Kate and she'll have the guys work to enhance it on our end."

"AB's sending it now. Also, this isn't your run-of-the-mill burglar. He had some sort of gizmo that disabled my brand new unbreakable alarm system."

"You and AB should try to get some rest. We'll keep an eye on the place."

"Yeah, your guys are sitting outside now. Thanks, Ben. Talk to you later." He disconnected and saw he had missed a call from Aunt Camille. He trudged up the steps and plopped on the couch. He returned her call and rested his head against a throw pillow while he chatted.

He ended the call with, "Sounds great, Aunt Camille. I'll bring AB with me."

She turned from her screen and gave him her high eyebrow look. "Where will I be going?"

"My house. Mrs. Henderson made a huge breakfast. They thought I'd be home from my shift and wanted to surprise me. Let's lock this joint up and go eat."

15

Coop and Gus met AB at the office in the early afternoon, refreshed from a huge meal, a nap, and a shower. Trevor, the guy Coop used for surveillance support arrived a few minutes later.

Coop greeted him on the porch with a handshake and Gus beat his tail against the wooden planks. Coop steered Trevor away from the house to chat near the sidewalk. "Hey, Trevor, thanks for coming on a Sunday. We had an intruder last night who bypassed our alarm with an electronic device. I need you to sweep the place for listening devices or cameras. I want to make sure he didn't leave anything behind."

Coop let Trevor work while he and Gus sat in the reception area. He and AB had agreed not to discuss the case until Trevor was able to complete the sweep. To mask any sounds, AB put the Christmas songs back on and played them throughout the house.

She opened the mail she had retrieved from the post office and after logging in the payments, printed a spreadsheet. She handed him the printout, which showed all but two of their outstanding accounts had been paid in full. He gave her a thumbs up. Gus couldn't contain himself and took to following Trevor through the office, nabbing a treat AB used to try to lure him to stay with her.

Trevor came out of Coop's office and gestured he had found something. He continued examining the rest of the building and concluded at AB's desk. He pointed to a plant in the corner by AB's desk and nodded his head. Trevor motioned to Coop to follow him into Coop's office. He showed Coop a tiny device behind one of the framed prints on the wall near his desk.

Coop led Trevor to the backyard and watched him inspect his Jeep and AB's car. Trevor shook his head indicating they were both clean. "Do you want me to remove the two in your office? Everything else is clean. Nothing in the phones, no cameras. Nothing on the exterior."

"Hmm, let me think about that. How far away do those microphones transmit?"

"They're slick. They have a SIM card and the listener programs it via a text message to a cell phone. The technology gives the listener the ability to listen from anywhere and the device transmits an alert whenever it's activated by a voice."

"What about my alarm? The guy used something to get past it."

Trevor pursed his lips and nodded. "Yeah, if the bad guys have enough money and resources, no alarm out there will keep them out. You have one of the best systems. It doesn't take long for experts in the criminal world to crack the systems. The good guys are always playing catch up. You were smart to have the cameras installed, otherwise you wouldn't have known you had a break-in."

"Glad I called you," said Coop, shaking his head in disgust. His eyebrows rose. "I need to talk to Ben and AB and brainstorm a way to use the bugs to our advantage. Are you able to retrieve the phone number they're connected to without alerting the listener?"

Trevor nodded. "I have the technology," he said with a grin. "I'll recover the number now and let you hash it over."

Coop followed Trevor back in the office and said, "AB how about I treat you to tea at that bakery you like? I could use a break." He gestured outside with his head and put his fingers to his lips."

"I can't refuse baked goods. Sounds great." She left the music on and followed him out the back door, with Gus on their heels."

When they cleared the house, Coop explained what Trevor had found and used his cell to call Ben. He reached his voice-mail and left a message. Coop checked his watch. "He's on the plane by now."

"I wonder if we could lure Featherstone to us, using the bugs?" asked AB.

"I was thinking along the same line. We could say we found the evidence we need, something vague."

"Set up a perimeter on the office and snag the guy who comes to steal the evidence?" AB nodded as she contemplated the idea. "Let's go to the bakery while Trevor finishes here. I don't want to stand around in the cold."

Coop drove them the short distance to Sugar Buns. Gus thumped his tail against the seat and panted with excitement. Sugar Buns was dog friendly and he always scored a few pumpkin dog cookies when they visited.

They settled in a cozy booth with Gus at their feet, busy munching on his own treats. After a few bites of his scone, Coop said, "I forgot to tell you, Ben said they located the Toyota sedan from last night. It was abandoned on Highway 40, wiped clean of any prints. No cameras in the area, so no way to know what vehicle picked them up or how many of them were in the car. He said they ran the VIN and found the owner, who had not yet found out his car had been stolen last night."

"Sounds like a dead end, or at least one on life support," she said.

"Yeah, they're going to search out cameras in the area and examine the footage for vehicles with extra passengers, but it's a bit of a long shot. Nothing from the residential area where the Toyota was stolen."

He checked the time. "Ben won't be able to call us for a few hours. They land in Seattle around eight-thirty our time."

"We could check with Kate and Jimmy and kick around the idea about trying to lure Featherstone to us."

Coop nodded and finished off the last of the tea. "Yeah, let's see what we can come up with. I want to get this sonofabitch."

When they arrived back at the office, they found Trevor waiting. Always one for details, he had documented the location of the devices with his video camera before he used his electronic expertise to decipher the information on the SIM card. He provided a written report of his findings, a copy of the video documentation, and the phone number associated with the devices. "It's not registered, so I suspect it's a burner phone. Call me when you want them removed."

After Trevor left, Coop and AB doused the music and closed the office, making excuses about being tired and heading home, for the benefit of the listener. They gathered their files and information and made their way to Aunt Camille's.

She was in the midst of her Sunday supper ritual and overjoyed to learn there would be another guest. Coop and AB established themselves in Coop's home office. He took his chair behind the desk and called Kate. He filled her in on the results of Trevor's work.

"I'll add that number to the list of the ones we're tracking and tracing and see what we can get on it. You haven't said anything in the office to alert the bad guys you found their bugs, right?"

"No, we were careful. Before Trevor got there, AB and I

watched the video and talked about it being the same guy at the mailbox, but nothing about the bugs."

"Good. I like your idea of trying to set them up, but rather than trying to make them come to you, how about we trace the phone and nab them?"

"Sounds less dangerous."

"You guys come up with a script that will keep them listening and I'll text you as soon as we have a trace."

"Give us until eight and we'll be back at the office."

"By the way, at the exact time you told Ben about your friend in the hoodie making a call, one of the burners went active. Called another burner, not Featherstone's."

"Makes sense. I'll text you when we get to the office tonight."

He disconnected and raised his brows at AB. "I take it we're setting a trap tonight?"

He grinned. "Yep. We need to come up with a conversation to keep them on the phone for a few minutes."

They contemplated possible discussion topics that would entice the perpetrators to pay attention and after a few back and forth exchanges they settled on a plan. "That should do it," said Coop.

She nodded and smiled. "Meanwhile, back at the ranch," she pulled a notepad from the stack of files she had positioned on the couch. "Yesterday I combed through four years of newspapers. I searched for any mention of Camden Academy and found articles about sports and school activities. Logan and Hunt were pictured in group photos like they were in the yearbook. There were articles about events and fundraisers and one focused on college acceptance decisions for graduates. Both of them were mentioned as star athletes throughout their time at Camden. There was also a series covering the study abroad program the year both of them went to Europe for one semester."

"Sounds mundane."

"Yep, no mention of either of them stood out. The only interesting item related to Mount Camden was the death of a young woman who worked an event at the school in 1980. They hosted a dance in conjunction with an all-girls school and the woman worked with the catering company. She was walking on the road late at night, after she got off work, and was killed by a hit and run driver. This was right before both of them graduated."

"Any connection to our guys?"

She wrinkled her nose. "Not that I could find. The only reason I discovered it was in searching the name of the school. No students were named in the article. I followed it through the papers and never found where the case was solved. She was a single mother of a toddler. Sad story. That's the only thing I found on the negative side with a remote link to Camden."

"Let Kate know and ask if they can dig into it." A knock on the door interrupted them.

Camille's face squeezed into the crack she had opened. "Supper's ready, you two."

They brought Camille up to date on the stakeout and break-in, while enjoying chicken and biscuits. Camille tsked and said, "I worry about you two. These hoodlums sound downright dangerous."

"We'll be fine," Coop said, patting her hand with reassurance. "We'll leave Gus here with you. Don't worry if I'm home late."

"We'll be in contact with Kate and she'll have units in the area. It'll be fine," said AB, with a smile. "How about dessert before we go?"

Camille's eyes sparkled. "Oh, yes. I made homemade brownies for brownie sundaes for y'all tonight." She hurried to the kitchen and Coop gathered a stack of plates and cleared the table.

After consuming sundaes the size of their heads, they headed back to the office in Coop's Jeep. Once they arrived, they positioned themselves in Coop's office. Coop set his phone to silent and texted Kate to let her know they were in position.

Once he received a confirmation from her, they eased into a conversation to activate the listening device. After a bit of chatting, Coop got the ball rolling. "So, I got a call from Ben tonight. They have some high-quality CCTV footage from downtown on our friend in the hoodie. He said they're enhancing it and are very optimistic they'll get an ID."

"Plus, the guy from our neighborhood who came forward. He got a look at the guy and is doing a sketch with the police. Not to mention our own video from the break-in."

"Glad we had those cameras installed in the office. I think it'll be enough to conclude it's the same dirtbag and with any luck he'll be in the system and they can get a name." Coop's phone lit up with a text from Kate. He nodded and smiled at AB.

"What about the car he got into?" she asked.

"It was stolen, but Ben said the crime techs found some physical evidence and they're analyzing now. Put all of it together and we should be able to find the guy." Coop continued to describe where the car was stolen from, adding they had found a witness who was being helpful in identifying the car thief.

His phone came alive and he gave AB a thumbs up. Kate's text reported they had a lock on the phone and another burner had been activated, along with Featherstone's. Units were on the way.

They continued the charade and kept talking until they got a text from Kate saying they had two men in custody and she would get back to them soon. Coop let out a breath.

The two of them stared at the white board, hoping a piece of data they had collected on the suspects would solve the puzzle. AB heaved a sigh and said, "I think we need a distraction. I need to get away from this for a few hours and let my mind work. How about a movie?"

"Sure, I could use a break." Once in the Jeep, Coop called Aunt Camille to let her know they were okay and would be at the multiplex in Green Hills. A spy movie was about to begin. They stocked up on popcorn and snacks and eased into the comfortable seats. Both of them focused on the film, a feature with a twisty plot and great actors.

The movie was at the midpoint when AB gasped and her buttery fingers clutched at Coop's arm. She leaned close to his ear. "We need to check something. I think I might know where Callie's envelope is."

"Do you want to finish the movie?" he asked.

"No," she whispered. "Let's go." They hurried through the aisle and when they got in the Jeep she said, "Go to the law library."

Coop's forehead wrinkled, but he steered them to Vanderbilt. "What are you thinking?"

"In the movie those two men used a dead drop to pass information. It made me remember when Callie and I were in law school. I had Professor Rhodes in the morning and she had him in the afternoon. She was having a hard time, so I used to stop by the library and leave her a note to let her know the topics on quizzes."

"You cheated?" He grinned as he glanced at her.

She huffed. "Technically, I guess. I didn't give her answers, just topics. She was so stressed out and I was just trying to be a good friend. Anyway, you're missing the point."

"I just can't believe Annabelle Davenport would cheat. You're the most honest person I know."

She rolled her eyes. "Again, not the point. We roamed around the library during the scavenger hunt. She was alone and could have hidden it. I want to check our book and see if she left the envelope there."

"What book?"

"We always used this obscure old reference book of court

logs from the 1800's. One of Arden's great-great-somethings was a judge back then, so we claimed it as our dead drop."

Coop shook his head as he pulled into the parking structure. "Seriously, a dead drop?"

"We didn't call it that or even know about dead drops. It was just a place nobody would ever look."

His phone vibrated with a text from Kate. He read it over and said, "Kate says they're going to work on the two guys they took into custody. They're not learning much yet, but are going to hold them overnight and play them against each other. Featherstone's phone was on for seconds and then dropped off. He's smart."

Coop pulled his access card out of his wallet. As a member of the bar, he had been issued a card for evening access to the library decades ago. They made their way to the entrance, through the barren garage. He held the card to the reader and the light stayed red. He removed it and tried it again. Nothing.

AB took the card from his hand and held it against the reader. Red light. "What the heck?" She huddled in her coat, longing for the gloves she left behind.

Coop looked at the glass doors and saw a small sign. *Closed for Winter Break.* "AB, they're closed."

She diverted her attention from the card reader. "Crap on a cracker." She plunged her hands in the pockets of her coat.

"I'll call in the morning and try to persuade someone to give us access. Kate will be able to get it, if we can't convince the school."

She thrust the card back to him. "Why didn't I think of this sooner?" They rushed back to the Jeep, escaping the frigid breeze. "I'm not sure I can wait until morning."

16

Monday morning Coop met AB at the gym, earlier than usual. As soon as they wrapped up their workout, Coop sent Kate a text to check on her progress with finagling access to the law library.

A quick shower later, with Gus in tow, he met AB in the Aunt Camille's kitchen. The office was still off limits until the listening devices were removed. The welcoming smell of his favorite coffee filled the air and he helped himself to a large cup. AB was at the counter, thrumming her fingers atop its clean surface. "Any news?" she asked, eyes wide with expectation.

"Not yet, but it's barely eight o'clock. Kate said she'd get in touch as soon as she finds somebody who could let us in." He took a large gulp of his morning brew and moaned after he swallowed. "They're close to getting our hoodie friend to crack."

He petted Gus and savored his coffee, listening to the tick of the clock, as they waited for word from Kate. He set his empty cup in the sink and his cell phone rang. "It's Kate."

AB perked up and listened to Coop's side of the conversation. "Uh, huh. Got it. We're on our way and will meet him there."

She had her jacket on by the time Coop disconnected. Since Camille preferred to sleep in and hadn't yet emerged from her suite and Gus gave them his saddest face, they agreed he could ride along. They hurried to the Jeep, loaded Gus in the back, and drove the few blocks to Vanderbilt. Coop parked in the same vacant garage and they crossed to the entrance. They stood at the glass doors for a few moments before a short balding man unlocked them.

"You must be Mr. Harrington and Ms. Davenport?" he asked.

"Yes, sir." Coop extended his hand. "We appreciate you meeting us, Mr. Conrad."

"The detective explained it was quite urgent and involved a murder case. I'm happy to oblige," said the soft spoken man, wearing a bowtie. He locked the door behind them and motioned them through the lobby.

AB looked at Coop and he gave her a nod. "We need to look upstairs in one of the historical logs."

"Whatever you need," he gestured with his hands, offering them free reign. "I'll be in my office on the first floor, just past the atrium."

Coop followed AB up the stairs and to the reading room. He watched her scan the shelves and remove a heavy leather-bound book. She placed it on a nearby table and took care opening it. As she did, it fell open to a page containing a modern manila envelope.

AB lifted her head, her eyes sparkling with anticipation when they met Coop's. "I was right." Coop handed her a pair of gloves from his pocket and she slipped them on. The envelope was hand addressed to Featherstone at the mailbox store.

She touched the envelope on the edges, despite the gloves, and examined it. Coop said, "Look, there's part of a label." He took out his phone and took pictures of the envelope before AB opened the clasp.

She slid the contents onto the table and separated the sheets with her gloved hand. Coop took more photos and then examined the sheets. "Here's our link, AB." He pointed to the sheet with Avery Logan's name and photos.

"So, Judge Hunt sent this to Featherstone. Why?" she asked, staring at the information on the papers, showing Logan's home and work addresses.

"That's the question of the day, AB." He put a call into Kate and explained they had evidence for her to collect.

He disconnected and said, "She's dispatching an evidence tech and said to wait until he's here and then meet her at the precinct. I want to pick up the rest of our files on the way."

Coop went downstairs to find Mr. Conrad while AB stayed with the documents. Coop explained the police would be coming and with a fluster, Mr. Conrad removed his keys from his pocket and rushed down the hallway to the lobby.

After handing off the evidence and filling out a report, Coop and AB retrieved their case files and made their way to the precinct. Gus meandered through the cubicles and plopped on the dog bed Ben kept in his office, just for him. Coop plucked two bottles of green tea from Ben's fridge. It was his latest alternative to coffee and Ben supported his healthy changes and kept it stocked for him.

Jimmy was at his desk. "Have a seat at the conference table guys. Kate will be right back." Coop slid a bottle of tea to AB and opened up the file folder. The large white board outlining the work done on Callie's murder stared back at them.

He thumbed through his reports and slid the screen on his phone. "The set of numbers left from the label on the folder you found match the shipment numbers assigned from Judge Hunt's system."

Kate and Jimmy took their chairs at the table. She sighed as she surveyed her notepad. "They're running the envelope for me now. Looking for prints or any physical evidence. Sounds like the label links it to Judge Hunt's office."

Coop nodded. "The most plausible explanation is this envelope contained all the information for a hit on Logan. It's just hard to believe Judge Hunt would be involved in something like this. He's well respected and up for another appointment."

"Maybe his appointment is the reason Judge Hunt is involved. Something to do with Logan might jeopardize his selection," said AB.

"Ben's calling us in a few minutes so we can run this by him. We want to make sure he's on board with moving hard on Judge Hunt," said Kate.

"Your hoodie friend, who we now know is Ricky Dunbar, is in the process of making a deal with the DA's office. He wants immunity for what he knows about Featherstone," added Jimmy. "He knows the system. Has a sheet. Burglary, fraud, assault. Been keeping his nose clean since his last probation. His friend was the driver who picked him up when you were following him, Coop."

"We need to get Featherstone before he bolts. Any more activity on his phone?"

Kate shook her head. "Ricky let it slip how careful the boss is with the phone. Ricky's got an appointed time to get in touch with Featherstone late tonight."

Jimmy added, "Featherstone told our boy Ricky to lay low, so the cops wouldn't be able to find him based on the phony conversation you two had. We, of course, haven't let on it was faked."

The phone buzzed with Ben's call. Kate put it on speaker. She brought him up to date on the current status. Coop and AB explained the connection between Hunt and Logan.

"If we're going after a sitting judge, we need to have this stuff nailed down. We can't implicate him unless we're sure. I'm having a hard time believing he would do this."

"He's been cooperative when I've talked to him. He acted surprised when Featherstone's information was iffy. I hear what you're saying, Ben, but my gut tells me there's more to this and he's involved."

The group deliberated and argued, with Ben getting the last word. "I don't want you moving on the judge until it's as close to one hundred percent as possible. If you get something to tighten it up, call me back."

The foursome at the table hung their heads as they listened to the dial tone. Kate flicked the speaker off and said, "You heard him. We need to establish a stronger link to the judge."

"Ben's got a tough job. Like it or not, he has to be politically savvy and he's the one who will take the heat, especially if we're wrong," said Coop.

"Did you get anything on the old hit and run case I told you about?" asked AB.

Kate shook her head. "Not yet. Sorry, it hasn't been a priority. If you want to dig into the file, I'll have it brought here."

AB nodded her head. "Yeah, that works for me."

"I think you two need to stay away from your office and the listening devices. We don't want to tip them off," said Jimmy.

"In theory we're closed for the next two weeks, so not a problem. We can work at home or here," said Coop.

Coop spread their files out on the table and scribbled on his notepad while they awaited delivery of the old case file. Once it arrived, they dug into it and created a new section on the white board with the significant data from the file.

The name of the victim was Patricia Redmond. She was a single mother of a toddler, Amy Redmond. Patricia's parents were given custody of the little girl upon the death of their daughter. Leads in the case were slim. No witnesses, no cameras back in that era. The detectives had scoured auto body shops for damaged vehicles, but got nowhere. Patricia had died instantly and was found the next morning along the side of the road.

AB searched the databases for Patricia's parents. They were still living in Nashville. She penned their address on a sticky note and handed it to Coop. "Let's go visit them and find out if they can shed any light on Patricia's death."

Coop signaled Gus and the dog followed them to the Jeep. They dropped Gus at Camille's and drove to the Redmond's house. They were greeted by an elderly woman whose face peeked out from behind the door. "Mrs. Redmond?" asked Coop.

"Yes," she gave them a wary look. "Who are you?"

"Ma'am, I'm Cooper Harrington and this is my associate, Annabelle Davenport. We're private detectives working with the police on a case. We came across your daughter's hit and run accident from 1980 in the course of our investigation and were hoping we could ask you a few questions."

Mrs. Redmond's eyes blinked in quick succession. "My Patricia?" She eased the door open wider.

"Yes, Mrs. Redmond. We know it's been a long time and we are so sorry to bring up what must be a painful topic."

She nodded, but opened the door and motioned them inside. "My husband isn't well. He's sleeping now." She led them into the dining room off the kitchen.

They took a seat at the table and Coop cleared his throat. "As I said, we're investigating a case with links back to Mount Camden in 1980. We were looking through old newspapers and saw the article about your daughter's accident. Did you have any theories about what happened?"

The woman rubbed her hands together and shook her head. "No, we never could figure out what happened."

"Did Patricia have any enemies or problems with anyone who would have wanted to hurt her?" asked AB.

Mrs. Redmond's eyes filled and she continued to move her hands together. "Oh, no, not that we knew of. Patricia was very kind and quiet. She was just trying to earn some money to support Amy. She took the bus and was walking to the stop. We couldn't afford a car for her to drive."

"We saw Amy was placed in your custody after Patricia's death. How is she?"

A twinkle flashed in her watery eyes. "She's wonderful. She was so young I don't think it registered what happened to her momma. We just loved her and raised her as our own. She's all grown up now. Married with children of her own." She moved from her chair and went to a bookcase where she retrieved several framed photos.

"This is Amy when she graduated college." She handed them another frame. "Her wedding." She held the last photo and smiled. "This is Amy with her family last Christmas." She set it down in front of AB. "She looks so much like her momma."

Coop studied the photos. "She went to Vanderbilt Law?"

Mrs. Redmond's smile widened. "Yes, she was an excellent student. She's a lawyer now. She works downtown at Bailey and Fulgram."

"They're an excellent firm," said Coop. "Annabelle and I both went to Vanderbilt Law."

The old woman glanced, with longing, at the photos. "Patricia would be so proud of her. We never had the money to send her to college and then when she got pregnant, it was out of the question." She shuffled the photo frames and returned them to the bookcase. "Amy was lucky enough to get a scholarship. She went to Magnolia Academy and then to Vanderbilt. Without the scholarship, we would have never been able to send her to either of them."

"Magnolia is the sister school to Mount Camden, right?"

She nodded. "That's right. It's the all-girls school. The school contacted us and told us Amy had been awarded a full scholarship. We never even applied or thought about her going there. It's so expensive."

"What was the name of her scholarship?"

Mrs. Redmond shut her eyes. "Oh, let me think. It was a strange name. They paid for her whole time at Magnolia and then paid all the way through law school. Every expense, even a monthly stipend for living expenses." She got up and went to a desk in the living room.

They heard drawers opening and closing and after a few minutes she said, "Here it is." She returned with a folder, yellowed with age. She pulled out a letter and read, "It says here, she's the recipient of a scholarship from the Corrigenda Apsconditus Foundation." She handed the letter to Coop. "We had never heard of it."

"I'm not familiar with it either. Very generous and I'm sure well-deserved." He smiled and jotted in his notebook before he returned the letter. "Please give our best to Amy, you should be proud of her." Coop stood and AB followed his lead.

"If you find out what happened to my Patricia, please come back."

Coop gripped her hand in his. "You have my promise. Thank you for talking to us."

They let themselves out and as soon as they shut the doors on the Jeep, AB turned the screen of her phone to face Coop. "I recognized the name of the foundation as Latin, but wasn't sure what it meant."

He squinted at the screen. "Just read it to me."

"Roughly translated it means concealed or hidden things to be corrected."

His eyes widened and his forehead creased as he steered them to the precinct. "We need to find out more about it." They picked up lunch on the way and when they arrived got to work researching the foundation.

AB tapped on the keyboard and frowned as she took bites of her sandwich. "Nothing on it. They aren't spending money advertising or seeking out applicants for scholarships. There's nothing showing on the Vanderbilt site where they list all the scholarships. Nothing on Magnolia either. All that pops up on a search is vocabulary help and Latin translators."

Kate walked by the conference table. "Any progress?" she asked.

"Maybe. You were looking into scholarships for the Logan kids. Did you find out anything?" asked Coop.

She opened the file and thumbed through the sheets. "Nothing. I put a call into Camden Academy and the University of Tennessee, but no call back yet. The wife was useless. Mr. Logan handled all the finances and she had no clue about the scholarships. Why?"

He explained what they had discovered from Patricia Redmond's mother and the generous scholarship from the Corrigenda Apsconditus Foundation.

Kate crinkled her nose. "The translation sounds like a secret penance or something."

AB perused the paperwork in Kate's file. "I'll try to raise somebody at the Magnolia Academy and follow-up with these other two schools and get more information."

Coop looked at his notes. "Kate, did you ask the wife about Logan's old yearbooks from Camden?"

She shook her head. "I can give her a call and ask if she has them." She flipped through the file and picked up the phone.

With both Kate and AB working the phones, Coop excused himself to Ben's office and used the phone on his desk to make a call. He emerged a few minutes later sporting a smug grin.

AB slammed the phone down as he took a chair next to hers. "Magnolia said they have no current records of such a scholarship. The woman I talked to said they don't retain scholarship files older than ten years."

Kate hung up her call and said, "Mrs. Logan is still a basket case, but she said we could come by and pick up the yearbooks, if it will help. I'll send a uniform to get them now."

Coop cleared his throat several times and wiggled his brows. "Would it surprise you ladies to know Judge Hunt has a foundation of his own that awards scholarships?"

The two women looked at each other and shrugged. Coop continued, "Well, he does. He's run the Corrigenda Apsconditus Foundation since 1988, when he graduated from Vanderbilt Law."

"I'd call that the mother of all coincidences," said Kate.

Coop and AB looked at each other and said, "There are no coincidences."

17

A flurry of activity followed Coop's revelation. Kate directed manpower to focus on locating personnel at each of the schools. The uniforms arrived with yearbooks from the Logan home. Jimmy concentrated on prodding the attorney who was finalizing the deal for hoodie man.

Coop and AB paged through the yearbooks and found Judge Hunt's signature and message to his friend, Avery. In each year, Hunt wrote a short entry implying a close friendship. In the last yearbook, they found an entry dated at the end of May, 1980. *Avery, Lucky to have a true friend like you. Enjoy your college years at Auburn. I hope we'll see each other on breaks. I'm forever in your debt and will never forget your devotion, both on and off the field. Your friend and Vanderbilt JD, Reese Hunt.*

Jimmy came around the corner and said, "We've got a deal with hoodie man. He's going to keep his appointment with Featherstone and keep him talking so we can get a location and pick him up. Ricky is Featherstone's right hand errand boy. As we suspected, Featherstone is an alias and Ricky knows him as Marcus. He's not sure that's his real name though."

Coop flipped the yearbook around so Jimmy could read it.

"This gives us our link to Judge Hunt. We need to ask him about Avery Logan and watch his reaction."

Jimmy nodded. "Let's run it past Kate. Also, Ricky admitted to being in the alley after the hit and run involving the bike messenger downtown. Featherstone sent him there to search for an envelope. He had expected a delivery by noon and sent Ricky to find it."

"What happened when he didn't find it?"

"Ricky said he called Featherstone on the cell and told him the envelope wasn't there and that's all he knows."

"Does Ricky know anything about the connection to Judge Hunt?" asked Coop.

Jimmy shook his head. "He doesn't know anything beyond his delivery duties. That's what he says, anyway. Hard to know how much to believe."

"So, he didn't know what was in the envelopes he retrieved from the mailbox?"

"Nope. He's just pick-up and delivery."

"Plus, a smidgen of breaking and entering. As in our office," added AB.

"Yeah, if his information doesn't lead to a conviction of Featherstone, our friend Ricky is looking at some hard time." Jimmy tapped his phone to read a message. "Prints on the envelope AB retrieved belong to our victim, Callie. No other prints."

Coop furrowed his brows. "I would have thought there would be other prints from Judge Hunt's office staff on the envelope." His thoughts were interrupted by the sound of his cell phone.

He squinted at the number he didn't recognize, with the screen indicating it was from Colorado. He remembered Hildie was on vacation and excused himself to Ben's office. He answered, "Coop Harrington."

A woman's voice said, "Mr. Harrington, I'm Sandie Coleman, Hildie's sister-in-law. I wanted to call you and let you know

Hildie is in the hospital here in Denver. I'm a nurse and the family thought I should call you. Hildie told us a bit about you."

"I'm sorry to hear she's in the hospital. What happened?"

"The doctors are saying she has toxic levels of digitalis in her system. She doesn't take digitalis, so we're trying to figure out how it happened. She complained about seeing auras and was lethargic and drowsy. I insisted she get to the hospital and when they ran blood tests, they found it."

"Is she going to be okay?"

"It's too early to tell, her levels were quite high. They're sending people to collect anything she may have eaten from the house. We suspect it must have been from a bottle of whiskey she brought with her. She was the only one who drank it. It was an office gift she had brought to share. None of us are big whiskey fans."

"So, she received it as a gift from someone at work?"

"I don't know for certain. The bottle is being tested now."

"Could you find out where the bottle came from? I'm in the midst of investigating a case with a link to Hildie's work at the courthouse and it could be important."

"Sure, I'll try. The hospital called the police, so I expect we'll be hearing from them."

"Give them my contact information and ask them to call." He also gave her Kate's name and number, knowing police are more comfortable talking to their own. "If you get a name of the detective in charge of the case, call me back and I'll call them myself."

"Okay, I'll do my best. Do you think Hildie was deliberately poisoned?"

"I can't be sure, but I think there's a strong possibility. That's why I need to find out the origin of the bottle."

He heard the sharp intake of her breath. "Okay, I'll be in touch soon."

"Tell Hildie I'm thinking of her. Please let me know how she responds to the treatment." He sent Sandie a text with all of his contact information and Kate's, just so she would have it on hand.

When he emerged from Ben's office, AB glanced up from the paperwork on the table. "Coop, what's wrong? You're as pale as your aunt's sheets."

He slid into a chair next to her. "It was Hildie's sister-in-law. She called to tell me Hildie's in the hospital in Denver." He relayed the conversation amid gasps from AB.

"Like you said, we need to determine the origin of the bottle," said Jimmy.

Kate came through the door and saw the solemn expressions around the table. "What happened? Why do you all look so miserable?"

Jimmy gave her the facts surrounding Coop's call from Hildie's family. Kate paced the room. "Now we have a great excuse to talk to Judge Hunt."

"I'd like to come with you," said Coop, his face still lacking its normal color.

"Yeah, that works. You're the one who talked with her family." She turned to Jimmy. "I'll go with Coop. You and AB keep working all the angles we have and try to get in touch with somebody in Denver to get more information about the bottle. Text me whatever you learn."

"I'll keep in contact with Hildie's family and give you any updates about her condition," volunteered AB.

Coop rode with Kate, who used her lights to get them to the courthouse in record time. They made their way to the sixth floor and found Sadie at the front counter of Judge Hunt's office.

Kate stepped forward and showed Sadie her badge. "I'm detective Kate Woodman and I think you've met Cooper Harrington. We need to speak with Judge Hunt immediately."

Sadie slipped her glasses down her nose and looked over them. "Is this regarding a current case?"

"No ma'am it's not about a case. It's an emergency and a police matter. I must insist we see him now," said Kate, using her I mean business voice.

Sadie let out a huff and punched a button on the phone console. She turned her chair and mumbled into the handset. She replaced the phone and said, "Judge Hunt is available now."

She pressed the buzzer to open the door and led them down the hallway. She knocked two quick times and then opened the door to Judge Hunt's chambers. Not giving Sadie a chance to announce them, Kate entered and Coop followed, catching a glimpse of Sadie's slack-jawed face before closing the heavy door.

Judge Hunt stood. "Mr. Harrington, what can I do for you? Sadie indicated it was an emergency."

Kate spoke before Coop could answer. "I'm Detective Woodman and we're here about your assistant, Hildie."

"Hildie's on vacation with her family. She isn't due back until January. I believe she's in Colorado."

Kate nodded. "Yes, she is. Mr. Harrington received a call from her sister-in-law in the last hour. Hildie is in the hospital."

The judge's eyes went wide and his brows rose. "What happened? Is she all right?"

Kate gave Coop a quick nod of her head. He said, "They're not sure yet. She's undergoing treatment for poisoning."

"Poisoning? How did she get poisoned?"

Kate retrieved her cell phone and then said, "We just received word from the Denver authorities. A bottle of whiskey she drank from was laced with digitalis. The bottle was one she received as an office Christmas gift. That's why we're here. We need to know more about it."

The judge brought his hand across his mouth and then

rubbed the sides of his forehead. "We tend to get inundated with Christmas gifts. I'm careful never to take any of them for myself, but let the staff take whatever they like. Cookies, chocolates, liquor. It's the only thing I can think of when you say office gift."

"Do you and the staff members exchange gifts with each other?"

The judge shook his head. "No, not formally. I always give the staff gift cards for their favorite things. I gave Hildie a spa weekend this year. My wife is the one who gets the gifts for them. She's better at choosing for ladies."

"So, do you know where the whiskey came from?" asked Kate.

"No, I'm sorry. Staff just puts all the items in the breakroom and people take what they like."

Kate stood and showed him the screen from her phone. "This is a photo of the bottle. It's a special limited-edition bottle made for the holidays. Do you recognize it?"

The judge looked at the photo. "No, I don't. I purposely don't get involved with the gifts. I don't want there to be any perception of impropriety and have tried to discourage gifts and used to return them all, but years ago we compromised with this practice of letting staff have them."

"Do you know of anyone who would want to harm you or your staff?" she asked, taking her phone.

He pursed his lips and she saw his eyes glint with tears. "That's a tough one. Many people who visit my court leave unhappy or end up in prison, so I'm sure some of them wish me harm."

"Have you had any recent threats?" asked Kate.

He shook his head. "Nothing comes to mind." He stood and paced to the windows. "Poor Hildie. I can't believe this." He rubbed the nape of his neck and then clasped his hands together. "She's a wonderful person. She doesn't deserve this."

Coop raised his brow and Kate gave him an almost imperceptible nod. "In the course of our investigation, we came across the name Avery Logan. Does his name ring a bell?" asked Coop.

The judge thrust his hands in his pockets and licked his lips. "I went to Mount Camden with Avery."

"Did you know he had been murdered?"

The judge stepped to his chair and sat behind his desk. He blinked several times and nodded. "Yes, I read about him in the newspaper."

"Were you still close with Avery after your time at Mount Camden?" asked Coop.

He shook his head. "No, we lost touch when we left for college. I went to Vanderbilt and he was headed to Auburn."

"So, you haven't been in contact with him since then? Like thirty years ago?"

He leaned back in his chair and Coop noticed his hands clenched the arms of the chair. "Yeah, that's right." The judge leaned forward with his elbows on the desk. "What's this have to do with Hildie?"

"Henry Featherstone," said Coop. "The envelope I asked you about. He's connected to Avery Logan."

Hunt's forehead wrinkled. "That's a strange coincidence." The judge checked his watch. "I'm due in court. Please keep me posted on Hildie's condition." He stood, all but dismissing the two visitors.

"We'll be in touch, Judge Hunt. Are you staying in town for the holidays?" asked Kate.

He opened a closet and retrieved his robe. "Yes, I'll be here. If anything changes, please call me at home. Hildie's been with me forever..." He didn't finish his thought as he put his arm through the sleeves. "I'll have my staff send her some flowers." Coop took note of his shaky hands fumbling with the zipper.

They showed themselves out and didn't speak until they were inside Kate's car. She looked at him and raised her brows in question.

"He's shook up and didn't want to discuss Avery Logan. I do think he was shocked to learn about Hildie. His reaction appeared genuine."

"I agree. I don't think he had anything to do with the poisoning."

"Maybe he was the target, not Hildie?"

She nodded as she steered the car back to the precinct. "Exactly what I was thinking. I want to put surveillance on the judge and determine where he goes."

"If Callie was killed for the envelope addressed to Featherstone, could be Featherstone is cleaning up loose ends. He's a careful guy. It means Judge Hunt could be next."

Kate put in the call for a team to stay on top of the judge until further notice.

They found Jimmy and AB where they had left them. Coop asked AB, "Any updates on Hildie?" She shook her head.

Jimmy hung up the phone and said, "That was the distillery in Kentucky. The bottle came from their holiday limited edition. Only 288 bottles, so they're going to send me a list of buyers. It's exclusive to the distillery store, so we'll have a complete record."

"Did Denver call us back on the specifics?" asked Kate.

Jimmy nodded and flipped through his notebook. "Preliminary lab results show the original wax was displaced and that's how the poison was inserted into the bottle. Then new wax, a slightly different red color than the original was put over the top of the whole thing again. Not noticeable until you get it to the lab."

"So Hildie wouldn't have noticed anything amiss when she opened it?"

Jimmy shook his head. "Probably not. The new wax seal

covered the old one. I doubt she would have noticed a bit more wax than usual. She would have had to cut the wax and then unscrew the lid. No easy pull tab on this one."

"Any fingerprints?"

Jimmy flipped a page in his notebook. "They said the bottle was surprisingly clean. Had Hildie's prints and one other set. They're running them through the system now."

"Considering the bottle had to be handled by the clerk who sold it, the person who bought it, Hildie, and any other staff in the office," said Coop. "Our guy must have wiped it clean before delivery."

"Call them back and tell them to run the set against Judge Hunt's staff. We can send them their prints from the database. If it's one of the staff members, it will save everyone time." Jimmy nodded at Kate and left the room.

Kate looked at her watch. "We've got several hours before Ricky is set to contact Featherstone." A voice from the doorway called her away.

Coop gave AB a blow-by-blow description of their conversation with Judge Hunt.

"Sounds like he was nervous. If you're right, he's figured out Featherstone is after him."

Coop bobbed his head. "We need to get him before this escalates further." Coop leaned back in the chair and closed his eyes. "We should give Ben an update."

Jimmy and Kate rejoined the two of them. Jimmy placed a list before them. He pointed at the yellow highlighted line. "Henry Featherstone was a buyer of one bottle of the whiskey. It was mailed to him at the mailbox store. Paid for with a money order he sent to the distillery with delivery instructions."

"And Ricky just confirmed Featherstone sent him to purchase a money order at a local convenience store around the time of the whiskey order. He claims to know nothing further about the whiskey or the poison."

The phone rang for Kate. She replaced the receiver and said, "Hunt is on the move. Looks like he's heading home."

Coop looked at his watch. "A bit early. I'd say he's rattled."

While they waited for the appointed time for Ricky to call Featherstone, Kate put in a call to Ben and the foursome sat around the speaker and gave him updates. "Go talk to Jeff in the DA's office. Run him through what we have so far and ask him if it's enough. I think we need to bring the judge in for questioning."

Jimmy took the task and left for downtown. As soon as he left, the surveillance team called in an update to Kate. The judge had gone home, but emerged after about an hour and was heading back downtown.

Kate received word from the Denver police and they confirmed the other prints on the whiskey bottle belonged to Sadie. One of the officers delivered bags of food and Coop attempted to eat a few bites, but couldn't tolerate the pungent smell or taste as his thoughts drifted to Hildie. Coop's cell phone rang as he was dumping his plate of Chinese in the garbage.

He answered and signaled for quiet. Kate and AB stopped chatting and listened. "Sure, Judge Hunt, I'm happy to meet you." He nodded his head. "I can be at your office within thirty minutes." Another pause and then, "No word yet. I've been checking and will let you know the moment I hear anything."

He disconnected and said, "I need to get to Judge Hunt's office. He intimated he might have some information related to Featherstone. He's distressed about Hildie."

"I'll put a call into the DA's office, they'll want to know about this. I'll pass it on to Ben," said Kate.

"No disrespect, Kate, but I'm going to get moving. I've got comms in my Jeep. You can use one to listen to what's being said and talk to me. I don't need to Mirandize him or get a DA involved. I don't want to spook him. I'll go in alone. He told me to use the intercom at the side entrance reserved for staff. He said he'd ask the security officers to let me in and up to his office."

AB followed him outside and retrieved the communication device for Kate. "Do you have your gun?" asked AB.

He grinned and patted his side. "It's in the Jeep. I'll put it on before I go in, since I'll be bypassing the metal detectors."

18

On his drive downtown, AB called. Hildie was expected to make it. The treatments were working and her heart rate was stabilized. Coop let out a sigh as he listened to the news. The tension in his neck and shoulders eased as he took several deep breaths.

He parked the Jeep and found the door Judge Hunt indicated. Before pushing the intercom, he spoke and made sure Kate could hear him. She was just leaving the precinct and would use her badge to get upstairs and wait outside the office until she heard Coop signal for the police. Should Coop encounter an unexpected situation, the two agreed on a distress word.

The uniformed officers in charge of security permitted Coop entry and directed him to the elevators. The building was buttoned up for the night and the only sounds were his footsteps on the stone floor. He arrived on the sixth floor and found the outer doors unlocked. The front counter was uninhabited and the lights were off. The door leading to the back offices was propped open.

Coop whispered his location and observations and continued down the hall. He heard Kate acknowledge his report.

He made his way to Judge Hunt's office and knocked on the door. "It's Coop Harrington, Judge Hunt."

"Come in."

Coop opened the door and saw the judge at his desk. The overhead lights were dimmed, but his desk lamp was on, as were several other lamps throughout the room. The lighting accentuated the strain on the judge's face. His eyes were red rimmed and glassy, his hands resting atop his desk.

"Sir, are you okay?"

He stared at Coop and nodded. "I've checked into you. I know you're a smart guy. I think you have your case figured out, but I need to tell you a few things you don't know."

Coop took a seat. "I heard from Hildie's family and she's going to make it. She's improving."

Relief flooded Judge Hunt's face. "Thank God for that." He let out a sigh. "This all began a long time ago. When you asked me about Avery, I knew it was only a matter of time. We were seniors at Mount Camden and I talked Avery into sneaking out of the end of the year dance. We drove down by the river and drank. Avery was afraid to drive back, so I drove his car. It was dark and I was hurrying to get back to school before they knew we were gone."

The judge held his head with both hands. "I didn't see her."

"Patricia Redmond?"

The judge nodded. "Yeah. We were both scared out of our minds. We left her there on the side of the road. She was dead. Avery's car was already a mass of dents. It was an old car he was constantly working on and never finishing. One more blemish wouldn't be noticed. He masked it with more filler and nobody was the wiser."

The judge sighed and took a breath. "Avery promised to never say a word and I trusted him. I told myself I'd make up for what I did. I tried."

"Your foundation?"

Judge Hunt stared across the room as a tear slid down his face. "I thought if I helped her daughter I could atone. I gave her a scholarship and sent her to law school. Amy's her name." A slight smile formed on his lips. "She's a successful lawyer."

"What happened?"

"Avery," he spat the name. "For years I'd been funneling him cash. To pay him back for keeping his promise. I didn't mind. We had plenty of money and I knew Avery could use the help. I provided scholarships so his kids could go to private school and college. Everything was fine, until Brad got arrested."

"For drunk driving and possession?"

"Right. Stupid kid stuff. Anyway, Avery was out of his mind. We had always used phony email accounts to communicate for the cash drops. I'd leave it in a park or a locker at a gym. He demanded a meeting in November. He wanted me to get Brad's case transferred to my court and then rule in his favor or dismiss it."

The judge sprang from his chair and stood. Coop's hand went to his side and rested on his gun.

Hunt paced back and forth. With a raised voice he said, "I told him I could give him more money, but I wasn't going to violate my oath of office. I had never had even the hint of a blemish on my judicial record and I wasn't going to do anything to jeopardize my appointment. I'm a fair judge."

He ran his hands through his hair. "He wouldn't quit. He threatened to expose me."

"So that's when you contacted Featherstone?"

"Yeah. He wasn't supposed to hurt anyone. I just wanted him to scare Avery and make him understand. Featherstone is a fixer. I connected to him through a person I knew from a case. I thought I had been careful and could remain anonymous, but look how it turned out." The judge opened a drawer in his desk and Coop's hand slid to his weapon.

Hunt slammed a cell phone on top of the desk. "This is the burner we used to communicate."

Coop's hand relaxed. "Tell me about Callie."

The judge hung his head and slumped into his chair. "A stupid mistake. I was sending Avery's information to Featherstone's mailbox. I came up with the ruse of him wanting me to speak at the event to use as a cover, should anyone ever ask about the delivery."

"And your intern lost the envelope, right?"

"I knew you were smart. Yeah, one of many small mistakes. Featherstone was expecting the delivery by noon and when he didn't get it, he called." The judge gestured to the burner phone. "Then the damn girl didn't get it out in the afternoon batch. And Billy got killed and caused another problem."

"That's why you insisted your staff recreate all the documents for the day. You needed that envelope delivered and it would be suspect it if was the only item you messengered with another service."

"Right again, Mr. Harrington."

"How did Featherstone know Callie had the envelope?"

The judge shook his head with disgust. "That was my fault. I was frantic when he called and said it wasn't delivered. I told him it would go out in the afternoon delivery. Then it got messed up again, so I called him to let him know it would be delayed. I explained our messenger had been killed on the street and we would be sending it with a different service. Featherstone went nuts. He thought there was a chance the envelope was with Billy and wanted to make sure it didn't get into the wrong hands. I tried to convince him it wasn't. I checked our logs and Callie was the only one who had picked up files that day, besides Billy."

The judge held his hands against his temples. "I was frazzled. I was trying to explain it to Featherstone and told him I could contact Callie and get the envelope back. That's how he knew it was her. I tried to reason with him, but he told me to leave it to him. He said if I tried to do anything, he'd go after my family. I begged him to just forget the whole thing, but he told me once he was contracted, there was no way to stop the job. He promised he wouldn't do anything drastic."

He shuddered with sobs and hung his head while murmuring, "I'm so sorry. Avery wasn't supposed to die and neither was Callie. I set all of this in motion, but Featherstone was out of control. And now Hildie. The poison was meant for me, but Featherstone clearly doesn't care who's harmed, so long as he's left untouched."

"Do you know Featherstone's real name?"

The judge shook his head. "No. I never met him in person. We communicated with the burner or via the mailbox."

"What about the person who connected you to Featherstone?"

His head snapped upright. "No, no. I'm done. I'm not involving anyone else or letting this go any further. It stops now." He wiped his eyes and stood. "I wanted you to know the whole story."

Coop watched as the judge turned and gazed out the windows, looking at the lights and reflection off the river below. "Tell them I'm sorry." Before Coop could react, he saw the glint in the judge's hand. Coop sprang from his chair as the sound of the bullet firing echoed in the room. The judge fell to the floor with a thud before Coop could reach him. Unmoving eyes stared up at Coop. He put his fingers to the judge's neck, but found no pulse. The sound of Kate's voice screaming in his ear shifted Coop's attention from the dark pool of blood forming under the judge's head.

"I'm okay, Kate. Judge Hunt is down. He shot himself."

"I'm just coming through the door downstairs. On my way."

Coop stepped back and away from the body. He diverted his gaze to the windows. The usual pristine view of the city below was interrupted by the spatter of blood and one long rivulet trickling down the glass.

19

Fast footsteps and Kate's voice calling for additional backup echoed down the hall to Judge Hunt's office. Kate took in the scene and asked Coop, "You sure you're okay?"

He was sitting in one of the chairs away from the desk and nodded. "Did you hear everything?"

"Yeah, we got it all and it's recorded." The sounds of hurried and heavy boots came from the hallway followed by the entrance of several officers. Kate took Coop to a conference room and asked him to write his statement. Technicians arrived with cameras and equipment to process the scene. He heard Kate order all the security officers to be held in the building, without access to communications. She didn't want the news leaking just yet.

Dr. Lawrence was on the scene within minutes and supervised the removal of Judge Hunt's body. Coop was finishing his statement when the squeak of the gurney wheels moving down the hallway pierced the relative quiet. Despite being several rooms away, the metallic smell of blood filled his nose. He was looking for tissues when Kate came through the door.

"You okay to drive home? I'm going to be here a bit longer."

"I'm going to go to the precinct and check in with AB. I'm fine to drive. Did you let Ben know?"

She nodded. "I called him." She took a chair at the table and Coop joined her. "He's worried. Thinks he made a mistake in not acting sooner. We're always focused on getting the case locked for a conviction in court and didn't anticipate Judge Hunt's actions."

"A well- respected judge as a murder for hire suspect is not the easiest tightrope to walk." Coop exhaled. "I should have done something more to stop him."

"I'm not sure you could have. I think he had made up his mind and had a plan. We found envelopes in his desk addressed to his family and one to Hildie."

"He must have decided after we told him about Hildie being poisoned."

She nodded. "Sounds like he knew we were closing in on his connections to Avery and Callie."

"He couldn't deal with the shame. In his mind he'd paid for the accident with Patricia Redmond. He justified the money to Avery and the scholarships as a way to compensate, but drew the line at judicial misconduct."

"His whole identity was wrapped up in being a good judge and this upcoming appointment." She picked up the file with Coop's statement and rose. "I've got to go tell his wife and the governor."

"I'm sorry, Kate. I wish I could have done something or realized sooner what he was planning."

She looked at her watch. "Ricky is supposed to contact Featherstone in about an hour. Jimmy's running the operation, but I'll make sure I'm back for it." She put her hand on Coop's shoulder. "You and AB should get some rest. We'll call you and let you know what happens. We're keeping a lid on this. I can't risk Featherstone getting wind of Judge Hunt's death."

"Just make sure you get the sonofabitch, Kate." Through a

swarm of uniformed officers, Coop made his way out of the building. He drove to the precinct and found AB waiting for him. She stood and embraced him in a long and silent hug. She removed her arms and said, "Let's get out of here."

He drove to a diner and indulged in a cup of coffee without AB's usual stern eye when he defied doctor's orders. They each ordered a piece of pie and struggled to unwind from the harrowing day they had endured.

"Tomorrow's Christmas Eve," said AB. "Hopefully we'll be able to call Callie's parents and tell them it's over."

"Yeah, I want to wait until they get Featherstone. He took another sip from his cup. "I need to tell Hildie."

She frowned. "Oh, yeah, that won't be easy. Better wait until she's stronger."

"I'll call her sister-in-law in the morning and explain the situation before I talk to her." He finished his pie and slid the plate to the side. "I've got my appetite back. Do you want to split an order of cheese fries?"

She grinned. "Sure."

They finished off the plater of fried potato wedges covered in cheese and bacon, left a generous tip for the hardworking waitress, and made their way back to the precinct. They found the conference table in the same condition as they had left it, littered with files and paperwork.

Kate and Jimmy were nowhere to be found, so they set about organizing the files and cleaning up the workspace. As they were finishing, Kate strode into the room. "Hey, guys. I thought you were home sleeping."

"Nah, we couldn't miss the grand finale. Did you get Featherstone?"

A huge grin spread across her face. "Jimmy's bringing him in now. Ricky did a respectable job and kept him on the line long enough for us to track the phone. We had units disbursed throughout the metro area and were able to get to him before he moved."

A uniformed officer stepped into the room. "Detective Woodman, we need you."

Kate nodded. "You two should get going now. We'll be tied up with interrogations and lawyers for hours. We'll know more about where we are with him in the morning."

"And hopefully his real identity," said Coop. "I'm exhausted," he added, scooping up their files.

Kate gave them a wave as she followed the officer down the hallway. AB yawned a number of times on the drive to Camille's. Coop cracked the window to let a cold breeze blow through, hoping to startle himself into a more alert state.

He pulled up to the house and said, "You're more than welcome to bunk in the guest room. It's still ready for you." He retrieved the files from the backseat and added, "We could regroup in the morning and get Trevor to remove those listening devices before we go in."

She nodded and yawned again. "Thanks, Coop. I'm too tired to even think straight, much less drive." She tiptoed down the hall to the guest room and Coop went through the door to his wing of the house. He found Gus asleep and flung his clothes to the floor before falling into bed.

Coop didn't wake until mid-morning. After a long shower, he joined Camille and AB in the breakfast room. He sipped from his coffee while Mrs. Henderson made him a plate of eggs benedict. "Any word from Kate?" he asked.

AB nodded. "I called and she and Jimmy had gone home for a few hours of sleep. They said she'd call you before noon with an update."

Camille twisted one of her hankies in her hand. "I can't believe Judge Hunt killed himself. And right in front of you."

"It was horrible. A tragic story," he said, taking his plate from Mrs. Henderson.

"AB told me it's not public knowledge yet, so I won't say anything at the beauty salon today." She checked her watch. "I better get moving. I've got a few errands to run after my hair appointment."

She stood and took her cup with her. "Remember it's our party tonight, so don't be late, Coop."

"I'll be here. Don't worry." He took another bite and said, "Oh, I need to call Trevor."

"Already done. He's going to meet us there at noon and said it would take a few minutes. A tech will meet us to take them into evidence against Featherstone."

"Did you sleep okay?" he asked.

"Like a rock. This case had been weighing on me. I'm glad it's over."

"I've got to call Hildie today and inform the Baxters of the outcome."

Coop's cell phone rang as he took his last bite. "It's Kate," he said, checking the screen.

"Hey, Coop. Just wanted to let you know we have an ID on Featherstone. His real name is Marcus Burns. He's a hitman for hire and is interested in trading us information on some other cases for a deal. The DA is still working out the details."

"He'll always be Featherstone to me. Do we have him on Callie's death?"

"Yep, the DA says it's solid. Avery's too. We'll have to wait until the agreement they're making is finalized. Not sure exactly what he has, but his lawyer is playing the hypothetical game right now. Featherstone said Judge Hunt contacted him through someone in the governor's office. He won't name names until he gets a deal, but sounds like it was somebody in the governor's inner circle."

"I'm going to call Callie's parents and let them know. I plan to talk to Hildie today and break the news about Judge Hunt."

"I don't envy you that one. His wife was devastated when I did the notification." He heard her inhale, "As was the governor. I didn't mention Featherstone's revelation about the connection to someone in his own office."

"Did the press get wind of the suicide yet?"

"Not yet, but they will today. Sounds like the governor wants to put a spin on it to give the impression Judge Hunt was facing a serious illness and took his own life. He doesn't want to be associated with any of Judge Hunt's offenses."

"Politicians never disappoint, do they? Always thinking about themselves."

"I feel for Hunt's family. They had no idea about the arrangement with Avery or the accident. He had kept it a secret all these years."

"Speaking of secrets, Mrs. Redmond deserves to know." He saw AB nodding from across the table. "AB and I can go and visit her today."

"That'll be great. Ben's leaving Seattle the day after Christmas. Jen and the kids will stay and come home later."

"Poor guy. I bet it was hell on him not being here for all of this."

Kate chuckled. "Yeah, he wanted to come home a couple of days ago, but I think Jen put her foot down."

"Have a Merry Christmas, Kate. I'm taking the next week off, so call my cell if you need anything."

He disconnected and AB suggested they go visit Mrs. Redmond on their way to meet Trevor at the office. AB took her own car and followed.

Mrs. Redmond opened the door and welcomed them, leading them to the dining room. "My husband is still not well, so let's sit in here, so as not to disturb him." She offered them tea and homemade cookies.

"We're sorry to stop by again unannounced, but have some news," said Coop.

The old woman sat on the edge of her chair, hands clasped in front of her. "Do you know what happened to Patricia?"

He nodded and caught AB's eye. "We do." He explained about the accident involving two boys from Camden Academy who hit Patricia. He did not go into the scheme Judge Hunt had concocted with Avery or the manner of Avery's death, but did tell her the identity of the driver. "He went on to become a lawyer and then a judge. He's the one who set up the scholarship and made sure Amy went to college."

Mrs. Redmond's watery eyes stared back at him as he went on to provide the details of Judge Hunt's suicide when confronted with Patricia's death and subsequent crimes he committed to keep it concealed.

"You were with him when he killed himself?" Her voice trembled when she asked.

"Yes, ma'am. I know his sorrow was genuine for what he did when he was eighteen. I also know it doesn't lessen your pain or loss. He tried to atone for Patricia by providing for Amy. It was the best way he knew to make up for his actions."

Her dry lips quivered and she nodded. "We were supposed to go to Amy's house for Christmas, but with my husband so ill, we won't be able to go."

"If you'd like me to tell Amy, I'm happy to contact her," offered Coop.

She shook her head. "No, she needs to hear it from family. She knew her mother had passed away when she was little, but I never told her the story of the hit and run until she was much older. Now I can tell her the rest of the story."

"Are you going to be okay, Mrs. Redmond?" asked AB, placing her hand atop the woman's.

Silent tears dripped from her face and she patted at them with a handkerchief. "So many lives ruined. Now Judge Hunt's family will suffer forever because of all of this."

"Would you like us to call Amy or someone else to be with you now?" asked AB.

The woman gave a weak smile. "No, Amy will be here soon. Since we can't travel this year, she's bringing Christmas to us."

"I'm so very sorry, Mrs. Redmond. If there's anything else we can do, please let us know. Feel free to give Amy our number, if she'd like to talk," Coop stood and placed a card in front of Mrs. Redmond. "I hope your husband improves soon."

She twisted the handkerchief in her hands and said, "I appreciate you coming back to tell me what you found out. I've been waiting a long time to know what happened to my little girl."

They saw themselves out and Coop noticed AB swipe an errant tear from under her eye as she walked to her car. "That was horrible," she said. "Heartbreaking."

He squeezed her shoulder and waited for her to drive away from the curb before following.

They parked behind the office, next to Trevor's van. Coop hurried to the door, "Sorry, I'm a few minutes late."

"No problem. I'll be out of here in five minutes." The evidence technician arrived as Trevor was removing the devices and collected them, giving Coop a receipt.

After they both left, Coop went into his office to put in a call to Hildie's sister-in-law. He reached her and was surprised to learn Hildie had been discharged from the hospital and was recuperating at Sandie's house. With her being a nurse, she had volunteered to take charge of Hildie's care.

Coop explained he had some bad news for Hildie and wanted to make sure she was strong enough to receive it. He didn't want to risk her finding out from the news or somebody else and Sandie agreed.

Hildie came on the line. "Coop, so thoughtful of you to call." Her voice was strong and unchanged.

"I'm so glad you're feeling better. I've got some news related to your poisoning and the rest of this twisted case." He went on to explain the entire sordid affair, starting with the hit and run over thirty years ago. He heard several sharp intakes of breath from Hildie, but each time he asked about her welfare she urged him to continue.

He paused after explaining she had been poisoned with the whiskey intended for Judge Hunt. "He wanted you to know how horrible he felt about you being harmed by all of this."

"This is all just horrific. I would have never thought Judge Hunt could be involved in anything resembling corruption." She sighed and asked, "What's going to happen to him?"

Coop fortified himself with a deep breath. "Hildie, I'm afraid Judge Hunt took his own life. I'm sorry to break the news to you on the phone, but I didn't want you to hear it elsewhere."

Her heard sobs followed by, "Oh, no, no, no." She moaned and wept. "His poor family."

"Are you okay, Hildie?"

"Yeah," she said with a soft voice. "I'm just devastated. He was a decent man, Coop. I know all of this makes him sound evil and awful, but he was an excellent judge and person. I would have never imagined he could do any of these things."

"What will you do now?" he asked.

She sniffed and exhaled a long breath. "I'm not sure. My sister and brother would like me to move to the Denver area. They'd like me closer. I told them I didn't want to leave Judge Hunt in a lurch, but now..."

"You need to rest and get well before you tackle any major decisions."

"I'll give you a call when I figure things out." She paused

before adding, "Thank you for calling me, Coop. I know all of this couldn't have been easy for you."

"You get better and I'll see you soon. Have a Merry Christmas with your family. I'm so happy you're out of the hospital. Remember you promised to meet me for a drink one night."

His reminder elicited a slight laugh. She chatted a few more minutes before disconnecting. He buzzed AB on the intercom and asked her to come in so they could call the Baxters together.

They reached Arden and Carter, who put them on speaker and listened as they explained the entire situation and how Callie had stumbled upon the connection between Judge Hunt and Avery Logan, leading to her death.

They were shocked, like Hildie, to learn Judge Hunt was involved. They thanked Coop and AB for their work on the case. Arden asked Coop to email a final invoice and promised to put a check in the mail. She excused herself from the call to attend to Christmas preparations, but Carter stayed on the line.

"Mr. Harrington, I want to thank you for helping John see the light. He has made the decision to divorce Winnie. It's been difficult, but I think his life will change for the better when he puts this behind him."

"And my dear Annabelle. Thank you for being Callie's friend. I'm so glad she had you in her life." His voice caught as he continued, "I'll always remember your kindness to my little girl."

They said their goodbyes and Coop hit the button on the speaker. "Whew, so far this day has been depressing."

AB dabbed her eyes with a tissue. "Not the best Christmas Eve I remember."

"Did you rebook your flight?"

"Yeah, tomorrow afternoon."

"Christmas Day?"

She nodded. "Aunt Camille invited me to her Christmas Eve

celebration tonight. Flights tomorrow were easy to get. Apparently, nobody wants to fly on Christmas Day."

"Makes sense. It'll be nice to have you there tonight. I could use someone in the under seventy age bracket."

"It'll be fun. Your aunt is a kick." She tossed her tissues in the trash. "I hung up a sign saying we're closed until January and put a message on the machine. I need to run some errands before the party tonight."

Coop nodded, "Of course. I haven't had time to do any Christmas shopping myself." He checked his watch. "I'll be home in a couple of hours." He stood and Gus jumped off his chair to follow.

He doused the lights and made sure the doors were secure before leaving in search of a few gifts he needed.

Camille's house was filled with chatter and laughter as six of her friends joined Coop and AB to celebrate the holiday. Christmas tunes filled the air and a sumptuous buffet had been laid out by Mrs. Henderson. A huge tower of fruit and other goodies had been delivered courtesy of Lola Belle and Daisy.

The women, dressed in sparkling holiday dresses, bustled about the formal living room and dining room, visiting and indulging in the extravagant feast and admiring Camille's decorations. Coop served as the bartender and kept the ladies supplied with whiskey sours, old fashioneds, and mint juleps. After all, they were proud Tennesseans and enjoyed their whiskey.

The ladies exchanged gifts and ended the night with champagne and a decadent selection of desserts, including Camille's famous brown sugar bourbon cake and a festive eggnog cake.

The limousine Camille had hired to bring her guests was summoned at the end of the night. Coop helped all the ladies with their fur coats and toted their bags to the driveway. They giggled in the back of the limousine, tipsy from their holiday imbibing. Once they were ensconced inside, Coop signaled the driver and Aunt Camille waved goodbye until the car was out of sight.

She took Coop's arm and they returned to the warmth of the house. AB was busy gathering dishes and tidying the kitchen. "Leave those be," said Camille. "I've got a surprise."

AB followed them into the living room. Camille presented an elegant gift-wrapped box to each of them. AB opened her box and found a bright summer dress and sandals, fit for her beach vacation. "Oh, it's fabulous. I can't wait to wear it." She hugged Camille.

"Go ahead, Coop, open yours," Camille urged with a sparkle in her eye.

He tore into his package and found a shirt in a tropical print, shorts, and swim trunks. His brow puckered as he continued to dig through the tissue and unearthed a large envelope.

He opened it and slid out a folder containing airline tickets and a reservation at a resort in the Bahamas. Camille was close to vibrating with enthusiasm as she watched him read the material. She couldn't wait for him to finish and blurted, "We're going to join AB and her family in the Bahamas."

Coop raised his brows at AB. "Did you know about this?"

"I can neither confirm nor deny my knowledge of the aforementioned event." She tried to contain a giggle. "After you told your mother you two were coming with me, Camille thought it was an excellent idea."

"We're set up in the villa next to AB. It's a grand place, right on the beach. We fly out with AB tomorrow. Mr. and Mrs. Henderson are going to stay in a guest room and take care of Gus and the house."

Coop smiled and stood to embrace his aunt. He plucked her

right out of her chair and twirled her around before setting her back down. "Thank you, Aunt Camille."

She shrieked and giggled as she regained her seat. "I thought you deserved a break from all this drudgery and chaos you've been through." She held his hand. "A change in tradition will do us both some good."

Camille brought out her new tropical wardrobe she had purchased for the trip. The three of them tried on their latest beach fashions and Coop draped his arms around his aunt and AB. Amid the twinkle of lights, he caught their reflection in one of the large ornaments on the tree. Instead of winter attire, floral dresses, shorts, and a bright pink sun hat atop Camille's white head signaled the beginning of their holiday this year. He dug his bare feet into the carpet and could almost feel the warm sand between his toes.

With a look of sheer joy, Coop planted a kiss on his aunt's cheek and gave AB's shoulder a squeeze. "This is going to be a great Christmas with my two favorite girls."

EPILOGUE

Deadly Connection is the second book in the Cooper Harrington Detective Novels. You'll discover a new case in each book in the series, but the characters you've come to know will continue

If you've missed reading any, here are the links to the entire series, in order.

Killer Music
Deadly Connection
Dead Wrong
Cold Killer
Deadly Deception

The books don't have to be read in order, but are more enjoyable when you do, since you'll learn more about Coop's backstory as the series unfolds. Continue reading to discover more whodunits that keep readers guessing until the end. If you're a new reader to Coop's books, you won't want to miss the other novels in the series.

ACKNOWLEDGMENTS

I love Coop and AB and had so much fun writing *Deadly Connection*. Like the first book in the Cooper Harrington Detective Series, it was challenging to construct the mystery and clues, but enjoyable. I like the puzzle of solving the case with Coop and strive to give the reader a fun read with lots of twists and surprises.

My favorite part of writing fiction is character creation. In this book the reader learns a bit more about Coop's background and gets a glimpse of his mother. I had fun with a few other minor characters, especially Audrey. As with *Killer Music*, this book is a departure from my Hometown Harbor Series in the women's fiction genre, but I plan to immerse Coop in another case soon.

As always, I'm thankful for my early readers, who are diligent when it comes to reading my manuscripts. Theresa, Vicki, Dana, and Jana were kind enough to read my drafts and give me valuable feedback and ideas. My dad is a great resource for expertise in all things crime, being in law enforcement for over thirty years.

I love my new cover branding from Elizabeth Mackey. She is a joy to work with a beyond talented.

I'm grateful for the support and encouragement of my friends and family as I continue to pursue my dream of writing. I appreciate all of the readers who have taken the time to provide a review on Amazon or Goodreads. These reviews are especially important in promoting future books, so if you enjoy my novels, please consider leaving a positive review. Follow this link to my author page and select a book to leave your review at www.amazon.com/author/tammylgrace. I also encourage you to follow me on Amazon and you'll be the first to know about new releases.

Remember to visit my website at www.tammylgrace.com or follow me on Facebook at www.facebook.com/tammylgrace. books to keep in touch—I'd love to hear from you.

FROM THE AUTHOR

Thank you for reading DEADLY CONNECTION. There are four books in the series, with more planned. Each features a new case, with the characters you've come to know.

For readers who enjoy women's fiction, you'll want to check out my Hometown Harbor Series. There are six books in the series, set in the picturesque San Juan Islands in Washington. Be sure and download the free novella, HOMETOWN HARBOR: THE BEGINNING. It's a prequel to FINDING HOME that I know you'll enjoy.

My new GLASS BEACH COTTAGE SERIES is also loved by readers. It is a heartwarming story of a woman's resilience buoyed by the bonds of friendship, an unexpected gift, and the joy she finds in helping others. As with all my books, the furry four-legged characters play a prominent role. BEACH HAVEN and MOONLIGHT BEACH are both available in this series.

If you're a fan of sweet Christmas stories, you'll want to check out A SEASON FOR HOPE and THE MAGIC OF THE SEASON, in my Christmas in Silver Falls Series. CHRISTMAS IN SNOW VALLEY is another stand-alone Christmas novella set in a cute small town. I've also written a connected series with five other authors, SOUL SISTERS AT CEDAR MOUNTAIN LODGE and readers love them!

I'm excited about my new releases for Bookouture, writing as Casey Wilson. A DOG'S HOPE and A DOG'S CHANCE are two emotional, but heartwarming books about the connection we have with dogs.

Speaking of dogs, I'd love to send you my exclusive interview with the canine companions in the Hometown Harbor Series as a thank-you for joining my exclusive group of readers. You can sign up here at my website.

MORE FROM TAMMY L. GRACE

COOPER HARRINGTON DETECTIVE NOVELS

Killer Music

Deadly Connection

Dead Wrong

Cold Killer

Deadly Deception

HOMETOWN HARBOR SERIES

Hometown Harbor: The Beginning (Prequel Novella)

Finding Home

Home Blooms

A Promise of Home

Pieces of Home

Finally Home

Forever Home

Follow Me Home

CHRISTMAS STORIES

A Season for Hope: Christmas in Silver Falls Book 1

The Magic of the Season: Christmas in Silver Falls Book 2

Christmas in Snow Valley: A Hometown Christmas Book 1

One Unforgettable Christmas: A Hometown Christmas Book 2

Christmas Wishes: Souls Sisters at Cedar Mountain Lodge

Christmas Surprises: Soul Sisters at Cedar Mountain Lodge

GLASS BEACH COTTAGE SERIES

Beach Haven

Moonlight Beach

Beach Dreams

WRITING AS CASEY WILSON

A Dog's Hope

A Dog's Chance

WISHING TREE SERIES

The Wishing Tree

Wish Again

Overdue Wishes

SISTERS OF THE HEART SERIES

Greetings from Lavender Valley

Pathway to Lavender Valley

Sanctuary at Lavender Valley

Blossoms at Lavender Valley

Comfort in Lavender Valley

Reunion in Lavender Valley

Remember to subscribe to Tammy's exclusive group of readers for your gift, only available to readers on her mailing list. **Sign up at www.tammylgrace.com. Follow this link to subscribe at https://wp.me/P9umIy-e** and you'll receive the exclusive interview she did with all the canine characters in her Hometown Harbor Series.

Follow Tammy on Facebook by liking her page. You may also follow Tammy on book retailers or at BookBub by clicking on the follow button.

ABOUT THE AUTHOR

Tammy L. Grace is the *USA Today* bestselling and award-winning author of the Cooper Harrington Detective Novels, the best-selling Hometown Harbor Series, and the Glass Beach Cottage Series, along with several sweet Christmas novellas. Tammy also writes under the pen name of Casey Wilson for Bookouture and Grand Central Publishing. You'll find Tammy online at www.tammylgrace.com where you can join her mailing list and be part of her exclusive group of readers. Connect with Tammy on social media by clicking on the icons below and liking her author pages on major book retailers.

facebook.com/tammylgrace.books
twitter.com/TammyLGrace
instagram.com/authortammylgrace
bookbub.com/authors/tammy-l-grace
goodreads.com/tammylgrace
pinterest.com/tammylgrace

Made in the USA
Monee, IL
10 April 2024